The SCHOOL of POSSIBILITIES

SEITA PARKKOLA

TRANSLATED BY ANNIRA SILVER AND MARJA GASS

The characters and events portrayed in this book are fictitious or are used fictitiously. Any similarity to real persons, living or dead, is purely coincidental and not intended by the author.

Published by Sourcebooks Jabberwocky, an imprint of Sourcebooks, Inc.
P.O. Box 4410, Naperville, Illinois 60567-4410
(630) 961-3900
Fax: (630) 961-2168
www.jabberwockykids.com

First published in Finland in 2006 by Werner Söderström Osakeyhtiö.

Library of Congress Cataloging-in-Publication data is on file with the publisher.

Source of Production: Sheridan Books, Chelsea, Michigan, USA
Date of Production: June 2010
Run Number: 12431

Printed and bound in the United States of America.
SB 10 9 8 7 6 5 4 3 2 1

PROLOGUE

I am Storm, and I am twelve. Not a bad age. But it could be the worst thing that ever happens to a boy. Worse than being kidnapped by body snatchers or being stuck in detention forever. Being twelve is like being in an eight-vehicle car wreck.

It's like being stuck upside down on a roller coaster.

This is my story.

It is also a story about India, who is a girl, not a country or a subcontinent, and about a derelict cookie factory that used to be a hospital.

I am not a bad boy, but I'm not a good one, either.

My thing is flying.

Many people want to fly, but not everyone can. You need wings.

I've got wings. I've got a skateboard.

When you want to fly, you must be fearless. I am fearless.

Maybe you've seen me around. I'm the boy on the bus with hair hanging over his eyes, with a board under one arm or in his bag. You'll never see me without my board or my board without me. We are one, as the saying goes. When I drop my board on the ground, lift my foot onto it, and kick off, no one can catch me. At least not by running or driving in a police car. Not anyone, ever. From time to time, the board gets wrecked, because in this game, you often fall off and sometimes fall over. Anyone who wants to fly shouldn't be afraid of bruises or broken bones. Quite a few skaters have had this or that split, like knees or insides.

I am starting at a new school this fall. The school is called the School of Possibilities. It is my last chance. That's what Mom, Dad, the headmaster, and a few others have told me. They've said that I had better believe it, because otherwise, I will be expelled, and after that, nothing good will be waiting for me in this life. There are places you can be sent to, even after you've been given your last chance, but they are talked about in whispers. They are meant for troublemakers who have no other hope. If you mess up your last chance, you get sent to the school for lost children, and your life will be ruled by the law of the jungle. In the School of the Lost, if you punch another child, you get a teardrop tattooed on your cheek. The worst kids have cheeks covered in tears. The School of the Lost is somewhere on the edge of the city—nobody really knows where. Children whisper about it in their yards and on the streets. It is said that there are no pictures on the walls there, and the students don't learn the rivers of Europe or the dates of revolutions and wars. They do time—a bit like in prison.

When this story begins, I only have one more opportunity before it's prison for me. If I fail, I will be Lost No. 101...or something like that.

After that, there is nothing.

I don't intend to fail.

Before I begin the story, I'll show you a place. It's a derelict factory. Nobody owns it. Nobody looks after it. It stands on the other side of the railroad tracks in the middle of a run-down neighborhood of wooden houses. It is as big as a castle and as black as a hole in a mountain. I liked it as soon as I saw it.

The factory is empty. Its windows and everything else inside it are broken. Even from the yard, you can see that it's a dark place—so dark that you need a flashlight or eyes like a rat's to walk through it. A tower stands at the side of the factory. It stands high above everything else, and you can almost see the whole city from it. You can only get up there using your sense of touch. If you were to use a flashlight, you would soon see that the walls of the tower are covered in painted pictures and writing. The place looks a little like a cave decorated with ancient markings:

> I WOZ HERE. I'LL BE BACK. TOM & TILLY. DON'T ALL ASLEEP. DON'T FALL DOWN. DON'T FALL OVER. FALL OVER ANYWAY.

When we get to the top of the tower, I'll hand you some binoculars. They are an important tool. My mother gave them to me on the day this story starts. Through the binoculars, you can see the harbor and my new school. You can see the building I live in when I stay with my father. It is the middle one of those three skyscrapers. Doesn't look like much, does it? You wouldn't want to live there. I live halfway up. The apartment has four rooms and a kitchen. It has a walk-in closet, a covered balcony, and a time slot in the basement sauna on Saturdays. There is a plaque on the door that says "Steele and Poole." My father and I are Steele. My father's new wife is Poole—Verity Poole. She is thin, although she eats nonstop. She is a bit like a spider that digs a hole and lies in wait for prey. Poole is also very good at a type of martial arts practiced by older people. She met Dad when she was eating goulash in his restaurant on the ground floor of our building. They fell in love.

Poole is a school counselor. You know, those people at school who look after children with problems—kids who are being bullied, or they are bullies themselves, or they are sick, or they have moved from somewhere else…or whatever. The counselor is the students' friend—that's the idea, at least. Verity Poole is a counselor at the school that gave me my last chance. You can probably guess the rest. She arranged for me to go to that school. It is thanks to Poole that I was given one more chance. She told Dad about the school. She really sold it to him. She said that the school was experimenting in new child-friendly methods, and that they would work even for me.

Verity Poole thinks she knows everything about boys, but she can think what she likes. The fact is that she knows nothing about boys. Her own child is a girl. The girl is called Mona, and she's in the eighth grade. When I saw Mona for the first time, she was standing in front of the mirror, combing her long black hair, and she called me little brother. "You look like a prince, little brother," she said, and asked if she could put some kohl on me. Kohl is a kind of pencil used by girls to draw on their faces. Mona wanted to pierce my eyes with it. That's what I think.

Mona has a white face, and she listens to dismal music. When you look at Mona, you instinctively expect a sudden spurt of blood to erupt from her mouth, like a vampire. She calls many boys "princes." She particularly calls boys whose eyes she wants to pierce "princes." Mona has the names of all these princes written on her arms and her pencil case. She describes them as tattoos, although she has drawn them with marker pens.

When you look out from the tower, you can also see the city center. That's where my mother lives. That's where I live when it's time to stay with my mom. You can see the tower from Mom's window. The tower is visible from almost anywhere in the city, just as you can see everything from the tower.

Now that you have seen all this, we can come down from the tower and run across the yard.

Now I'll begin.

This is the first day.

This is where it all starts.

THE SCHOOL OF POSSIBILITIES

1.

The School of Possibilities was a metal building behind a tall fence. Its windows were vast, and its walls were metal. The School of Possibilities was a bit like an aquarium or a large television screen. Only decent children and ambitious teachers moved throughout its corridors. Its caretakers and cooks were dedicated. Once in a while, one of the school's students would try to get out, but he would always be returned to the flock. Breakouts were not attempted often. That's how it was. The school was called the School of Possibilities, but it was also called Last Chance.

When I walked in through the gate on the morning of my first school day, I saw it all at once—all of it. At least that's what I thought then. The school was transparent—a bit like a crystal ball. The day began with a talk in the headmaster's office. I had to sign a paper that said: *I, Storm Steele, choose the future.* It was school procedure. Everyone was there voluntarily. No one was forced to be there. The paper listed a horrendous number of things that I was agreeing to once I had signed. Many things were forbidden, and many other things were considered my duty. Although parents normally made the decisions regarding their children, the students themselves also had to make a commitment to their education. This was a requirement.

I went to the school with Mom and Dad.

"Welcome," the headmaster said to us when we stepped into his office. He first shook Dad's hand and then Mom's. He nodded to Verity Poole and squeezed my shoulder. "We are here for Storm," he said. "We will take care of him." The squeeze he gave my shoulder was military-strong—crushing even.

There was a round table in the room. We sat around it with straight backs like the knights in that ancient tale where everyone comes to a sticky end. I sat there with Mom; Dad; the headmaster; Counselor Poole; my new teacher, Daisy Cutts; and Rob Reed, assistant to all the students and the headmaster's right-hand man. "It won't work," I wanted to say, but I didn't. Instead I inspected the group more closely. Rob looked a little like a policeman. Mom looked better than Verity Poole. The headmaster was fat and loved Danish pastries. There was a plateful of them on the side of the table. The teacher looked as tight as a balloon about to explode. Everyone was nodding and waiting for the headmaster to finish saying his piece, which took some time. The headmaster droned on and on:

"The School of Possibilities is a school without any long tradition, as yet. That is how new it is. It is a place that promises each year to offer a chance to a few desperate children and to prevent them from ending up in institutions where children easily become thieves and murderers. We don't have a long tradition, but we do have a long line of trophies for our work as educators. Storm is one of the lucky ones. He can thank our energetic counselor, who with good reason can be said to embody the school's spirit."

Dad smiled at Poole. Mom snapped a pencil in two.

Then the headmaster read from a paper describing me as an unthinking child who kept running away, scrawled and defaced, and didn't understand the consequences of his actions. He told us that I was not evil, however, and that I was a very suitable boy for placement at the School of Possibilities. "All of us on the governing body of the school believe that there is hope for Storm, and that after getting through the sixth grade, he will be ready to move up to the seventh. One day he could become someone important like a doctor or an architect, for the School of Possibilities has developed strict but constructive methods that enable us to weed out bad habits from the most uncontrollable rascals and to get them to realize how sensible it is to invest in the future."

When the headmaster finished, he gathered up the pile of papers in front of him and looked at me.

"Yet there is a price for everything," he said. "In order for Storm to achieve the best results, he must make some small sacrifices..."

A silence followed during which everyone waited for the blade to fall.

I waited for it, too. I could feel it hovering over me, above the table, and over this whole situation, and it would soon drop. I waited and waited, and then the headmaster spoke again.

"Storm must not have any contact with his former friends, school, or hobbies," he said. "Storm must sever all his ties with the past. He must no longer...no longer..."

"Skate," Poole interrupted. "He must give up his skateboard."

The headmaster nodded, and then he said, "You must not hang around with that crowd."

I took hold of the table and tried to catch my breath—like you do when someone kicks you right in the stomach and all your breath escapes from your body. Perhaps my favorite place to practice was on the steps of an art school by the river. The others who frequented the art school were older and had been skating there for years; but there was always room for me, and I learned things from the bigger boys. It wasn't just hanging around.

I needed a time-out now, because my heart was sending out the first symptoms of a heart attack. The most astonishing thing in all this was that Mom and Dad, whose only task—whose actual duty—was to defend their son, were nodding approvingly like battery-operated souvenirs and showing every sign of agreement as the headmaster was speaking.

The headmaster again turned to look at my parents.

"Storm's mentor here at school will be his supervisor, Rob Reed. He is the school's specialist in working with impossible children and has been doing it for years. Mr. Reed is a genius and understands boys. Miss Poole also takes care of student welfare. She deals with both model and problem students. She has promised to support Storm's father and make sure that the rules are adhered to at school and at home. As I already said, Counselor Poole is a woman of pure gold. She embodies our school's spirit and direction."

Poole nodded, and I gave Mom a meaningful look. I thought that she would surely oppose all this, but to my surprise, she nodded, too—maybe a little tensely but clearly accepting the arrangements.

"Mom," I said, but she avoided my eyes.

"For your sake, Storm," she said to her hands, which were resting in her lap.

"That's the right attitude," the headmaster said, thanking her. "Parents must also commit. Without parental participation, we wouldn't have the success we do."

"I object..." I interrupted, but then Rob Reed thumped me on the shoulder.

"Don't worry, Storm. We'll get along," he said and winked in a way that only a person with no sense of occasion would.

When, at the end, Mom asked if they had ever failed, the headmaster was overcome by some kind of a coughing fit, and together, Rob Reed and Daisy Cutts whacked him on the back. As the situation progressed in this way, I picked up a pen off the table and stuffed it into my pocket.

"It does occasionally happen," the headmaster said when he was again able to speak. "*That*...cannot be avoided. There are always children for whom our methods are ineffective. I wouldn't worry about Storm, however. He will succeed."

When the briefing was over and he had taken leave of Mom and Dad, the headmaster confiscated my skateboard and put it in a special glass cabinet which looked a bit like the School of Possibilities, only in miniature.

"This is for your own good," he said and then added that now I was part of the group and would have opportunities for all sorts of other hobbies at this school. I would soon forget about the board.

"You are here to get better," he said and guided me into the corridor. "Now you can get to know your new class. Rob Reed and Miss Cutts will take you there."

I kept looking at the glass case over my shoulder as we walked away and it receded into the background. It was full of all sorts of things confiscated from the other children. The board hung there a bit like the crest of a vanished kingdom. If I forgot it, would that mean I would forget about flying? Would that even be possible? When I closed my eyes, I saw the board grow wings and flap its way out of the glass case and out the school window.

My imprisonment had begun.

2.

W*hat kind of a child gets a chance at the School of Possibilities?* you might be wondering at this point. *What bad thing has the boy in the story done? Has he robbed a bank, driven the car he stole from his father through a store wall, or liberated the cats from the pet shop? Or has he done some other peculiar thing?*

No, no, no to all that.

I was accused of running away.

It all started when I decided to take a trip one day. At that precise moment, I didn't think I would ever come back. It was one of those days.

This is what happened.

I was practicing jumps on the railroad station steps when the stationmaster came to tell me off. "Skating is not allowed here," he said, and I stopped to watch people boarding the train with their dozens of suitcases. There were single men and women, whole families, children, dogs, and even a parrot. It all looked fine, and suddenly, I started to imagine that I was someone else, like an orphan who was sent off to start a new life, all of his possessions stuffed in a duffel bag.

That was when I decided to get on the train. At first I thought I would just get on and jump back off onto the platform straight away, but once I had taken a seat, I didn't get up again. At some point there was an announcement that the train was about to leave and that all those who were not intending to travel had to get off, but I didn't stand up or get off. I stayed in my seat, clutching my skateboard and staring out of the window. Then the train shuddered into motion, and I was on my way somewhere—perhaps to a city bigger than this one or a completely new country. I looked out the window and acted like someone with a serious destination, someone with some important reason for traveling. Of course I had no money, and the fare collector reported me. Mom and Dad came to pick me up from a station somewhere en route between two cities. They were no longer together and fought every time they saw each other. They fought all the way home that day.

I made the same journey three more times. At last a man who knew about these things was called to my school. "I know why children keep running away," he said and then asked me all sorts of questions. He also tested me and said that I was impulsive, which meant unpredictable. It was a bad thing—or that was what I reckoned anyway, because Mom started crying right away, and Dad sighed heavily.

"We have to set boundaries for you," the man said. "Be careful, or you will come to no good in this life. You can't just do whatever you like. You need boundaries and a place where they will be enforced."

Then in the summer, Dad found Miss Poole, or Miss Poole found Dad. At the same time, they found me a school that specialized in boundaries and in enforcing them. That was how I came to be in this place, and that was why I was now walking behind Rob and Miss Cutts toward my first lesson.

"Here no one screams or sticks gum on the walls or on other students," Rob explained. "We don't push, jump the line, or trip others up. We don't have bullying."

I nodded vaguely. I was sure he was lying, and later—quite soon, in fact—I was proven right.

The light in the corridor was so bright that it reflected off all the surfaces, blinded your eyes, and then scratched them. You almost couldn't see in front of you, it was so bright. On the surface, there was nothing strange or peculiar about the School of Possibilities. It was like any other school. It looked a bit like Castle Mount Primary School, where I had attended the fifth grade, or Spruce Lane School, where I had attended the fourth grade, or a few others from my past.

I pulled the headmaster's pen out of my pocket and tried to scrawl my signature on the wall, but before I could get anywhere near the tiles, Rob got hold of my hand with the speed of a predator, and the pen fell on the floor.

"Marker pens are forbidden, my good man," he said, the whole time keeping up his overly friendly smile.

This was the beginning of my life at the School of Possibilities.

The next thing I knew, Rob had pushed me into a classroom and then up onto the podium.

"This is Storm, your new classmate," Rob said, pointing at me. "Storm is a boy who has been given an opportunity. He is an impossible child, but he has decided to redeem himself."

"Storm chose the future," Miss Cutts echoed.

"Opportunity," as Rob pronounced it, or "future," as the teacher said it, sounded like the brightest medal in a prestigious contest. I stared at the class in the mirror covering the back wall of the classroom. It showed twenty-six heads and then me. I had very black eyes. When I was little, Mom always called them *the eyes of darkness.* "I don't have to be afraid of the dark, because my son has the eyes of darkness," she always said, and I would giggle senselessly the way little children always do the world over—maybe even right now. Other things have been said about my eyes: I look as if I have just done something forbidden or I am planning my next move, which in this context means pranks and all sorts of naughty things. I also have interesting hair. I have fuzzy, flaxen dreadlocks—maybe you know what they look like or maybe you don't. The hairstyle was Mom's idea, as most of the attempts at being different are in our family. I acquired the hairstyle around the same time that Dad decided to get together with the Pooles. It was Mom's way of retaliating, and I was in the middle. Verity Poole detests my hair.

As Rob left the room, the teacher nodded at the closing door. She turned to look at me. "Storm is not as lucky as all of you," she said. "Storm has two homes. Storm has had problems, but now he wants to reform. We will support him in this. Does the class agree?"

Twenty-six pairs of eyes stared at me, unblinking, and the students nodded.

"To be on the safe side, keep your desks locked for now, and keep an eye on your bags. Storm is only at the beginning of his journey, so a chance to commit a crime could trip him up."

I stared at the floor, scarlet-faced.

"Is the boy allowed to keep that hair?" someone in the back row asked. "Isn't it against the rules?"

"An appropriate question," Miss Cutts said. "Storm's hair is untidy, but we won't force him into anything. He will cut it once he has been in our healing company for a while. He will realize himself how ridiculous he looks. We will give Storm time."

Then the teacher squeezed my shoulder and pointed at the boy who had just spoken. "This is Will," she said to me. "Will is going to be your student mentor, your best friend chosen for you by the school. Stand up, Will, and say hello to your friend."

The boy stood up. He straightened his back like a soldier. We looked at each other. Something flashed in the boy's icy eyes. He didn't like me.

Just then, in the middle of the proceedings, there was a knock at the door, and Rob's head appeared in the doorway. "The headmaster wants to see you," he said, summoning the teacher. The teacher told the class to wait and disappeared into the corridor.

I was left alone on the podium, thinking that things were now going to get out of hand. They always had on these occasions in my previous schools. But no one went wild. Everyone looked at me and waited. I looked back. I can stare quite a while without blinking. It's a skill you can develop with practice. I can also hold my breath.

I could hear the headmaster's constant droning.

The atmosphere in the classroom was completely lifeless. It was like staring at death. In the end, I had to blink.

"He'll fail," a boy next to Will said. He didn't say it to me. He said it to Will and the rest of the class. "This guy won't make it through the year. Believe me."

My supposed best friend nodded. Someone laughed.

Then the door opened again, and the teacher stepped back into the classroom. She took hold of my shoulder. "Go and put your things into your desk," she said, pointing at an empty place by the window.

"Is the boy going to take India's place?" a girl sitting in the front row asked and then pressed her hands to her mouth.

The teacher frowned.

"India does not exist any more," she said.

"But—" the girl started, and the teacher raised her hand as a signal for silence.

"We do not discuss that subject," she said and opened the geography book. "We are now moving on to talk about the German economy. Turn to page twenty-five and the paragraph on industry."

3.

The morning was uneventful. After a couple of lessons, it was lunchtime, which we spent in the classroom. We sat at our desks with napkins on our laps and stared at the chalkboard, on which the teacher wrote *tikka masala*. It was the name of the food loaded onto our plates, at least in the teacher's opinion. "A staple international cuisine," she said, although the portion was all rice. I pointed this out to the teacher, but she replied by drawing a curved line on the board.

"Execution hill," she said and looked at me. "Who will explain to Storm? You, Alexander!"

The boy behind Will started to speak. "An execution hill..." he began. "The idea is from a game called hangman, which consists of a leader and players who have a number of guesses. Every time you guess wrong, the gallows grow a little. The one who is the first to be hanged loses the game."

Of course I knew the game. The leader draws a line representing each letter of a word. The words are usually long and complicated, such as *monogram* or *kaleidoscope*, and every time the player guesses a wrong letter, the gallows grow by one line. Each player has his own gallows, and the person who is the first one hanging on the end of the rope loses the game.

"What happens to the hanged?" I asked.

"Tell Storm," the teacher said. She had turned to another boy. "You, Anton!"

"You get punished," Anton answered.

"But what kind of a punishment?"

"A useful one."

The teacher kept raising her arms like an agitator at a mass meeting.

"Examples, children. Give examples. Tell Storm."

"Painting," said someone.

"Cleaning," said another.

"Demolishing," said a third.

"Building," said a fourth.

The teacher kept nodding. "Or working for the school after school hours," she said and signaled for us to return to our plates.

With my mouth full of rice, I stared at my empty execution hill, which was only empty for the time being, and wondered how much demolishing and building I would have to do before the year was over and I would get to the seventh grade. What would happen if I refused to accept the "useful punishment"? Would I immediately fall down an abyss where perhaps not a sea monster lurked but a punishment center for children who had lost the game waited? But again I reminded myself that I had decided to stay. Other gallows apart from my own had been started on the board. Some had only the hill. Others had the hill and a support beam. Some had flowers. Underneath every construction was the name of a student. On Alexander's hill, there were already a couple of upright beams. In one corner was an assortment of gallows, with a rope hanging from each. It looked a lot like a site of mass execution.

Under every one of the gallows, it said—

"India," Alexander replied before I had even asked.

I leaned in closer.

"India?"

"India!"

"She must have had a lot of punishments."

The boys glanced at each other. Anton looked quickly at the teacher.

"The most impossible child of all time," they whispered.

"Impossible like me?"

Anton shook his head. "Too impossible," he said.

"But where is she now?"

The boys shrugged their shoulders. "We don't know," they whispered. "We don't talk about her, and she's never coming back. You heard what the teacher said. She doesn't exist."

"But—" I started, but Alexander pressed his finger to his lips meaningfully.

"She once tried to break into the glass case," he whispered to me.

I raised my eyebrows. "The glass case?"

"The glass case in the corridor."

I looked at the forest of gallows and then at the desk that was now mine, where India had once sat. Through the window, I could see the playground, the railroad tracks behind the fence, and the decayed part of the city beyond the tracks. I could see a building, some sort of a factory, with all its windows darkened or boarded up with plywood. That was what India had looked at as she sat here. What had she been thinking about? Where was she now?

When it was time to go home, Will was waiting for me at the gate.

"I will be walking to and from school with you," he said.

"What? Why?"

"School rules. So you won't be tempted into crime."

I laughed, because it sounded like a joke, but it wasn't. The headmaster or Rob Reed had given Will this task—thank goodness neither of *them* wanted to accompany me.

This sort of thing made me realize how serious the situation was. Believe me.

We walked toward my home without speaking. When we got there, Will stopped. I carried on to the door.

"We will help you," he said behind my back, somewhat mechanically.

I turned around and was about to answer, but I was dumbfounded when I saw the nastiest flash I had ever seen in Will's previously expressionless eyes.

"You will fail," he mouthed at me—or that was what I thought he mouthed. The expression came and went in an instant, and I couldn't be certain whether I had even seen it at all.

"Did you say something?"

Will shook his head and said, "I will wait for you here tomorrow."

"What if I don't show up?"

Will shrugged his shoulders.

"Your choice, but...if I were you, I would."

I stopped to stare at the boy's back as he walked away. Was that a threat? Or how should I take his comment?

"I'm not going to fail," I whispered.

Before Will disappeared around the corner, he stopped. "Remember, soccer training today at the field! Be there!" he shouted without turning his head.

Soccer training? Frowning, I thought for five seconds or less and then forgot the whole thing as easily as some unknown person's birthday. Soccer training was the easiest thing in the world to forget. I was not the type to chase around after balls.

4.

In the evening, as we sat at the table, Dad said: "Here we are, the whole family around the table, celebrating Storm's first day at his new school." Then he placed a saucepan containing some steaming concoction in front of us, and Verity Poole clapped her hands. They looked at each other over the pan, as proud as two alchemists who had just discovered how to make gold.

I picked up my spoon. Mona picked up hers.

We pushed them into the pork stew and then into our mouths. All the time we were staring at each other. We swallowed simultaneously.

And then it started again—the same battle every evening. Mona kicked me. She kicked me really hard. If you imagined that step-sisters only did this sort of thing in films, you would be mistaken. Mona did it, too. She kicked like a horse.

Of course I kicked back. I did it instinctively. It was also easy to kick a bit harder than I originally intended. This evening's counter-attack caused Mona to splatter the stew everywhere. She looked even more like a vampire now than before, with a shred of beet hanging from the corner of her mouth like a piece of intestine. The sight of her nearly made me choke on my milk.

Mona started to shriek.

"The prince is kicking me," she yelled, almost in tears.

"You are not kicking Mona, are you?" Poole asked me.

I shook my head vigorously, without averting my gaze from Mona. I tried to guess what she would come up with next. She always thought of something. My appetite was gone. The scene was typical of this recipe for disaster that Dad called a family and I called a horror show.

Dad had gotten it into his head that a family made a person whole. He didn't say it in order to joke or impress. He meant it, and that would have made anyone feel uncomfortable. In all honesty, we were not a family but rather four pieces of a jigsaw puzzle that wouldn't fit together, and we would never be anything else. The only unifying factor was Verity Poole's love affair with my father's food. However, all steel rusts when you sink it into a pool, as the saying goes.

It was also thanks to Verity Poole that Dad was now *Vladimir*. He used to be John—plain John without any Russian ancestry. Dad became Vladimir when Verity Poole got the idea that concoctions prepared by Vladimir would sell better than those prepared by plain old John. I have to confess that she was right. The restaurant had now started to become successful. Dad trusted Poole, of course. He was a nice guy but also naïve and trusting. For example, he didn't understand that establishing a family was difficult. It was definitely no picnic.

I pushed my spoon into the stew again and told Dad about the gallows. I had imagined that he would be shocked, but Dad just thought it was funny and that the teacher was a great comedian. Miss Poole laughed along with him, a little too enthusiastically.

Of course I was not amused. The teacher had managed to draw three lines on my execution hill within a rather short day.

"I need a skateboard, Dad," I said then.

Dad just sighed. "How can you need a new skateboard?" he asked in a surprised and rather weary voice. He was trying to remember something, probably the fact that I was not allowed skateboards.

"They took it from me at school."

"Did they?" Dad said, still a bit surprised.

"It has been confiscated from him. Don't you remember, Vladimir?" Verity Poole butted into the conversation. "We do not approve of skateboards. The School of Possibilities believes in hobbies supervised by adults. Children need guidance. They cannot be left to themselves."

I stared starkly, my dark eyes pointed at Poole.

"What if you started to play soccer?" she suggested. "Soccer is a military hobby."

Dad's face brightened then. "That's a great idea," he said. "Did you hear, Storm? We'll get you a soccer ball."

"I don't want a soccer ball," I said dourly. "I want a skateboard."

Dad looked at Miss Poole, helpless.

"Your father cannot get you a new skateboard if it is forbidden by school rules," Poole said.

"Dad?"

"I can't, Storm," Dad said, and then he dug a piece of paper out of his pocket and pushed it in front of me. "This contract, signed by me, says that the child must be supported, and that the rules must not be broken. Breaking the rules will lead to expulsion from the school and fines."

"That's how it is," Poole verified. "If you break the contract, the future is canceled. You can't want that to happen!"

I shook my head vigorously. No, of course I didn't want that, but I did still want to fly…and become the world's best skater. I still wanted to move to a city with seven—no, eleven hills and a huge number of rails and steps just right for skating.

And then I lost my train of thought when the doorbell rang.

I ran to answer it.

Mom stood in the corridor in the dark.

"What an awful shirt you're wearing!" she declared immediately and gave the hem of my shirt a tug. "Where did you get it from? It looks like a tablecloth."

"It is a Ukrainian tunic and a sort of national costume. Some people don't know anything about other nations' folk traditions," Verity Poole said. She had appeared at the kitchen door.

Dad stood next to her. He didn't say anything. He stared at the floor.

Mom started to pull the top off me.

"I came to collect Storm," she said. "I've got a surprise for him."

"Do something," Verity Poole snarled at Dad and poked him with her sharp elbow. Dad moved stiffly.

"It isn't a changeover day," he said with uncertainty. "It's Wednesday."

To be on the safe side, I said nothing.

"I've got something exciting for you," Mom said and pressed my cheek. "You'll love it. It's a starting-school present."

It was a present. Mom loved presents. The usual days for giving them were not enough for her. She wanted to give presents almost every day of the year—whenever possible, really.

"Give me the present on Friday," I said cautiously.

Mom pursed her lips, offended. "You'll need it before Friday," she said. "This surprise is an object, but it's also a lot more. It's a new hobby."

I sighed deeply. The present was a hobby? It was another new hobby? My mother had a vivid imagination and used it to think up new hobbies for me all the time.

"Storm has been forbidden from new hobbies," Verity Poole said.

Then Mom straightened her back and looked triumphant.

"This hobby will also suit the school program splendidly. I called the school and asked the headmaster."

"Who's that?" Mona interrupted, appearing in the hall.

Then everyone started to argue, and I dived under Mom's arm into the stairway.

"See you," I called over my shoulder and pushed the door closed behind me.

"The boy's escaping!" Miss Poole screamed.

"Storm!" wailed Mom and Dad.

"That got rid of him," Mona celebrated.

At this point I was already on my way downstairs. I ran to the yard and down the street that went around our building and led to the harbor and far beyond. En route, it passed the sports field and the school, too.

At the school gate, I stopped to catch my breath. Behind the enormous windows, the school's long, empty corridors and coat-less hooks stared silently at me like they would in a nightmare.

5.

"Nice of you to come and see us. We've been waiting for you, haven't we, boys?"

I looked up to see Rob Reed hovering over me, and behind him was a group of students. Rob was clutching a whistle and looking energetic. He was wearing sports gear plastered with sports shop logos.

"I'm not planning on playing soccer," I said, panting, still out of breath.

Rob nodded approvingly.

"First you'll have to raise your fitness level," he said. "If a mere walk makes you that exhausted, you won't make the team. On the Team of Possibilities, you will only make progress with an iron physique. Now I'm going to give you a nice surprise. You can still join us. You can do something for us."

Rob then handed me a broom.

"When climbing a tree, you have to start from the bottom, not the top," he said. "Your task is to clean the players' changing room. It's over there in our brand-new sports hall at the other end of the schoolyard. No shortage of trash there."

"I can't," I said, shocked.

Rob raised his eyebrows inquiringly.

"I'm on my way to see the doctor," I quickly continued.

"At this time?" Rob exclaimed. "I don't suppose doctors ever have a rest."

"I know," I said and rolled my eyes.

"Why don't you go to the changing room anyway and start cleaning? It's only ten hours since you signed the contract," Rob said and forced the broom into my hand. "You voluntarily agreed to keep our school rules. I hope you haven't forgotten that."

I took the broom and marched through the gate into the schoolyard.

The sports hall resembled an aquarium, like everything else in the school complex. A dazzling metallic light shone from its windows. Synthetic turf gleamed behind the glass. On the wall hung a plaque stating that the city had built the hall for the School of Possibilities' sports department in recognition of the school's success in its work with children.

The changing room was already quite tidy. I gave the tiled floor a sweep. The place seemed new. It smelled fresh—not at all like the changing room hellholes in my previous schools. There were no signs of the carvings, scratches, or other marks left by the studded shoes that the children wore.

I swept the floor and sat down on a bench.

I didn't have to wait long.

"We have come to inspect," Alexander said at the door, a couple of other boys from the team peeking out behind him. "What do you think? Will he do as the team cleaner?" he asked over his shoulder.

The boys snickered.

"Looks pretty bad, in my opinion," one of them said.

Then Will pushed his way into the room. The other boys made room for him. Every single one of them kept their eyes trained on him. Will walked around the room with sometimes a stern look and sometimes a blank look on his face. He looked at everything. He inspected the whole place. After this had been going on for a while, Will signaled to Alexander, who disappeared out of the door with two other boys. When they reappeared almost immediately, they were carrying buckets. At once the room started to smell disgusting.

You can probably guess the rest.

Will signaled again, and the boys tipped up the buckets, which were full of trash. The trash spread all over the floor, and because it was some sort of decomposing and rotting compost stuff, the place immediately began to stink like a dump.

"Yuck!" someone shrieked.

"He's messed up the changing room," another one said.

Then Will stepped toward me, pointing. "Start cleaning, you pig," he commanded.

He wasn't laughing, but the others laughed for him. They held their noses and backed out toward the playing field, where Rob was already blowing his whistle. What was it he'd said? Here at the School of Possibilities, there was no bullying? Yeah, right.

I stared at the floor, frozen to the spot, and tried not to vomit. It was perfectly clear to me that I was not going to clean up the mess. When the boys were far enough away, I slipped through the door and ran out of the hall and away from the schoolyard. I left the lively din of the game and the fence they called the "guard dog" behind me.

I carried on running even when I could taste iron—or blood—in my mouth. I ran along a railroad track, and when I heard the train hooting, I still carried on running. I was on the railroad track for a really long time, but then, mercifully, I jumped onto the embankment and carried on alongside the train. My shoes sank deep into the mud. A few children's hands were waving to me through the train window, all sorts of faces pressed against the glass. Then I stopped and yelled as loudly as I could amid the racket of the passing train until my throat hurt. If you had looked at me then, you would have thought I was crying at first, but quite soon after that, you would have realized that you couldn't see any tears.

And suddenly, there it was in front of me—the empty factory, the place that changed my life. The story could begin at this moment.

The factory was large and complex. It was like the body of a giant prehistoric lizard or a wounded monster. Its towers were like horns and its windows like the pecked-out eyes of a large animal. Low outbuildings leaned against the sides of the factory. The place looked as if it could take off on its wings at any moment.

"Wow," I said aloud.

When I stepped closer, stones broke loose and rolled away from under my feet along the railroad embankment. Immediately a massive flock of black birds—who knew what sort of birds—took off from the yard. On one corner of the factory were burnt signs of a previous fire. Or maybe there had been an explosion at some point, as things were strewn here and there. There were charred walls, pillars jutting out askew, barrels split open, bits of building and, of course, huge amounts of broken glass everywhere.

I jumped from the embankment down to the yard and strode past wrecked cars and barrels toward the building. Yet another train clattered on the railroad track behind me on its way to the harbor.

I slipped inside and turned on my flashlight. I never went anywhere without my flashlight and my jungle knife. Well, it wasn't actually a jungle knife—just an ordinary pocketknife.

On the wall, there was something written in bright letters, so I stepped closer to read them. The writing read: AMUSEMENT PARK.

Amusement park?

That was what it said...and in a most extraordinary style, too. You could have skated along the letters. You could have climbed up them, and you could have jumped off them. The paint was bright red, orange, blue, and white. Later I found out that red is never just red, but rather red ochre or alizarin red, that yellow is Naples or bile or cobalt yellow, and that white is titanium, lead, or French white. I also found out that asbestine and aurum mussivum are colors, and that colors have dozens, if not hundreds of names. It matters a lot which colors you choose. The painting was excellent, and I memorized it down to the last detail. I would have liked to paint something similar on my own wall.

I pushed through the door and immediately screwed up my nose. The painting had smelled of fresh paint, but once inside the factory, I was hit by waves of all sorts of worse smells, like damp plywood, metal, rust, grain, just plain dirt, and who knew what other substances made up the bizarre colors? I swept my flashlight's beam around the walls.

Sounds were coming from the corners—all kinds of sounds, like creaking, water dripping and running, wind whistling in the tin structures, and rats, birds, and bats rustling. I aimed the light at each corner and found heaps of useless stuff. Otherwise the place was empty. Its tall windows had at some point been covered with chipboard, but now the boards were only partially in place.

And then I heard a sound. That sound—it was somehow quite familiar.

It was a slam.

It made me freeze on the spot.

It was followed by another, and yet another slam.

I hastily turned off my flashlight.

My heart was pounding, of course, and my blood curdled. The fine hairs on my skin stood up. I listened to the sounds with every nerve strained. I was terrified. My hand sought the pocketknife. The knife was only meant to scare people. I could never hurt anyone.

As I started to feel that I wasn't the only one listening and that I would be standing there for the next ten or twenty years, someone shrieked and broke the silence. At first I thought of hungry ghosts, and although I didn't believe in ghosts, I got incredibly scared. Still, I didn't turn around and run away. To be honest, both options felt equally good and bad at that moment, but it was easiest to stay put.

"Who's there?" I shouted. I tried to make my voice sound threatening and deep, but I only achieved a shrill squeak. I sounded like a scared kid, easy to frighten and even easier to swallow.

When there was no answer, I decided to check things out. I crept deeper into the darkness. The first room I explored was followed by another and yet another. The floor under my feet was precarious. I felt my way forward and found a corridor. There was light at the end of it.

I continued to stumble, and when I got to the end, I was in a room which was not as dim as the others—but neither was it light. Perhaps it was more of a hall or an assembly room rather than just a room. Dotted around the place stood damaged pillars with bits kicked off them—pillars reaching for the ceiling. The light came in through windows where the boarding had been ripped out and through all sorts of cracks and other holes in the walls. Large puddles of water had pooled together on the floor from rain that had seeped in through the holes and cracks in the roof. Spray-paint cans were floating in the puddles like people on holiday relaxing in a hotel swimming pool. The water was yellow and looked toxic.

I was not alone in the room.

A boy was bustling about in there.

He was doing something familiar. He was building a ramp. He had already piled the trash up into a fairly high heap onto which he was now rolling a barrel. When the barrel was in place, he dragged a large box on top of the heap. Then he ran to pick up his skateboard, raised his foot onto it, and kicked it into motion.

He started to practice.

I stepped closer into the shadow of a pillar. I stood there with a dreadlock between my teeth. I had an absurd habit of gnawing on my hair. I also ate coat and sweater sleeve cuffs and all sorts of other things that hung down.

When the boy pushed up into the air, I nearly bit my tongue and choked. He was good—that was for sure. Truth was, he was *really* good. I watched the jumping for a while, but soon I couldn't contain myself any longer and stepped forward bravely. Of course, the floor creaked underneath me. If you haven't noticed before, floors, stairs, and doors always creak in these sorts of situations.

The boy now noticed me. He flipped the board into his hand and waited for me to get closer. I went up to him.

"Hi," the boy said.

"Hi," I said.

The boy frowned.

"I was wondering how long you were going to spy on me," he said.

I bit my lip, surprised. The boy had known I was there. He had noticed me ages ago. Maybe he had known about me even when I stepped inside the factory and stumbled in the dark to watch him skate.

"Can I have a go?" I asked and pointed at the board.

I was quite direct and impolite, but truthfully, I could already see myself up in the air doing extremely complicated tricks and couldn't wait any longer. My insides were fluttering, as if someone were inside me playing some mysterious instrument. I missed having a board underneath me with all of my being.

The boy looked at his board for a while with a wrinkled brow, like people who are deep in thought often do, considering causes and effects and who knew what else. He was copper-colored, with messy hair, and looked a bit like Mowgli in that jungle cartoon. Luckily he soon handed me his board and smiled.

"There you go," he said. "Do you want me to show you? It's a bit—"

"I know how," I interrupted him and took the board confidently.

I dropped it on the ground and jumped on. Then I started toward the ramp.

The boy stood behind me the whole time.

When I tried to get onto the ramp, I fell. I think I even swore a bit, but then I tried again. Actually I attempted the jump several times without succeeding once. It felt like the boy had put a spell on the ramp. I couldn't even manage the tricks that were normally child's play to me.

In spite of this, the boy didn't laugh at me. He just looked at me with his hair over his eyes.

I fell all over the place.

"I can't understand this," I snapped. "I'm not really this pathetic."

"That's what they all say," the boy said and took the board from me. "It's difficult if you're afraid."

Now I really started to feel irritated. "I'm not scared," I grunted.

The boy shrugged his shoulders and then executed a jump that looked easy.

I gulped and snatched his board again. As I was setting off, the boy whistled, and I fell. It didn't matter that I fell onto my belly into a toxic yellow puddle of water. It didn't matter that I was hurt. I still lost my temper, and suddenly I did something I shouldn't have done. I smashed the boy's skateboard.

I jumped on it, and it snapped—just like that, as easy as a wood shaving or cracker bread. I didn't do it on purpose. For some reason, I felt like saying it was an accident.

The boy didn't think it was an accident.

"No! Stop!" he shouted and lunged for the board. He pressed the halves into his lap. "You shouldn't have done that," he said.

I hung my head. "Sorry," I whispered sadly.

"I have to go," the boy said and got up.

"Truly, I didn't—sometimes you just can't help it."

"I have to go," he said again and ran into the shadows. Quite soon all I could hear was his footsteps.

"Wait!" I shouted and ran after him. The boy ran ahead of me nimbly, as if he were born in the damp, dirty factory. He clearly knew the place. It was difficult to keep up with him.

"Hey, wait!" I yelled again.

I wanted to make amends somehow. Thousands of ideas whirled around in my head like an upbeat music video. None of them was very useful.

"Who are you anyway?" I shouted. "Who are you?"

He didn't reply.

When we got to the yard, it was already dusk. I wondered what darkness would look like if it were not darkness, but an object. I didn't want to think about the broken skateboard, but I couldn't help it. The boy was still clutching it, and then suddenly, he pushed it into my arms.

"You can have it," he said.

"What?"

The boy glanced over his shoulder at the thicket growing at the edge of the site.

"You'll need it," he continued. "Don't lose it! Don't show it to anyone. I'm going now."

"Boy, hey, wait!" I called after him. "What's your name?"

Then he turned around. He gave me a long look with his head tilted and laughed. "You think I'm a boy? You must be blind."

He pushed the hair off his muddy face and wiped it with his sleeve, which only resulted in more mess. I squinted, and then something happened. The stranger started to look like a girl. Of course, she wasn't the kind of girl I was used to—not the kind of girl I met at school, and especially not like the girls in the School of Possibilities. But she was certainly a girl.

Before I had a chance to think this through, a train thundered by us. I glanced at it, because that was what I always did, and almost right away, I turned back to the girl.

She had disappeared.

"Where did you go?" I shouted. "Where are you?"

But the girl didn't answer or reappear. The only thing in the yard reminding me of her was the skateboard in my hands.

"Sorry!" I shouted. There was no reply. I peeked inside the factory again. "Sorry!" I shouted through a crack in the door, but no one answered. Then I picked up the skateboard and took a better look at it. It had been a fine skateboard, but now all it was good for was spare parts. I pushed it into my bag.

All around was darkness. The trash heaps had turned into shadows, and the factory looked like a black hole that could suck you in. The whole place began to terrify me, and then, of course, I started to think about home. But because I had two of them, for a while, I couldn't decide which one to think about, let alone which one to go to. That made me feel a bit weird, and I almost stopped being scared. I decided to go to Mom's. Before I left, I scrawled a tiny signature on a rotten piece of wood, and then I sped off.

6.

Mom lives downtown in an apartment building at least a hundred years old. The stairway often smells of all sorts of food, like chicken or sausage. There is an empty shop in the basement where bands often practice. You can hear right away that no one really knows how to play and that playing is just an excuse to hang out in the basement. When you meet the "musicians" on the stairs, they are usually pale and wearing sunglasses. They always wear shades, even in winter and at night. Apart from them, there are only old people on Mom's staircase. Quite a few of them play organ music from morning until night and sing in frail voices, as they were doing that day.

Thankfully, I had a key to Mom's apartment.

When you step inside, you have to push your way deep into a jungle, because the hall and other rooms are thick with wedding dresses hanging from the ceiling. They are long gowns with trains and wide skirts, netting, and frills. I pushed them out of the way as I headed for the kitchen. The dresses swished and rustled around me like reeds made from silk.

"You came!" Mom shouted. The shout was a bit muffled, because she had pins between her lips.

A woman stood on the table. She was large, but the dress made her look even larger. I felt a bit sorry for the table, which groaned underneath her and the dress.

"I was worried about you," Mom said a little accusingly, and a couple of pins fell to the floor. Then she thrust a pair of binoculars into my hand. "This is the surprise. You can see in the dark with them."

"Binoculars!" I exclaimed.

Both women looked at me intently, as if they were waiting for something. I said thanks and bowed a little.

"Don't look so miserable," Mom laughed. "These are very special binoculars. They're real, not a toy. You can look at the stars with them. Do you like them?"

I weighed the binoculars in my hand. "They're really great."

"The best you can get," Mom assured me enthusiastically. "Just what you need when you're looking for brightness in the sky at night. They bring the stars closer."

I didn't want the stars to get any closer.

"Must have been really expensive," I said cautiously. "Can you afford something like this?"

Mom immediately looked uneasy. I guessed that the binoculars were bought on credit and that Mom couldn't afford them and would be eating cabbage soup for the next few days.

She smiled at me tensely. "Don't you worry about that," she said, although, of course, I couldn't just stop thinking whenever she ordered me to.

The tulle-clad whale moved on the table. "You have a nice mom," she said.

I put the binoculars to my eyes. Immediately the bolts of cloth in the corner of the kitchen, weighing tons, were brought closer. Mom was a seamstress and loved fabrics, but she loathed wedding dresses and colorless white tulle.

No, let's rewind.

Mom was a dress designer who could also sew. She would have liked to design clothes herself and make special garments with trimmings, unusual materials, colors, and details, which would make an outfit almost a work of art. Because there were so few grand parties and even fewer masked balls, such clothes were hardly ever ordered, and so Mom had to make wedding dresses. The wedding dresses were often all the same. For some reason, women wanted to look like princesses at weddings. Mom hated wedding dresses, which did not surprise me in the least. Clients

often changed their minds many times before the dress was finished. Then Mom would lose her patience and want to stick a pin into the clients.

I flopped down on the floor to adjust the settings on the binoculars. Although the present was a good one, I was a bit wary of it, as I was of all presents. They always led to complications. Now, for example, Dad might be offended and feel left out. "Don't you get everything you need from me, Storm?" he might ask.

This sort of thing happened all the time.

The truth was that presents were dangerous—a bit like ticking bombs. I wouldn't be surprised if murders had been committed and limbs cut off because of presents.

I put the binoculars to my eyes and looked at things in the room.

At first I pointed them at the kitchen door and saw a heap of dirty dishes in the sink, a map of the London Underground, a photograph of me on the refrigerator door riding a tricycle at three years old, and wedding dresses hanging from the curtain pole, ceiling light, cupboard door, and plant hanger. Then I saw sleeves and bodices cut out of white silk in a heap under the table, and patterns and pins on the floor.

I turned to look at Mom. Of course the binoculars made her bigger, too. The pores of her skin were like craters on the surface of the moon, and her mouth was full of teeth like boulders.

"Thanks," I said.

"Do you like them?" Mom asked again, and I nodded.

Finally Mom's client left, and we ate ice cream.

"Rita is a good client. I'll make a lot of money for this," Mom said and fingered the hem of the wedding dress lying on the table. There was more fabric in that garment than there was in a four-man tent. "Rita wants to look like a princess."

"Don't they all?" I said, rolling my eyes, which made Mom laugh. "Why do you make wedding dresses? Why don't you make costumes for space movies instead?

Mom ruffled my hair and said, "They never make space movies in this country; but most people want to get married, and they don't worry about counting the cents."

I pointed the binoculars at the harbor. There was the tower, standing, waiting. It stood in darkness, just a black shadow beyond the roofs.

"You're smiling," Mom said and hugged me. "I always know when something's happened to you. Tell me about it."

I quickly moved the binoculars away from the factory and pointed them toward the black sea. It wouldn't be sensible to tell Mom about the girl and the factory, because at least the factory—and maybe the girl, as well—would frighten her. She would try to prevent me from going there again. And I wanted to go back.

In any case, I had an idea. I decided to take the binoculars to the factory.

"Are these on the approved list at school?" I asked Mom.

Immediately Mom nodded eagerly. "The headmaster approves of binoculars. When I called your school, he was quite excited about them. He said that you could join the Possibilities' Observers. It's a kind of—"

I interrupted Mom by bursting out into laughter. "What do they observe? Possibilities?"

Mom nodded. "It's astronomy," she said. "Every star is a part of the universe and, in a way, like a small possibility. That's what the headmaster said, and it sounded quite beautiful."

I raised my hand. "Stars are not possibilities, but the past," I said. "The light shining from them is millions of years old."

"What on earth are you talking about now?" Mom laughed.

"Just that the stars we can now see with these binoculars probably expired a long time ago." I then picked out a star and looked at it very carefully. "Even that brilliant star there may have collapsed millions of years ago, but we can still see it."

"Don't try to be so smart," Mom said. "The astronomy club leader is that nice young man."

"Meaning who?" I asked, worried.

"Mr. Reed, of course. Don't you like him?"

"He's better than Poole, but only by a whisker."

"He seems quite multitalented," Mom said and looked funny, almost as if she was dreaming. Right away I was worried.

"Even so, you better not fall for that guy," I said quickly.

Mom fell for men really easily—too easily. Anyway she was now shaking her head and laughing. "No, I won't," she said. "And in any case, I don't think Mr. Reed would have the time for anything like that."

This was too vague an answer for me.

"Do you promise?" I demanded.

"I promise," Mom said, holding up her hands. "Everything will be all right. Believe me."

"Perhaps," I said. "Now I have to call Dad."

7.

The following day we had to choose our hobbies. Rob Reed was the leader of almost every group. He didn't lead the girls' ballet group, but he coached the soccer players and taught porcelain painting, bird behavior, making and sanding bread boards, medieval jewelry making, and guitar playing.

All this and more became obvious when he handed the list out to the class. "Everyone must choose at least two hobbies," Rob said encouragingly.

Quite soon, however, I noticed that my hobbies were already marked on the list. I didn't shout out any objections. I was still crushed by the morning. The day had started miserably. Right after morning assembly, the teacher had drawn three new lines on my gallows as punishment for the messy changing room and for not turning up at the meeting place where my new friend Will had been waiting for me. I had also been ordered to clean up the changing room, which had taken at least two hours and turned my stomach, as well.

At some point Rob noticed my gallows. "Seven lines means that punishment is approaching," he informed me, smiling. "The first set of gallows always goes up faster than the ones that follow. The human animal is a fast learner."

I concentrated on my list so I wouldn't have to look at Rob's endless smile. At the top of the paper, it said: *Useful ways to fill one's time.* Halfway down the list came porcelain painting. *Getting to know the equipment. Drawing skills not necessary. The themes are floral arrangements and...*

I put my hand up and then asked, "What use is painting floral arrangements onto porcelain plates?"

Rob calmly interlaced his fingers and looked at me. "It develops concentration, and concentration increases the ability to learn," he said.

Porcelain painting was not marked on my list. That was good. If I had a brush in my hand, I would have painted foxes in a hen-house on my plate. I looked out to the yard and through the fence at the factory. I thought about the girl. Who was she? Was she at school now? Which school did she go to? All children went to school, so she must surely go to some school.

"As you have probably noticed, you don't have to choose," Rob's voice interrupted my thoughts. "Your parents have enrolled you with the Possibilities' Observers and Friends of the Fish."

I had noticed this and said, "I don't like fish."

"You will," Rob assured me. He tapped his finger on the list where it said that fish were delightful. "Your father will tell you more about that subject."

8.

After school I crept to the glass case where my skateboard was imprisoned. It lay there among other confiscated items like an object whose purpose had been forgotten an eternity ago. I pressed my finger against the case.

"It's armored glass," said the cleaner who was polishing the floor around me. She poked my feet with her brush, and I jumped out of the way. The lock on the case was as big as a demolition ball and looked pretty strong.

"There are security cameras, as well," Will's toneless voice said behind my back. He had followed me. The guy walked around right on my heels, as if we were connected by an invisible thread. "Shall we go? Hanging around school gets you a line on the gallows, and you can't afford that."

On the way out, we wrote our new hobbies on the school's communal notice board that hung on the corridor wall. I stared at the schedule for a long while. My life was changing into a list of times and dates. The new school not only had a schedule for lessons but also one for leisure activities. Today I would go and examine the stars for the first time, and tomorrow's program was about fish.

We soon headed home. Most of the time, we didn't speak. Will's hobbies were soccer, stargazing, and porcelain painting. He must have been the weirdest boy I had ever come across. I walked as fast as my legs would carry me in order to get rid of him. "See you tonight at the Observers," he called before he disappeared around the corner.

When I got home, Dad was leaving for work. I pointed the binoculars at him.

"What's that?" Dad asked.

"A present from Mom," I answered cruelly, because I was angry with Dad about the fish club, which he had something to do with.

"I have a present for you, as well," Dad replied with equal cruelty and gestured for me to accompany him. Dad's present turned out to be an aquarium. The mystery of the fish club was solved.

"You enrolled me in that club," I noted, raising my eyebrows.

The aquarium rested on the desk between us. It was so big that it left no room for anything else. "You'll get your own goldfish," Dad answered. "Or even two. A whole shoal."

"The goldfish is not a shoal fish," I said. "I don't want to be friends with a fish. I want to skate."

Dad placed a big shell on the bottom of the aquarium. "Fish must not be left for long. They have to be looked after," Dad said. "Fish are like small children and need someone to take care of them."

"Thanks, Dad, really nice of you," I said.

"The aquarium is on the list of approved hobbies," Dad said. "The headmaster thinks that a difficult child needs things to love. It calms him down."

"You can't love fish."

Dad looked astonished. "Every living creature needs love, Storm."

I couldn't be bothered to argue with him. The fact remained that I could never love a slimy, brainless creature that kept opening its mouth and looked stupid, which it was. "Who looks after the fish when I'm at Mom's?" I asked.

"Mona can do that," Dad said and put his hand on my shoulder. "I do think, however, that it would be best for you to be here as much as possible to take care of the fish yourself. I wouldn't trust Mona. I don't think she would have the patience to dish out the right amount of food. She doesn't seem to like fish. It would almost be like letting a cat get its claws on the aquarium. Perhaps some days, instead of going to Mom's, you could stay here and look after the fish."

I frowned and stared at the aquarium. Eventually I said, "I don't know."

"Think about it."

Then Dad went into the hall and put on his shoes. At the door he bumped into Verity Poole. Poole stepped past Dad into the hall and fixed me with her eyes. She had extremely sharp eyes. Obviously I had done something, and it would soon become clear what it was. "You have continued to deface," Poole said, forcing her voice to stay calm.

Dad turned to look at me. "Have you been defacing again?" he said and sighed.

"Defacing?" I repeated and shook my head. I didn't understand any of this.

"What has happened, Verity?" Dad asked, concerned.

"Our staircase has been defaced, and I can think of no other culprit than your son," Poole answered.

I followed her into the corridor.

Welcome to the amusement park, it said on the wall. The text was surrounded by a beautiful sun colored yellow, red, and blue.

I had seen it all before. I was astonished. It was hard for me to control my expression. Although the sun was only paint, it was lighting up the dark corridor, in a way. The girl from the factory had been here. She had been here a moment ago and knew where I lived, which was strange, to say the least.

"Well?" Poole was waiting and tapping the floor with the toe of her shoe, her hands on her hips.

I shook my head. "I didn't do it," I answered.

"Who then? The blind pianist from the third floor?" Poole's voice rang with a mocking tone as she said, "I'd say the boy is lying."

Dad started to cough, and I shook my head vigorously and said, "I didn't do it. I didn't. I didn't. I didn't!"

Poole stared at me. "I am going to watch you, Storm," she said and turned to look at Dad. "We are going to watch him, Vladimir. If this sort of thing continues, I will have to report it to the school."

When Dad left for work with Poole close behind, I knew what to do.

Welcome to the amusement park? The graffiti was an invitation. It also meant that I had been forgiven—or at least given the opportunity to make amends.

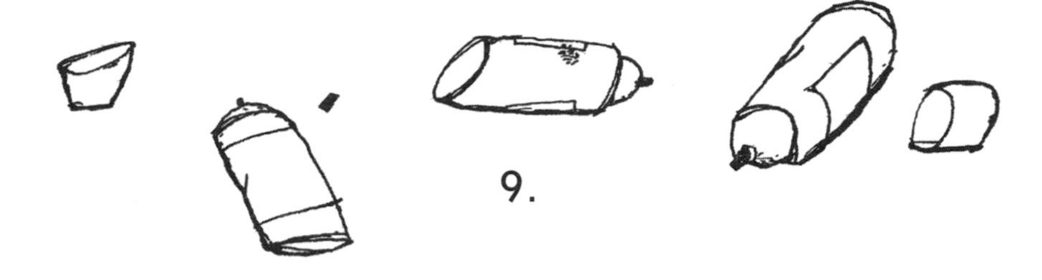

9.

The girl wasn't at the factory when I got there, but she had been. New pictures had appeared on the wall, one of them being a huge open mouth smiling. The colors of the pictures were freshly painted and still bright. I saw a heap of empty paint cans on the floor.

It was quiet.

What if the message on the wall of our staircase was a threat? *I can see you. I know where you live. Beware!* I shook my head. It wasn't possible.

I picked up one of the cans. It said "Desert Yellow" on the side. I shook it and pressed the button on the top. A spray of paint hit the floor. Luckily it wasn't empty.

WHO ARE YOU? I sprayed on the picture, and as I remembered the binoculars in my backpack, I added underneath: DO YOU WANT TO SEE THE STARS? I signed my name: STORM.

I had to use the leftovers of five different paints. Then I hung the binoculars on the wall and ran out of the factory.

10.

My gallows were complete, and I suffered my first punishment.

"I am your new girlfriend," a voice said behind me, and someone took me firmly by the elbow.

A girl with a pointed nose had appeared next to me. It took me a while to realize that she was from the same class. Her coordinates were something like the following: the desk at the front, window row. Description: a keen math fan. The hand went up for every question. Motto: "Me, me. May I answer, ma'am?"

"I'm Bridget," the girl said. "You can take me out for an ice cream today."

We stared at each other for a moment. I was speechless—almost.

"Listen here..." I said. "What was your name again?"

"Bridget," she replied.

"Listen, Bridget," I started again, slowly and deliberately so that she would really get the picture. "There's been some misunderstanding here. You're mistaking me for someone else. I don't date under any circumstances."

My student mentor and supposed friend, Will, then appeared behind Bridget. "Your gallows are complete," he said.

"Your gallows are complete," the teacher also said during the next lesson. "Punishment number one is a new girlfriend. We experimented with girlfriends for the first time a year ago, and the results have been promising. Before you protest, listen to this. The punishments certainly won't get any lighter. If you have any questions, go and see the headmaster in his office. You'd better take note, though, that the headmaster believes in the power of feelings, fish, girlfriends, and pets. No complaint has ever been accepted. The headmaster especially believes in this girlfriend we have chosen for you."

I slumped back into my desk.

"The girlfriend will help you with your homework and keep you company. She will also look after you. In a couple of weeks, you will realize that you can hardly manage without her."

I stared at the teacher in disbelief. This wasn't real, was it? It couldn't be. In my previous schools, they sat quiet students next to disruptive ones. The disruptive ones were usually boys, and the quiet ones were usually girls. There was never any mention of love. The idea was simply that the quiet ones would calm the disruptive ones down. It didn't work very well.

"But I don't even know this...this..." I managed to say, searching for the name that I had forgotten again. "I don't like her."

"Liking will come in time," the teacher said and started to spread her papers out on her desk. "Move over and sit next to your new girlfriend. We are now going to talk about the French Revolution."

The teacher motioned to Will and Alexander to help me. They pushed my desk into its new position right next to Bridget's. Luckily this was also right by the window. I sat down and felt sort of giddy and panicky. My new girlfriend opened up my history book at the right place and underlined a sentence in it.

Amid all this great despair, I had a new idea. "Teacher!" I called out and waved my arm so hard that it nearly fell out of its socket.

"Would someone tell us where the revolution began? What can be considered to be the starting point?" the teacher asked. "Do tell us, Storm! Nice to see that the revolution interests you."

"I can't have two girlfriends!" I answered.

The teacher put her book down on the desk and stared at me.

"I already have one. In this country you can only have one girlfriend at a time." I smiled triumphantly.

The teacher wasn't interested in revolutionary slogans any longer. "All relationships are broken off when you join the School of Possibilities," she said.

"But we only met a couple of days ago," I said. "We look at the stars together," I added hastily, bending the truth.

The teacher continued to stand still and stare at me. In fact, the whole class stared. It was one of those things you could feel on your skin. Then the teacher got out her phone, sent a text message, received one in reply, and said, "Rob Reed is waiting for you in the office."

Rob Reed was tapping the edge of the table with a pen. He wanted to know who the girl was and where I had met her and whether or not I understood that the school would provide me with friends. "You will not be left alone here," he said.

To me it sounded more like a threat than a consolation, which was what it was meant to be.

At first I said nothing, but in the end, I lied and said that I had made up the story about the girl, that I didn't really know anyone, that I had gotten the idea into my head because of the desperate situation from which there seemed no escape. Rob appeared to swallow my story. Part of it was actually true, as it always was with a good lie. I didn't have a girlfriend. I buried my head in my hands. Rob patted me on the shoulder.

"I understand," he said and handed me two free tickets to the movies. "Take your girl out. It's a start."

I took the tickets and shoved them into my pocket. I didn't want anything to start. I didn't want to go out with a girl chosen by someone else because my gallows were complete. When I stood up to leave, Rob reminded me not to forget about the Friends of the Fish. "You didn't join us to plan our fall trip to the star observatory," he said and looked displeased. "You'll have to be more careful with fish. Stars will wait. Fish won't. On the weekend, we are going upstream, fishing with lures."

"Yeah, yeah, yeah," I said and jumped up.

"Before you go, could you kindly return my pen you took a moment ago? It has sentimental value," Rob said.

I was pretty sure he had extra eyes in the back of his head.

I threw the pen across the room, and Rob caught it. As I closed the door behind me, I thought that I had lost another round, that I had been tricked by the rules.

11.

Of course I ended up sitting in the shopping mall ice cream parlor after school at three o'clock, doing homework with my new girlfriend. I kept my hood firmly over my eyes in case any buddies—or enemies—from my previous school were around. Both were often here hanging out. I used to hang around here myself before my move to the School of Possibilities.

I didn't know what the homework topic was: subject, predicate, trading ships, peace treaties, or turnip growing. I said, "Yeah, yeah, yeah," to everything and was unable to concentrate. I spun around in my chair as if I were riding in a carousel and looked at the people around me. There were a lot of them, and they were everywhere. They charged here and there, dangling bags, backpacks, briefcases, and children in their hands. They dodged each other, and every now and then, they collided like balls in a game.

And then I saw the girl again.

She was standing in front of the hamburger bar among the green leaves with her hair over her eyes. It was quite an awesome sight. I thought that the shrubs were plastic—they looked plastic, anyway—but there was nothing fake about the girl herself. She was a bit like a hungry tiger stalking the crowd in the shopping mall.

I wondered what the girl was doing here, and evidently I seemed distracted, because Bridget soon started to tug at my sleeve. There is nothing more irritating than people who tug at your sleeve.

"What is it, Storm?" she asked.

I looked at her with sleepy eyes, as if I had just woken up from a coma, and laid a hand on her book. "I just remembered something extremely important. I have to go."

Bridget jumped up. "But the movie!" she cried out.

"Take some friend of yours," I suggested and thrust the crumpled tickets at her. Then I threw my books into my backpack and, with a rather stylish leap, I bounced over the ice cream parlor railing.

"Storm!" Bridget called after me. "Stooorm! Come back!"

Comeback? There was a dog called that in some movie. In one scene, when they wanted the dog to go away, they said to it, "Go away, Comeback."

At this stage I was already hurtling furiously toward the fake plants outside the hamburger bar.

The girl did not stop to wait. She, too, had started to sprint.

"Wait!" I shouted. "Don't go!"

There was something on the floor on the spot where the girl had stood a moment earlier. It was a lollipop. I picked it up and started to stride in her direction. I caught glimpses of her fuzzy hair.

It's not easy to run in a crowd of people—not if you are twelve. You get hit by various objects, all sorts of stunning blows from umbrellas, bags, and elbows all the time. Anyone can batter a twelve-year-old. In this tidal wave, I drifted toward the girl, and every time I thought I had lost her, I saw glimpses of her among the coats, trouser legs, and boots. This carried on until I tripped. It just happened—a bit like trips in the movies. The hero always wants to catch someone but does a belly flop by accident. I fell and slid into the wall between the elevator and the trash can. I hurt my knee, my side, and both elbows.

"Kids! Always charging around," someone big and hairy said above me in an angry voice.

I didn't care.

I stared at my tripper.

There were two of them. They looked misleadingly like mirror images of each other—two small boys in baggy trousers and hoodies, two boys so alike that, for a moment, I thought I was confused by the bang on the head and had started to see double.

"Hi, hi, hi," they greeted in stereo.

"Yeah, hi," I said and glanced around me, but the girl had disappeared. "Did you see…?"

The boys looked at me with their bright eyes. "Yes, we did," they said.

I turned around to look at them again, more closely this time. "What did you two say?" I asked.

The boys looked at each other, and then one of them took me by the hand. He squeezed it, and for some reason, I trusted him.

"What's the matter? What do you want? Have you lost your mom?" I asked.

The boy looked at his brother and made some sort of a happy victory sign. Then they both turned together to stare at me again. They looked seven or eight years old at the most. "India told us to give you this," one of the boys said and handed me a piece of paper.

"India? Did you say India?"

Both nodded enthusiastically.

"India, India!" they said. "She was here just now."

"I know that name," I said, amazed.

The boys glanced at each other and smiled. "We know it, too," they said.

I shook my head. Were we really talking about the same girl? "Is India…is she the skater girl?"

The boys nodded. "India is our friend."

"And who are you?"

"That's Moon, and he's my brother," one said.

"And this is Ra, my brother," the other said.

"We are *moo*-dy," Ra said.

"*Ra*-ging," Moon added.

"We are also twins," they said in unison.

Then they both beat their skinny chests like little monkeys. They knew something I wanted to know—and would find out if only I knew how to ask.

"Can we have some of those?" Ra said and tugged my sleeve. He had noticed the doughnut shop. Underneath a glass dome, there were dozens of doughnut rings and hearts covered with pink, black, and brown icing and sprinkles on top.

"I don't have any money," I said and snatched my hand away.

Suddenly in the crowd, I saw something familiarly red and heard someone call, "Stooorm!"

"Who's that?" the boys asked and looked around.

"Bridget," I replied.

"Who, who? What Bridget? Is she someone dangerous?"

"Very dangerous. Run!" I hissed, and we did, really fast.

When we had reached safety in a jeans shop, we hid between two clothing rails.

"Are we saved?" Moon puffed.

I took hold of his shoulders and squeezed him. "What do you know about India? Tell me right now!"

The boy was holding a box that his brother immediately opened. It contained a batch of doughnuts. Ra picked out a doughnut decorated with pink icing and pushed it between his brother's teeth so he couldn't answer my question.

"Lovely," Moon said when he was able to speak again.

Ra also took a large bite out of the doughnut. "Doesn't taste of carrot," he said.

"Or potato," Moon added.

"Where did you get them?" I asked.

"I found them," Moon said, his mouth full and its corners covered in sugar. "They were lying on a table, and no one wanted them. Do you?"

I shook my head. The boy had swiped them from a customer, of course, and now we had an angry customer, as well as my new girlfriend, and goodness knew who else, after us. "Stupid kids," I cried out. "Don't you understand? I'm going to get into trouble over this and maybe get—" I thought for a moment and then continued, "a new girlfriend who can run faster, a real leech."

"Wow!" the boys said.

I grabbed hold of Moon's shoulders again and shook him. "Tell me about India. Who is she?"

"India's in our gang," Moon answered.

"India knows how to trap," Ra added.

"She's a hunter."

"She can see in the dark."

My eyes rolled. They really did.

"Where is she now?" I asked.

"On a raid," Ra said. "Getting food."

"And a new board," Moon explained. "Someone broke the old one."

"We suspect an enemy."

"There are lots of them."

"Everywhere."

"Did India say so—that it was an enemy?" I asked rather quietly.

Moon and Ra glanced at each other and shook their heads. "India sent this for you," Moon then said and pushed a crumpled piece of paper into my hand.

I opened it with impatient fingers.

CLIMB THE STAIRS was all that it said.

"Nothing else?" I asked.

Moon pushed his head closer.

"What does it say?" he asked.

"Confidential," I said. I scrunched the paper up in my hand and shoved it into my pocket. Suddenly I saw something that made me go cold. Verity Poole was approaching the rack under which we were crouching. Mona was walking next to her. For a moment I considered a lightning retreat, but they had both already spotted me and were striding closer.

"Moon? Ra?" I hissed, but the boys were nowhere to be seen. They had vanished.

All that was left was an almost empty doughnut box on the floor.

"Doughnuts?" Poole said and picked up the box. "Where did you get the money?" She speared a doughnut with her long finger and lifted it up into the air. "No, don't answer that," she said. "I can guess. You stole them."

I shook my head.

The only thing missing from the scene was Bridget, who soon arrived.

"I called your mother," she said. She was out of breath after she had to chase me around the shopping mall.

"You called my mom?"

Bridget glanced at Verity Poole, who nodded.

"I mean, your stepmother. I told her that you disappeared and—"

Verity Poole lowered her hand on Bridget's shoulder.

"No need to blush, child," she said. "You acted correctly. This is exactly the task you have been chosen to do. A girlfriend must always be alert. This sort of thing frequently happens with impossible boys. It will decrease with time."

I went to the movies with Bridget. In fact, Verity Poole and Mona walked us to the movie theater and made sure that we stepped into the dimness of the theater.

The movie was boring and meant for kindergarten kids. In the film, animated fish were busy doing something I couldn't concentrate on, and every so often, there was singing. I thought about the stairs the whole time.

Climb the stairs. Climb the stairs. What did India mean by that?

I thought about those three words so feverishly that when Bridget tried to push her hand into mine after the movie, I instinctively said, "Climb the stairs," to her by mistake.

"See you tomorrow," she said and waved when we parted.

"Until tomorrow," I said lamely with my hand on my forehead, as if I were a soldier who was about to be shot in a hail of bullets.

Some might have called my situation a trap.

12.

The next day was difficult, mainly because Bridget was on my heels the whole time. She seemed to have completely abandoned her former life and friends. She only had the patience to stay with them for about five minutes, after which she rushed to me like a gun dog that had picked up the scent of blood. Will also kept a close eye on what I was doing.

When I went to Rob at lunch break to report on my first date, my obedience was rewarded with complimentary tickets to an ice-dancing performance. *Disney on Ice. Experience an unforgettable magical journey.*

"The School of Possibilities gives young love an opportunity," Rob said and winked.

"Who's the third ticket for?"

"Will is going to be a chaperone."

"A chaperone?"

"He will see that things don't get out of hand," Rob said and winked.

Get out of hand? The man must have been crazy.

I was relieved that Will would be with us, but I didn't let on. I kept a perfect poker face. If Rob didn't realize that Will would protect me from Bridget's attempts to kiss me, I wasn't about to enlighten him. Don't get me wrong, I didn't dislike kissing or girls—not all of them, anyway. I didn't actually kiss that often. To tell you the truth, I'd never kissed anyone. I would maybe kiss a girl if a suitable occasion or a suitable girl came along, but I would absolutely want to make the decision myself. It was important to make those sorts of decisions yourself.

I shoved the tickets into my pocket and made a quick exit. *Experience an unforgettable magical journey*. Indeed.

Both my guards were excited about the ice theater. Afterward they walked me back to my neighborhood. Before I entered the stairway, I glanced over my shoulder and saw Will sending a text message—probably compiling a report to Rob Reed. At home I was met by Dad holding a transparent bag with some fish swimming around in it and Mona filling the aquarium. Dad was in the middle of giving a lecture about fish, and Mona was listening. She listened because she knew it would annoy me. I was not jealous of Mona, but in my opinion, people should always stick with their own parents.

"These fish will fall in love with me and forget all about you, prince," Mona said after Dad had closed the door behind him. She smiled at the fish through the glass of the aquarium. If I were a fish, that kind of grimacing would drive me mad.

"I'm completely indifferent to those fish. You can eat them, if you want. The main thing is that you buzz off."

I wanted Mona out of the room. I wanted to study India's letter in peace. Of course Mona didn't leave. Mona was not the type who could be easily gotten rid of. She often reminded me of those resistant viruses that spread like wildfire and keep their victims out of action for weeks.

"Go!" I ordered. "Clear off, and get out of my sight! Thank you."

"I can't. The fish will miss me."

See, I couldn't get rid of her; she had to be thrown out, so I threw her out. It wasn't easy, because I was quite small, and fourteen-year-old girls are big and difficult to shift—at least when they don't want to be moved. I tried all the techniques I knew, and Mona did everything she could to thwart me. She tried to cling onto everything in the room and succeeded.

"Fatso," I hissed.

Hearing that, Mona answered with her fist. Mona's fists are no joke. They are really hard, because she wears a ring on every finger, and they work a bit like brass knuckles. Did I mention that Mona also strangled me and bit my arm?

"I'll tell your dad!" she yelled through the door when I had gotten her out and managed to shut it between us at long last.

"And I'll tell the veterinary surgeon that you have rabies," I yelled back.

We both hammered the door.

"You'll get to feel my fists yet," she threatened.

"You'll be put in quarantine," I replied.

When Mona finally calmed down, which took a while, I propped a chair in front of the door and spread India's piece of paper out in front of me on the windowsill.

CLIMB THE STAIRS, it said.

What did it mean?

Climb?

I stared out the window, and then it occurred to me—the tower. Yes, of course. I slammed my fist down on the sill. I had solved the puzzle. India had climbed up the tower to look at the stars and wanted me there.

There are many ways to tell this story. Now it sounds like a love story, but believe me, it isn't. I was not in love. I was not talking about that. Or...I don't know. Maybe I *was* in love, though I didn't know what with. Maybe with the factory. It was so amazing and outside of everything. I thought of it as freedom.

Suddenly I was in a really good mood and full of energy.

I waited patiently for supper, and when it arrived at the table, I tried to tell everyone something vague about my class soccer training, and my buddy who was the captain of the team waiting for me in the parking lot. I described Will as a solid friend, which was actually a bit rich. Dad, however, suspected nothing and was so pleased for me that I almost felt bad about lying as I scurried into the stairway after the meal.

13.

There wasn't much light left in the factory yard when I finally got there. Rain was slashing down horizontally, and the sky was a sickly gray. I had thought about an action plan all the way there. I needed to find those stairs, at the very least. Without them I would make no progress.

I circled the factory like a burglar hot on the scent of loot and finally found some steps by the wall. They were almost hidden among overgrown vegetation and actually turned out to be part of a ladder. The ladder was so badly rusted that it could barely support the weight of a falling leaf, and definitely not a twelve-year-old boy—not even a pretty light boy like me.

The factory windows stared at me, black and broken. It seemed a bit like the place was saying, *Run away, boy. You don't belong here. We don't need you. No one needs you. Go. Run. Vanish.* I didn't listen, but instead, I peeked inside the factory through every possible hole and crack. It was so dark that I needed my flashlight again. When I shook it, it came on, and when I shook it some more, it finally stopped flickering so that I was able to light the room opening up in front of me.

The factory is such a peculiar place that inside it, you instantly lose all sense of direction and proportion. You stand still for a moment, no longer sure about where you are going or where you have come from. The factory is a world of its own. There are no such sounds anywhere else.

When I found a sturdier ladder inside, I decided to climb it, although the rungs were also rusted and broke in my hands. I wedged the flashlight between my teeth. Any amount of light was never enough in a place like this. The flashlight lit up the walls, on which were written things: DON'T FALL ASLEEP; I SEE DEAD PEOPLE; THEO & MIMI; JENNA; JAN; TIM; I WAS HERE, and then various dates scrawled underneath the names. Judging from the dates, the place had been empty for a long time—twenty or thirty years. During that time all sorts of children must have climbed up to write on the walls and smash their fists through the windows, then grown into adults and disappeared.

I wrote my name there, too.

I wrote, STORM WAS HERE—STILL IS.

I also drew my tag.

Then I continued upward. I hauled myself up rung by rung. At every pull, the floor fell farther behind, and I didn't want to think about what would happen to me if I fell—something horrendous, anyway.

The factory around me was quiet. The air was full of frightening possibilities. The sound of climbing could also be heard, and then, the whistle I was forced to let out, because otherwise all that darkness and silence would have been too much for me.

I kept climbing higher and higher. Suddenly my foot slipped, and then the other one did the same. I was left hanging above a void, and my heart was beating like crazy. I clutched the rung tightly with both hands, and my feet thrashed about helplessly. The flashlight fell down, of course, and clattered away somewhere. I started to yell for help. That was what people did in these situations, even though no help was at hand. Then someone grabbed my wrist and yanked. It was a surprisingly strong hold, and it pulled me up.

"Why did you use that one?" a voice puffed into my ear, and then I heard something crack away from the wall and clank into the depths.

"India?" I yelled out loud, and a hand pressed tightly over my mouth. It smelled of dust, rust, and abandoned factory—in other words, exactly what you would imagine oblivion to smell like.

"Hush," the girl hissed. "Be absolutely silent. Don't even breathe."

I saw her face. She had big black eyes and lashes like fans. Her eyes had an alert look, a bit like a wild animal. From looking at her eyes I could immediately see that her ears were listening, and that not a single rustle—absolutely nothing—would go unnoticed.

"This is dangerous territory," India whispered into my ear and switched on a light. "You move carelessly."

I looked at her, astounded.

"It's impossible to be quiet here," I said quite angrily. I was not in a good mood after the recent scare, and my wrist was almost dislocated from all the yanking.

India took hold of my shoulder. "You make as much noise as a herd of bison," she said and shook her head so that the bones and

lollipops lodged in her hair snapped and rustled. It was the most unusual hairstyle I had ever seen, except in cartoons.

"Was there something else? Because you came and scribbled on our staircase."

Sometimes I can be nasty. I didn't really think of India's pictures as scribbles. As far as I was concerned, she could have covered all the walls of the stairway and the elevator with suns and other heavenly bodies. It wouldn't have bothered me at all.

"I think I'll go," I said instead.

India looked a little sad. "Don't go," she said and took hold of my arm again. She clutched it tightly. Suddenly I noticed Mom's binoculars hanging around her neck.

"You've got them," I said, happier than I had been before.

India nodded. "They've been useful," she said and lifted the binoculars to her eyes. "You can see in the dark really well with them."

She focused past me at the yard.

"What can you see there?" I asked and looked in the same direction.

Then I knew—or guessed, at least—what India was looking at even before she lowered the binoculars and answered me. On the edge of the yard stood a battlement. It was a scrappy, lumpy structure hunched in a thicket, hulking and gloomy—so dark that it disappeared into the shadows.

"The Wall of the Lost. That's what it's called," India said.

I flinched. The Wall of the Lost? Was that what she had said?

"Do you mean that...is that the place where they leave the failed children?"

India spat over the railing. "Who says that the children have failed?"

I was unable to answer.

"What if they have been especially successful?" India continued. "What if they are the most successful of all...and the luckiest? That battlement is only a wall, really. It is a house wall, and there really is no battlement."

I couldn't see the house. I only saw the wall and, of course, the thicket.

"Where is the building?"

"There it is," India replied and pushed the binoculars over my eyes.

I couldn't see anything. It was too dark. There was too much mist and debris.

India looked at me with her head tilted and said, "There are passageways under those old cars and the grass. They are everywhere underground. This is a bit like a big winged creature, isn't it? The walls form its spine and a lot of thin bones twist under the ground. Its wings are spread, and it's asleep. This was a hospital sometime long ago. The patients were pushed along the underground passages from one wing to another on metal trolleys. Then it became a factory, and they started to make cookies here. This place has had many purposes. Now we are here."

"Who are *we*?" I wondered and still couldn't make out the hospital ruins lying beneath the walls of the tower in the twilight. I could only see a mess.

"Me and the other children. The ones you called failures," India answered. She lifted up the binoculars again and looked out. "I take care of us. I am the guard."

I was silent and looked into the night. "You are a guard? You are a hunter? What do you hunt?"

"Is that what they said?" India laughed. "Maybe I do hunt. This here is a fortress, and over there is my forest." She pointed at the city spreading out in front of us, sparkling almost like a mirror image of outer space. It probably could have also been called a desert or a jungle.

Then she became serious and took me by the shoulder. "But listen…thanks for these," she said and raised the binoculars. "You can see…as I said, they make things easier."

"Did you look at the stars?" I asked.

India looked at me as if I was especially stupid. "What would I need stars for? I was looking at the city and the school, of course. But now I really have to go."

I shoved both hands deep into my pockets and stretched them. "Is that why you invited me here? You wanted to thank me for the binoculars?" I asked.

I was disappointed, and India must have noticed. She looked at me very seriously.

"I would like to see those passages," I said. "Take me with you."

India shook her head vigorously. "You shouldn't be here. This is not a place for play."

"But you asked me to come," I said, offended.

India nodded.

"I wanted to tell you that if you ever needed help, and you might, give me a sign, and I'll come."

"A sign? What sign?"

"The skateboard. When you put the pieces in your window, I'll know you're in trouble."

I had thrown the skateboard on the closet floor among other junk, not thinking that it would serve another purpose than spare parts. I hadn't realized that I would still need it.

India was already glancing at the darkness.

"Why would you help me?" I asked. I had taken hold of her arm almost instinctively, because I was scared that she would disappear again. "I broke your board and..." I said, hesitating for a moment. "Why would you help?"

"I'm like that," India said.

"I don't like heroes."

"Me, neither."

We were silent for a while, and I wondered what it was that India was guarding, if this was a place where no one wanted to come.

"There are other things in the world apart from those you can imagine," India said then. "You not understanding everything doesn't make it magic. If you need me, I will come. Don't forget that."

She patted the binoculars hung around her neck.

Then India showed me the stairs, which opened up behind a blanket spread on the wall, and we started to feel our way down. The stairs were sturdier than the swaying bits of junk I had climbed up a moment ago. Even so I held tightly onto the handrail. I had decided that this time India would not slip away, but she did anyway.

14.

The next day a new execution device began to rise up on my hill in the punishment corner. This time it was a guillotine, because the teacher had decided to take advantage of the situation and teach the class about historical punishment methods. “When torture was stopped in France in 1791, a law was passed for all the accused to have their heads cut off mercifully and without causing pain, so the guillotine was born,” she said, drawing the frame on my hillock in red chalk.

We also learned that the head was severed in a fraction of a second and rolled into a basket. Flowers grew and butterflies flew in between the execution hills drawn on the chalkboard. They were drawn as rewards for having done something exemplary. Bridget had a whole swarm of elephant hawk moths on the board. She had earned some of them for going out with me: five moths for patience, to be exact. I had no insects or plants yet. I had only collected supporting beams and pillars on my execution hill.

After the teacher had admired the sprouting guillotine for a while, she told us to write about a place we wanted to go and about one we hated and wouldn’t want to visit under any circumstances.

"Get to know yourself," she urged and told us to close our eyes. "Think, and start writing when the music stops."

I closed my eyes and immediately started to think about trains and traveling on them, about the scenery that slides by and the places that you could see here and there from time to time: all the buildings, sheds and other hovels, small wooden villages and apartment blocks on their outskirts, outbuildings, tractors, places where people lived, and places with shutters on the windows. Once on a train, I mistook clouds for mountains. That was an extraordinary moment. The black mass of cloud looked like a chain of mountains undulating on the horizon. I imagined that there were dark passes, brightly sunlit peaks, caves, and avalanches you would have to fight to avoid being buried under by the snow and freezing to death. Then I began to think my favorite thought. It was about a city, a dream city in which I would live one day, where there would be hills, hundreds of steps and railings, thousands of ramps and ledges, and dozens of statues with pedestals suitable for skating—and not a single guard or police officer anywhere in sight. Then I moved on to think about my own city and the places inside it that were suitable for skating, which weren't many and were now all forbidden to me. And then I started again to think about the girl called India and the battlement that was really a wall, and the skateboard that was a sign, and—

As soon as I opened my eyes, I started to draw all sorts of things on the paper so fast that my pen was almost smoking.

"What have you written?" the teacher asked then and startled me. "Are you doing this task, or are you asleep?" she asked, waiting for an answer.

I wasn't quite sure. "I'm doing it," I said anyway. "My place is an amusement park."

"An amusement park," the teacher repeated. "That's right. All children want to go to the amusement park. Does anyone else have something to say about this?"

No one said anything, and I didn't say that I meant a very particular amusement park, either.

"This looks a bit like scribbling," Will said then. He had sneakily snatched my exercise book and was now scrutinizing my work. I tried to snatch the paper back, but the teacher got there first. She did not look pleased—anything but. She was frozen to the spot, staring at the drawing.

"I think it's beautiful," Bridget said in a voice that trembled with fear for some unfathomable reason, endangering her elephant hawk moths.

The teacher did not say a word.

"What's wrong now?" I asked.

The teacher looked at me seriously and asked, "Are you planning on defacing some place? This is clearly a plan for defacing."

The teacher waved the paper in the air. I looked at the drawing on it. It looked good. It resembled the graffiti India had painted on the factory wall.

"You told me to—" I began.

"Ma'am," the teacher corrected.

"Ma'am, you told us to write about places. My places are colorful."

"This is a geography lesson, not a corner for hatching criminal plans. I have heard that scrawlers always take pictures of their scribbles and collect them in a book. They call this a black book. I know. In the School of Possibilities, we are strictly against vandalism and defacing." Then she marched to the execution corner and drew the fourth line of the day on my guillotine.

"Can I have my paper?" I asked. Suddenly it felt very important to get the paper back.

The teacher, however, shook her head. "I am keeping it as evidence," she said.

"It's mine," I said with my hand stretched out and stared at the teacher.

"If you have a complaint, go and discuss the matter in Rob Reed's office."

My shoulders shuddered, and I felt helpless and damned angry. When I got out of the classroom, I drew my tag on the door as a hint that I would get my revenge somehow.

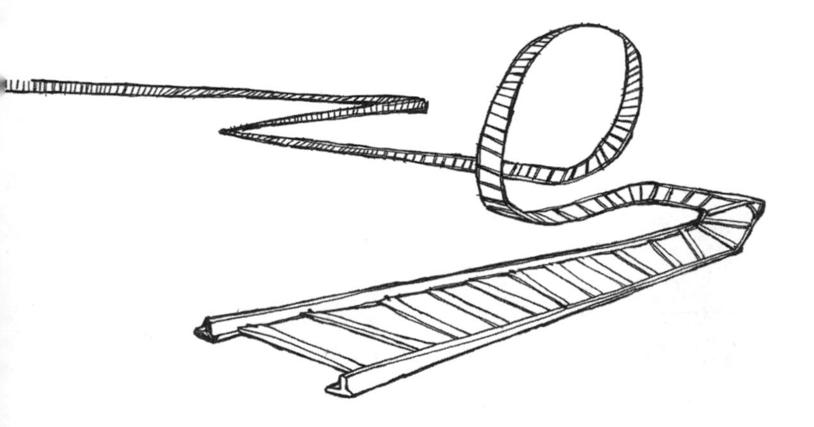

15.

As soon as I opened the front door when I came home from school that day, I knew Mom was there somewhere, because the corridor smelled of wedding dresses. Trust me—I had lived with their smell all my life. They smelled of dust and sometimes of mothballs.

"Mom?"

"Storm! Is that you?"

"What are you doing here? It's Thursday."

Mom lifted her finger to her lips. "Let's be quiet so the harpy won't hear us," she said and scratched the air with her fingers, as if they formed the long claws of a bird of prey. Of course I knew right away whom she meant, and we both laughed. Verity Poole had kicked up a dreadful stink about Mom's last visit.

"I came to tell you something." I stepped closer. Mom looked worried. "The wedding dress sales are not profitable," she said. "I could slave away night and day, but there aren't enough clients. I may have to close the business and think of something else."

"What would you like to do?" I asked quietly.

Mom laughed, almost cheerfully. "I'd like to go and try my luck in some other city. Or why not abroad? I could start a business in Paris. Paris is a romantic city. People get married there all the time—there are huge numbers of brides."

"But…you wouldn't leave me?"

"You would come with me, of course, silly," Mom said and squeezed my chin.

"What about Dad?"

"Don't you remember? This is only a dream, darling. Really, I'll have to think of some much more boring idea."

A cold fist closed up inside me. I suddenly felt lonely, and then I felt tired. I almost wanted to curl up on the corridor floor and fall asleep. I bit a tuft of my hair. I didn't want Mom to be worried or dream of Paris, which was somewhere far away. You may not consider dreams to be very dangerous, but I know that is what they are—they are extremely dangerous. For instance, I lived with the Pooles because Verity Poole had long dreamed of a Russian chef and a little brother for Mona.

"What are you planning to do?" I asked Mom and wished that every woman in the city would decide to get married this second and rush to Mom to order a wedding dress. The dresses would need a lot of work—there would be no skimping on materials and no expense spared—and they would have all sorts of special attachments like ledges, feelers, tubes, and tails. Mom would get money from all this, and with the money, her worries would disappear as if they had been sucked down a drain.

Mom didn't have an answer. Instead she started to bite her nails. She always did this when she was thinking hard. "Your school is quite expensive," she said then. "If you don't obey the rules, the fees will go up sky-high. Parents also have to pay for the punishments and the supervisors. It costs an awful lot for you to have a best friend and a girlfriend."

"I didn't want them. I hate them both."

"I know. I know, darling," Mom said and continued to look thoughtful.

The scene could have ended there, but it didn't, because next thing we knew, Dad appeared in the corridor with Verity and Mona close behind him. All three were carrying full shopping bags and were animatedly saying things like *zdrahstvuy* and *harasho*, which sounded like Russian. When Poole noticed us, the expression on her face became judgmental and almost triumphant, like a security man who had snapped up a shoplifter. The corridor soon filled with angry voices. It paralyzed me. I almost forgot to breathe.

"You have to choose," Mom said and gripped me like a life vest, which was ironic in a way, because I couldn't float. Hell, I couldn't swim, either. I went completely white then. "It is so cruel and simple," Mom said.

Miss Poole then started to pull me in another direction, and I felt as if I were being torn into two pieces—I probably nearly was.

"Do not disturb our life anymore, or else we will get a restraining order, and you will never see your son again," Verity Poole whispered, and Mom looked as though she would start biting her nails again.

At this point a whole crowd of curious neighbors had also appeared in the corridor. The noise attracted them. They were like flies that couldn't keep away from fresh droppings. I was now in Poole's pincer hold and couldn't get away, although I tried, for as you remember, Poole was a master in some karate-type sport. She must have been a black belt, because I wouldn't have lost to a weak opponent. It was unlikely that anyone would have been a match for her—not even a kung fu master—unless he chopped the hag's head off first.

Mona watched what was happening with glee and switched on the stairway light every time it went out. The neighbors were also involved in the situation like an English soccer crowd. Everyone called out advice: "Get the boy under control!"

"And what's that woman doing here?"

"Blood on the playing field!"

I tried to see Mom past all the arms and the chaos.

When the situation got too unbearable, I bit Poole's arm and tried to escape, but before I had even gone a few steps toward the front door, Mona tackled me. She stuck her foot out in front of me so that I tripped and flew onto my stomach on the hallway floor.

"I got him!" she shouted and jumped on my neck. Her bony knees pressed down on my spine.

"Storm!" Mom shouted.

"Run," I told her, for I was afraid the people in the corridor would do something to Mom. They were the kinds of maniacs who would have frightened you, too. When the door closed behind Mom, they started to cheer, as if they were at a boxing match.

I had lost the game and was detained in my room. I felt so lousy that I almost started to cry—almost.

16.

The torture methods included in Poole's detention were an exceedingly bright light and isolation. They were means that had been originally used in times of war. Then later they had been prohibited as inhumane, and new and kinder methods of destroying the enemy had been adopted. It was more hospitable to blow up your opponent right away than keep him waiting in light or darkness—or so it was thought, anyway.

Except that Poole did not think so.

She implemented the torture like this: The light bulbs in my room were removed and replaced by more powerful ones. Sixty watts became 120 watts, and finally the light switches were unscrewed so that I couldn't turn off the lights when I went to bed. At suppertime I received a meager ration in the doorway, after which the door was locked again. At bedtime Dad called from the corridor in reconciliation, "Try to understand, Storm. It's all for your own good," to which Verity Poole added, "Leave him be. The boy will learn manners with the light treatment."

Mona then said, "I spat on your bread under the cheese. Enjoy your meal."

I pulled a face at the door and served the supper to the fish. The cucumber slices stayed afloat on the surface like life vests adrift. The tomato disintegrated, and the cheese settled among the little fish and the slimy, waving, water grasses. If I tried to find some good points about the situation, one was that the detention had saved me from the first meeting of the fish club and the company of my official girlfriend.

After the fish had their supper, I sat on the desk and set the skateboard pieces on the windowsill in front of me. It was so light inside that the window was like an enormous mirror from which my own image looked at me. But the tower was there somewhere and stood dark by the railroad. At its foot was the factory, which had once been a hospital and then a place where bread and cookies had been made. India and India's secret were also there, for she certainly had a secret.

I picked up the board, inspected its worn pictures, and thought about what I actually knew about India. The girl had been thrown out of the school because she had been so impossible. She had failed, or so they would say at school. And like India, there were other children, as well—the twins and maybe some others. India had laughed mockingly when I spoke about failure. She certainly seemed to manage quite well without school. But if this was so, why didn't she want me with her? Why had she shown me the hospital walls and told me about the passageways when she didn't want to take me to see them? She had talked about guarding, and she really did protect something. But who did she protect, and from what? *I take care of us*, she had said.

I stared at my image in the window. I pressed my hand against its reflection and imagined that there were two boys who looked

alike and were the same age, that the hand in the window was my brother's, that we shared everything, and therefore, I would never be alone. Gradually the image slid into a mist, and my eyes closed. I started to dream, and in the dream, I saw India; the two boys who looked alike, Moon and Ra; Bridget; Will; and a forest where white gowns hung from every tree. They looked like wedding dresses sewn by Mom, but they might have been something else. I was cold, really cold, and when I woke up, I knew I had been asleep for a while, because my arms were numb. It wasn't morning by far, because it was still dark. I knew, as one sometimes does, that I had not woken up without a reason, but that something had roused me. It took a while to realize that the room was now dark and that the window was no longer a mirror.

Beyond the dark roofs where the tower was, something was visible—a light flitting about restlessly. At first I thought it was a fire, but then it occurred to me that maybe someone was dancing in the tower holding a light.

17.

In the morning Mona woke me. She stood beside me with a fish in the palm of her hand. “You killed Charlie,” she said. Then her voice cracked.

I was still half asleep and couldn’t understand what she was talking about.

“Charlie was floating belly-up between two slices of cucumber,” Mona continued.

I took a look at the fish on her palm. “It’s dead, all right,” I said and whistled, impressed. The dead Charlie didn’t differ much from the live one. The same vacant stare was still present in its eyes. I stretched out my hand and tried to take it. Mona yanked the fish farther away from me then.

“You will not touch him again,” she hissed. “Isn’t it enough to have poisoned him?”

I held up my arms in surrender. You have to act calmly with lunatics. They must never be agitated or provoked. It isn’t worth veering onto a collision course with them.

“I was only going to help you and take it away,” I said kindly.

“Away? Away where?” she asked suspiciously.

“To the trash can or the bathroom. Wherever you take dead fish.”

Mona looked at me, shocked.

"The bathroom?" she cried out and tried to slap me. I managed to slip out of the way. I was quick in such situations. People tried to slap me almost every day, so I had some practice.

"I'm going to bury Charlie," Mona said, sniffling.

I sighed very deeply. People who thought that the death of a fish was a catastrophe comparable to an earthquake were incomprehensible to me. "It's a fish, and fish don't live very long. They catch diseases and get eaten by other fish. That's the life of a fish."

"We will bury it together," she announced in a tense voice. "You will help."

"Whatever," I said. "Have you chosen a suitable flowerpot yet?"

Mona glared at me and looked as if she was about to shove Charlie up my nostril. Just then, the door opened, and Verity Poole invadcd my room.

"There's a call for you, Storm," she said. "What are you doing here, Mona?"

"I'm allowed to be here," Mona said defiantly. "You brought me Storm. That's what you said. I'm bringing you a surprise. I'm bringing you a little brother."

That kind of talk delights no one. No one wants to be like food brought to chicks by the mother bird. Birds digest the food first and then puke it up for their chicks. In the world of birds, you get eaten twice over. It is a hard life.

I ran into the hall and shouted into the receiver, "Who is it?" I didn't know what I was expecting, but it was Rob Reed on the line.

"Good morning," he said. "The fish were upset that you didn't show up last night."

"I know," I said. "One of them has died."

"What?"

"Nothing," I said and looked at Mona's reflection in the mirror. She was wandering into the kitchen bearing Charlie on her palm.

"Your girlfriend is also upset," Rob said emphatically. "But that is not why I'm calling. I have decided to give you a special tutorial. Today's program is an exercise in self-control at the railroad station. We'll meet there at nine."

I mumbled, "Yeah, yeah, yeah," into the phone and put the receiver down.

I went to the railroad station. It was quite near—only a couple of blocks away. It was a bright day, and the station was busy, as it almost always was. People came and went. Bags were pulled, pushed, and carried. Looking brisk, Rob stood on the platform. Then again, Rob always looked brisk. He didn't have bad mornings. He didn't get out of bed on the wrong foot, because he only had right feet.

"Welcome to special your tutorial," he called out as soon as he noticed me. He was smiling, of course. He smiled with both rows of teeth. A dental practice or a toothpaste company probably paid him to display his teeth. He could have earned a fortune from smiling.

I didn't greet Rob, because I was busy staring at the train at platform two. It gleamed in the sun. Trains can be really beautiful.

The stationmaster was standing next to the train I had my eye on, guiding passengers inside. He looked at tickets, directed people and lifted baby strollers into the cars.

"Are you going on a train?" he asked when he noticed me. Almost right away he looked at me again, alert. "I know you from somewhere," he said. "I've seen you. Where is your mother?"

I was about to answer when Rob intervened. "No problem," he said and patted my shoulder. "The boy is not running away. He is under my supervision."

The stationmaster nodded and concentrated on dispatching the train. New faces appeared in its windows all the time.

"You might have noticed that the man recognized you," Rob whispered. "Maybe you didn't know that all stations have been warned about you."

I glanced at Rob, unbelieving.

"I'll show you," he whispered and gestured for me to go with him.

I followed him into the station building.

There, he showed me a poster. It hung on the notice board among advertisements for concerts and yoga. It was a picture of me. I didn't yet have dreadlocks, and I looked startled or surprised. The picture had been taken against the police station brick wall in the spring, when I was caught running away the first time. The poster said: *If you see a twelve-year-old boy in the vicinity of the station, contact one of the numbers below. The boy may be running away. He is not dangerous, but he has criminal tendencies.*

"That last thing is a lie," I said.

Rob looked at me with a smile on his lips.

"I don't think there is any proof of that," he said and concentrated again on the poster. "There is one of these at all exit routes: railroad station, bus station, airport. It probably isn't worth trying to run away. That is today's lesson."

I looked after the departing train and nodded. The train, the platform underneath me, the smell of the rails, the sounds, and the familiar announcements had made me think about escaping and trying my luck elsewhere. Those dreams were now useless. I would never get farther than the platform.

We sat on the platform, and Rob lectured me on how to lead an exemplary life. I listened with one ear and watched as men, women, and bags entered another train.

"All this attracts you," Rob said and jumped to his feet. "I'm now going to leave you here on the platform for a moment, and we will do a kind of experiment to test your willpower. Can you manage not to get on a train? I will be observing you, but I'll leave some distance—an opportunity if you like. Otherwise there is no point in doing this."

I nodded faintly and sat down on the bench by the stationmaster. Rob thought I was pretty hopeless.

The stationmaster had already forgotten who I was.

"I'm the boy in the poster," I said, and because I couldn't think of anything else, I chatted about trains and told him that I liked them.

"I hate trains," he replied morosely and was obviously in need of some cheering up. That was why I decided to tell him all sorts of things, like how I would become an architect when I grew up and would build a city with lots of levels, thousands of railings, rails, ramps, stairs, and pedestals. Some people needed to be told about these things.

"It would be easier to skateboard than walk in this place," I said and explained that trains that looked like airplanes—cigar-shaped with panoramic windows—would run on rails in the streets, and that there would be no obstacles to skating, no red and yellow prohibition signs. In my city it would be impossible to drive a car. Everyone would be skating, including the police officers, teachers, nurses, and firefighters. Mothers would take their children to day care on skateboards, and children would learn to skate before they even knew how to walk. I was getting quite carried away as I chatted, and in the end, I suggested that he could become a stationmaster in my city. I could teach him to get by on a skateboard then.

Suddenly, in the middle of my torrent of words, things began to happen at the station. First an alarm went off, and then a girl shot out of the station hall. She was wearing a white lace dress, which she had shortened by tying knots in its hem. People turned to stare at the girl, unsure about what was happening. She zig-zagged between them, leaping over suitcases as nimbly as a hurdler, and jumped onto the rails in front of a departing train. Of course the brakes of the train began to screech, and the girl's pursuers, who had appeared on the platform, stopped in their tracks for an instant. Someone was screaming, although it was as clear as day that the girl had escaped and was speeding away on the rails out of the reach of her pursuers.

Then the engineer emerged from the cab, gesturing that everything was all right, and the train left. After it was gone, I saw the girl on the other side of the station yard. She ran wild like the wind. There was a long distance between her and the station already, and her pursuers didn't seem to have any chance. But they started to clamber onto the rails. At the last train, the girl jumped up and climbed between two boxcars to the other side. At the same time, my focus sharpened, for the girl was no longer alone. More shapes rose up from among the rubble—one, two, three. I squinted, because it looked as if the rocks had come to life for a moment and were now crawling to escape from underneath the train. The boulders looked surprisingly familiar. I recognized the two boys and, of course, India.

"Criminals," puffed the stationmaster and tore off his hat. "Just hooligans and monsters, all of them."

Rob appeared on the platform just in time. He stared goggle-eyed at the events unfolding in the station yard. "What's happening?" he asked the stationmaster.

"The kid robbed the magazine stall," the man said.

Rob turned to look at me. Of course his first thought was that I had performed a conjuring trick and committed the robbery in spite of all the close supervision.

I shrugged my shoulders and tried to look as normal as possible.

"I don't know anything about it," I said quickly. It was almost true. I knew—or at least suspected—that the children would now be running toward the harbor, hidden by stationary trains and bushes, and that they would dive into the messy yard of the factory and disappear into the ugly building with all its hiding places. I didn't look in that direction.

"It's strange that whenever you are around, this sort of thing happens," Rob said, wagging his finger. "I'm just wondering how we will report this at school."

Again I shrugged my shoulders innocently.

We went inside the station just in time to hear the police officers questioning the eyewitnesses. No one had seen anything much. Rob listened attentively. We both did. The girl had appeared from nowhere and had snatched the contents of the station buffet cash register.

"A sweet girl," the waitress said.

"She was suddenly there, and she vanished just as suddenly," said a passenger, bent under the weight of his backpack.

"Magic tricks," insisted a cleaner, leaning on a mop.

"Sleight of hand," huffed an elderly man with a stick.

When we set off for school, Rob watched me the whole time, his head tilted to one side. I could tell that he was thinking hard. He believed that I had something to do with the events. He also believed that I was lying when I said I didn't know anything. I looked up to the sky and saw all sorts of airplane trails and other cloud formations. This time I had almost told the truth. I didn't know anything about the children, but I knew that I wanted to find out more.

18.

On Friday evening after school, I went downtown with my official friends.

And then suddenly things started to happen again.

The three of us were standing around and browsing through some CDs in the shopping mall when someone appeared beside me. Before I had time to realize who it was, I got severe palpitations.

"Oh, dear! Are you planning to steal something, boy, even though you know that I have eyes everywhere?"

The voice belonged to Verity Poole. It sounded like Verity Poole.

I swallowed so loudly that the noise I made could have cracked nuts. Poole was following me again. How that was possible—who knew? Of course the CD fell out of my hand, and my legs wanted to run away. All of a sudden, a small scratched hand appeared from somewhere behind me and picked up the CD.

"CD players are few and far between where I come from," a voice said, quite different from the voice just before. "But I will say this—even if we had a hundred of them, we wouldn't listen to this sort of junk."

"India!" I whispered, excited. "It's you. I imagined…I imagined that—"

She was standing next to me, her arm almost touching mine. She peeked at me from under her hood. I could only see the smile but not the eyes.

"What did you imagine?" she asked.

"What trick was that?"

"What trick?" she asked, looking innocent. "I came to say hi. Or would you rather spend time in their company?" She peered at my personal security guards from under her hood and screwed up her nose.

"Of course not," I snapped, and I also glanced at Bridget and Will, who were efficiently rummaging through the CDs. "But what was that? How did you do that voice? It sounded just like—just like Poole. I was scared that the old hag was on my case again."

"I'm quite good at that sort of thing," India said and laid her hand on mine. Then she performed the trick again. "I don't think it's very nice that you have a girlfriend at school," she said, sounding exactly like Mona. "You were supposed to be mine, only mine, my little prince. Did you hear me? Mom brought you for me."

She mimicked Mona so perfectly that I forgot to wonder how she knew her, and instead I burst out laughing. Of course my personal guards immediately turned around to look, and I had to press my face really close to the CD rack to stifle the laughter. I rifled through the covers feverishly, as if they were edible and I hadn't eaten for months.

"What is it now, Storm?" Will asked.

"Some band with a ridiculous CD cover," I replied.

"Storm is really childish," Bridget said quite loudly to Will, and then they both turned to look at their own rack again.

"They didn't notice you," I whispered, giving India a sidelong glance.

"You can't blame them for that," India said. "Do you want this?" She pushed a CD into my hand.

I shook my head. I didn't want Cuban rain songs.

"You can have it anyway," India said and shoved the disc into the pocket of her hoodie with a movement faster than the fluttering of an insect's wing. She dropped a lollipop into the space left by the CD. "Let's go."

"But—" I started and glanced at my guards. They weren't looking at us. Bridget was here to choose some background music to help our studying, and she had just found something.

India crouched down next to me and dived under the CD rack. When I felt my pocket, I realized that she had just taken my wallet and bicycle key and replaced them with a couple of lollipops, and that I had better run after her if I wanted to get them back.

"India," I hissed.

We sprinted out of the shop, one after the other.

Outside I grabbed India by the sleeve.

"Give them here. I know you took them," I said angrily.

India started to laugh and handed back the items.

"It's worth guarding anything you don't want to disappear," she said.

I pushed the things back into my pocket and said, "I think we lost those two."

India nodded. "It was quite easy," she said. "Disappearing isn't magic. It's melting into the background. You have to be inconspicuous. That's all. Adults don't see everything. They see something, and then they forget a hundred other much more interesting things. It's easy for a child to disappear."

India took off her hood. She had tied her hair into a knot again and pushed lollipops into it. "Now we'll spy on your friends," she said. "The little monkeys will lead us to some people we know."

From the cover of some plastic palm trees, we observed Will and Bridget's movements in the shopping mall. They sent someone a text message and then sat down at a café table. Soon Rob Reed strode in, followed by Miss Cutts and Verity Poole with Mona on her arm.

I chewed a dreadlock, agitated. "Do they really have nothing better to do than run around after me?"

India shook her head emphatically. "The little monkeys are informants," she said, "as is everyone in the School of Possibilities. I suppose they still have the detective club, where they teach spying, trailing friends, and snitching on them?"

"I don't know," I said. "I bet I'll have to pay for this escapade."

"Listen," India said seriously. "You will have to pay in any case. They won't give you any other opportunities except the opportunity to fail."

I clutched her arm. "What if I came with you to the School of the Lost?"

India shook her head so hard that one of the lollipops came loose and fell on the floor. "It's not quite that simple," she said, picking up the lollipop and putting it in my pocket. "It's quite final—a bit like drowning. Do you understand?"

"No, I don't," I said.

"A boy wanted to know what it was like at the bottom of the sea. He asked the mermaids playing on the shore about it. One of them said, 'Come on. We'll take you with us, but remember that once you have breathed in water, you can never return.'"

"Fairy tales," I snapped, my eye still on the group at the table.

"Come," India whispered. "I'll show you something."

We got out of the shopping mall and slipped into the concrete inner courtyard of an apartment block. India punched a code into the door entry panel and yanked me into the stairway.

"Do you live here?" I asked, reading the names on the board hanging by the street door with interest.

"Sometimes," India replied.

We took the elevator to the sixth floor. India rang the doorbell of the door marked *Hill.* An old woman with white hair and freckles came to answer the door.

"Well, good morning, Vera," she said. "Come in. Who is your friend?"

"He's just a buddy," India said. "William."

William? I raised my eyebrows, surprised.

"Hello, William," the granny said.

"Hello," I said, trying to catch India's eye. After I failed to do so, I smiled my charmer's smile at the old lady—what Mom called my polite smile, which I flashed occasionally. "You can be the most charming child in the world," she always said on those occasions and squeezed my cheek. Sometimes she also addressed me by pet names that she had used when I was a small child. They all sounded like the names of mushrooms or fungi: *Stormling*, *Stommy*, *Stompy*, and *Stomsy*.

"Would you like some hot chocolate?" the old lady asked, and she limped into the kitchen ahead of us. Of course we did. We also wanted the cinnamon buns and ginger cookies she put in front of us on a china tray. The picture on the plate depicted a blue battalion of soldiers attacking another battalion in some war, the name of which was obscured by buns and cookies.

"Is she your grandmother?" I whispered in India's ear.

"In a way," India whispered back.

"How do you mean...*in a way*?" I asked.

"In a way, she is. Don't ask so many questions," India whispered. She looked at me severely, and I snapped my mouth shut. I could be obedient when I wanted to, although no one believed that I could.

The old lady showed us some photographs. I wondered which one of her children was India's mother or father. There wasn't much of a resemblance.

19.

After visiting India's granny, I went straight to Mom's house. There was a smell of food in the stairway, as always, and someone was banging drums. Inside the apartment there were boxes in crooked piles.

"Where are all the wedding dresses?" I asked, although I knew they were in the boxes. I was stung by the thought that today I had broken the rules and that every crime had its cost.

"I've been making preparations," Mom replied.

That is a word you don't like to hear. You immediately start to fear the worst when you hear it. *Preparations*? I suddenly felt really lonely.

"What's going to happen?" I asked tensely. The kitchen and the whole apartment looked strange without hundreds of dresses hanging around.

Mom looked at me nervously and started to bite her nails. "At first I thought that nobody would want them, but then a department store bought them," she said. "They're taking the whole stock. But—"

"But?"

"They are paying next to nothing for them."

In the evening, on Mom's sofa bed, I thought about adults and how greedy they were. I thought that I would never become like that. I would rather go and live at the bottom of the sea and start to breathe water like the boy in India's story.

When I woke up the next morning, Mom's apartment was full of bustle. A lively tune was playing on the radio, and the front door was open. Workmen went in and out. They were carrying the boxes Mom had packed. Mom was standing in the hall, watching the men with her arms crossed. She was wearing one of her favorite wedding dresses and sunglasses.

"What's happening?" I asked, surprised.

"The wedding dresses are going," Mom replied, adjusting her shades.

When I looked at them quizzically, she said, "I don't intend to snivel about it now." Immediately a tear rolled down her cheek from somewhere behind the dark glasses.

I went to turn off the radio. "But it's great that they've been sold," I said briskly.

"They'll cut them up into rags. The styles are old-fashioned."

I stared at the men, furious. The last one got her to sign the papers and slammed the door shut behind him.

"What now?" Mom asked, and I was unable to give her an answer.

THE BADGE

20.

I'm warning you now. My story is about to get more sinister. I had been at the School of Possibilities for precisely forty days. We were in the kind of messy season when fall changed into winter. It rained constantly, and everything was gray. The leaves and the birds had performed their annual disappearing act, and all sorts of things like the ground, snakes, and frogs had started to freeze. I loathed the fall.

Sometime around then, things started to happen.

A series of events took place. I was sentenced, and Mom did the same as the birds—she disappeared. She left without leaving an address.

That was how it went.

And yet all that was just the start.

But let's start at the beginning. It was my fortieth day, and the teacher started it by talking to me about the punishment corner. She had a piece of chalk in her hand, and she kept tossing it up in the air like a softball.

"Your guillotine is now finished," she said, looking at her

drawing of an execution structure on the wall, quite pleased with herself, though it was not a very good drawing. If you had seen it, you would have given her four out of ten for her drawing skills. The parts of the guillotine sprawled crookedly, and the neck-cutting blade was bent. Seeing a guillotine like that immediately made you pleased that the teacher didn't go around subways painting pictures on the walls.

I was thinking about these things as I was standing there by the door. I was a little frightened, too. Then the teacher gestured for me to take my place, and I did. I waited to see what would happen next and whether the punishment would be worse than the previous one or not. Did anything worse than a girlfriend actually exist? I was vaguely aware of the teacher telling the class how the new, fast, and effective executions had been at least as important a factor in the French Revolution as its message: liberty, fraternity, and equality.

"All four pulled the cart we call the revolution," she emphasized. "Punishments are also important in our revolution against children's indiscipline."

Next the teacher said that death by the guillotine blade was a humane punishment, by which she meant that it was a kind way of taking a person's life. There was something contradictory about this notion, although of course, there were worse ways to die. In any case this particular topic was the teacher's favorite. She talked about it often and at great length. On this occasion, when she had talked about it enough, she got to the main subject, which turned out to be me, and told the class about a small event to be organized on that same day in the school sports hall after the end of lessons. It would be a trial which the entire school was going to attend.

I would have the starring role. I would be the accused and the sentenced.

"Storm has brought shame on the class," the teacher said. "We had earned respect, and the achievements of our model students had been admired. But now our reputation has been tarnished. The trial, which will start soon, will be filmed, and it will be shown in classes next week. The purpose is to remind the school's students about the consequences of disobedience."

The teacher made the punishment sound pretty awful. I listened attentively, waiting for more details. The humiliation must be something even worse than having a girlfriend, since it was being publicized in this way. It was a little difficult to imagine what this new punishment could be, because the worst thing I could think of at the time was having a blabbing snitcher hanging off my arm for the rest of my life. After all, Bridget had caused most of the lines on my punishment hill with her conscientious tattling.

When the school bell announced the end of lessons that day, Rob Reed appeared in the classroom. "I've come for Storm," he said. "Are you ready?"

I nodded and stood up. As I walked to the door, I realized to my horror that my legs were shaking.

"Is everything all right?" Rob asked and pressed his hand to my shoulder.

I shook it off and stepped into the corridor. I couldn't stop the shaking.

The teacher hastily arranged the class into a double line behind us, after which we all started to march toward the sports hall. I walked at the front. Rob, the teacher, and the rest of the class followed behind me. The rest of the students were standing in the corridor waiting for us to pass by, and after we had passed them, they joined the tail of the growing procession. No one spoke or called out, but the hundreds of marching shoes made a rhythmic thundering noise. There was something ominous in that sound.

All the floodlights in the hall were trained on the playing field. Lights swept it. Cameras watched it. As I stepped closer, pushed by Rob, I saw the men behind the cameras—only they weren't men, but boys and girls from the school's camera club.

This was the place where the sentence would be announced. Here it would be implemented and immortalized.

I stumbled onto the playing field, straight on the center line. One of the cameramen immediately ran up to me and put me in a better position for the spotlight. There was so much light—the spotlight was so bright—that it was impossible to see into the stands from the field. But from the drumming sound of steps, I could guess that they were filling up all the time. The heat of the lamps soon made me sweat, and my legs started to shake even more. I felt like a creature in outer space, like a boy floating without gravity, without a radio link to the mother ship, waiting to be picked up or waiting for everything to end—whatever that ending might be.

When the loudspeakers started to send out a deafening screech, the hum in the hall subsided. I wiped my wet forehead. It would not be long before I would have water running out of me like I was a bathroom faucet.

"Does the accused know why he is here?" a voice thundered from the loudspeaker. I thought there was something familiar about it, but I couldn't be certain.

I swallowed.

"Yes," the voice continued. "At least he should know. Look at him! Look carefully! This boy, Storm Steele, has shown contempt and disregard for the rules and has broken the trust placed in him. He has scorned the efforts that those who have tried to help him have made for him. The trial here today in this prestigious hall and the sentence Storm will be given will be based on witness statements from his closest friends, his teacher, his tutor, and the counselor. This is his second punishment within a short time. With a third, he will lose his last chance. We have been sympathetic and understanding educators, reasonable supporters, and patient with our encouragement. However, if this is not enough, there are other things we can do. We can hold up our hands and give up. We can say that the child is hopeless. There is another place waiting for every unsuccessful child. There are no more chances there."

The voice continued to preach. At some point I began to believe that it would never stop, that I would have to remain standing in that spot for days and weeks to come. I felt faint, and my hands were tingling. The bright light burned my eyes and made them water. Water ran down my back. I felt stiff, but changing my position didn't make me feel any better. Any breathing or clattering sounds from the stands were covered up by the scratchy screeching of the loudspeaker.

"We sentence you to shame," the voice declared. "From now on you will wear a badge. It will serve to remind you, your classmates, and your family that a marked child will soon be lost. It is not a long journey, and half of it has already been made."

The badge was shameful. What did it mean?

I tried to understand—to think clearly—but the heat confused my brain and turned my thoughts to porridge.

Next the girls' arts and crafts teacher walked onto the playing field. I barely recognized her, because the water was now pouring from my eyes. The woman was wearing the school team shirt. She held up her hands and showed something to the spectators.

"I am Maria Karma, and I mark this boy," she announced and leaned over me.

The audience began to drum the floor of the stands rhythmically.

I wiped my eyes with the hem of my coat and saw that Maria Karma was holding a needle, a thread, and a piece of fabric. My heart gave several extra beats. For a moment I imagined that the teacher would start to poke me with the needle, like Mom did with her awkward clients. But then luckily she just squeezed my arm and sewed the piece of fabric onto my coat. It didn't hurt at all, but I still felt strangely cold. It felt a bit like something inside me was screaming and resisting, but that something was far away, deep inside me, and didn't surface.

After the teacher had completed her task, she received applause and left the field.

I glanced at my sleeve. The badge looked harmless.

"You are marked," the voice said. "You may go!"

I started to walk toward the edge of the playing field, my legs wobbly. I staggered to the yard. Rob accompanied me with his hand on my shoulder. "Can I go home?" I asked. My throat was dry, and my voice cracked. Probably no one heard it. Rob didn't hear it. I didn't even hear it myself.

At first everything seemed normal. As I stepped out of the door, a train was just passing the school on its way to the harbor. People emerged from the hall and wandered out of the gate. No one looked at me, pointed, or laughed—nothing. Neither of my bodyguards hurried after me.

With my legs still shaking, I walked toward home. I was near the sports ground when I received the first blow on the side of my head. The second one hit me on the back of the head.

"Penalty!" Will shouted from the field. "Throw-in. Shoot! Now!"

More blows followed: a third, fourth, fifth, and sixth.

I threw myself on the ground.

"Stop!" I yelled and protected my head with my arms.

I was being stoned. Was I being stoned?

No, not stoned...but something else.

Trash was being thrown at me: rotten tomatoes, plums, and black, swollen bananas.

"Stop it!" I shouted again.

I tried to get a look at my attackers. There were several of them—at least ten or more. Some of them were from my own class, like Will, who was standing in the middle of the group and holding an orange.

I had rotting fruit in my eyes, and it wasn't easy to see.

Will stared at me. I stared at Will. As he lifted his arm to throw, I feinted and dodged the other way. I wasn't hit by an orange but by a tomato. Red goop was spread all over my face, and I couldn't see anything anymore. I pressed my face against the ground and started crawling to escape. I rubbed my eyes with my sleeve, and I knew that the ditch I could make out ahead would save me. How far was it?

I dragged myself toward the sanctuary, not bothering to dodge the missiles any more. There was a place that I thought about then. It was a beach where I would sit with Dad and Mom. The tree branches reached the water, and some of them were under the surface. Maybe there was a boat, as well. Or perhaps there wasn't. At the very least, I was certain that Mom and Dad were there and that they looked after me. I was very little, not yet lost. I hadn't gone astray then. I hadn't yet betrayed anyone.

It was a long way from there to this moment.

Then I reached the spot where the road ended and the ditch began. I was hit for the last time, rolled off the road, and fell down.

21.

I sank below the surface.

My eyes were open, and I could see that there was water in the ditch, with slimy leaves floating on the surface and below. *Drowning must be like this*, I thought. It was easy—a bit too easy. Soon I would start to breathe in the water and leaves, and then I would become a fish. That was what I was thinking, and then suddenly someone yanked me by the arm and stopped me from falling in any deeper.

"Hell," she said, and I spat leaves onto the bank.

India's arm was wrapped around my shoulder, and with her other hand, she was thumping me on the back. She had saved me. She seemed to be saving me all the time, as if she were a guardian angel, not a child.

"That'll do for now," I heard Will's voice in the distance. "The marked one has received his punishment."

His shout was drowned out by the jubilant cheering.

My shoulders were trembling.

"Don't be afraid. It's over," India whispered. "They were only throwing vegetables at you. They had stored them up. Pails full of rotten fruit and vegetables for handing out the punishment. They knew this was going to happen. Just ask me. I know."

"I stink," I said, screwing up my nose.

"Yes, you do," India agreed. "You stink worse than a pig."

I was thinking about Dad's face when I'd get home. I also thought about Mom.

"I can't go home like this. To either home."

India looked at me with her head tilted to one side.

"I have an idea," she said.

We went to the restroom at the shopping mall to get a wash.

I looked at my reflection in the mirror and drew a sharp breath. I looked like a monster. My hair was slimy, and my face was blotchy. My cheeks were red and yellow, my eyelashes green. India also looked at me critically.

"You need a complete wash and fresh clothes," she said. "I'll go and get you some. Wait here. Don't let anyone in. When I come back, I'll tap on the door five times. That means three quick and two slow. In the meantime, you get washed. Take those off," she said, pointing at my wet pants.

"These?" I hesitated, and the worst thing was that I blushed. I didn't have sisters, and I was not really used to undressing with girls watching. I was a bit shy about these things.

India evidently realized this, because she laughed, mocking me. "Don't start to chicken out now," she snorted. "I've seen half-naked dirty kids before. It's nothing new and definitely doesn't interest me."

Then she left, and I pulled my clothes off, slimy with rotten fruit goop. For a while I considered washing them, but then I shoved them into the trash can. I would have to explain the disappearance of the clothes somehow at home, but I didn't worry about that now. Instead I pushed my head under the faucet and started to wash my hair. Dreadlocks don't dry very quickly, so I never liked to wash my hair, especially on cold days.

Once I had got my hair and the rest of me washed, I had nothing else to do, and I started to feel cold. By the time India came back, I was already shivering uncontrollably, and I was only just capable of opening the door.

India looked at me and grinned.

"Much better. You're clean. Now we can get you dressed," she said, briskly dumping a pile of clothes on the floor. She rummaged in the pile and pulled out pants and shirts of various sizes, all absolutely hideous. I didn't know what museum she had cleaned out, because the clothes were historical and faded from hundreds of washes—from the sun and wind of past centuries—and all they were good for was a rat's nest or cutting up into rags.

"Put these on," India said and threw me a pair of pants and a shirt. The pants were the kind of formal ones that men wear to the office or to a funeral, and they were so long that I was forced to roll the legs up ten times. The shirt had blue and yellow stripes. It was the ugliest I had ever seen.

"Was there really nothing else?" I asked in desperation.

"Stop whining," India sighed. "You should be pleased that I actually bothered to save you. It was easiest for me to snatch some clothes for you from the collection bin at the flea market. They aren't guarded."

I pulled a face when I realized that India had randomly filched a plastic bag from one of those Salvation Army collection points behind the shops into which people threw all the rags they had gotten tired of and hadn't thought up any other use for.

I held out my arms as a sign of surrender and pulled the clothes on. When I was ready, I looked at myself in the mirror and confirmed what I had already guessed—namely that I looked like a clown in a cheap circus.

"Wait," I said. I looked at the trash can. "I have to take the coat. It's got the badge on it. If I leave it here, they'll sew a new one on me and the whole thing will have to be repeated."

India looked at me thoughtfully.

"It's your decision," she said. "I wouldn't bother, though. You have no more chances in that place."

"You can't know that," I said, but I felt a shiver, because I knew she might be right. Up until now, everything at the new school had turned against me—all my good efforts, everything I had tried.

"I've been thinking," she said. "Maybe you should come with me, after all."

That was such a surprise that I felt as if the roof had opened and ice-cold sleet was falling on me from the sky. It made me realize that India had suggested something that went past a certain point and wasn't a game. Going with India would mean giving up everything normal like Mom and Dad. That was why I dashed to the trash can to rummage for the coat.

"I think I'll keep on trying," I mumbled with my head in the can, my earlobes burning red. I dropped the coat into the plastic bag, which I then placed in my school bag. I was careful not to look at India, because I was quite ashamed.

"As you like," India said, and we left the restroom.

We ran until we warmed up. At last we stopped to catch our breaths at the shopping mall's glass-covered square, among the large-leaved palm trees. The square was surrounded by a tropical thicket growing up from clay pots, with the aromas of roasting nuts and sausages wafting from the stalls and a constant stream of passing shoppers milling around. Light shone brightly through the glass dome, and I didn't feel cold anymore.

"I see," a girl's voice said behind me. "So here he is. This is the brat who's been hidden away from us. The guy looks like a stray dog."

I spun around fast and saw a girl in front of me. She was thin and very white. She had piercing, icy-blue eyes that made you think of all sorts of things. She was wearing a slightly ragged wedding dress, the hem tied in knots. I had seen it before. Behind the girl stood Moon and Ra. They were holding hands.

India stared at the girl and looked as though she had been caught.

"You do know the rules?" the girl asked.

"Of course I know the rules."

The girl raised her eyebrows. "Then you also know that no good will come of this."

"He's been marked," India said. "I saved him. You know me."

Again the girl raised her eyebrows. "Has he been marked?" she asked.

India nodded, and the girl now looked at me more closely. She rolled her eyes at the twins, who were peeking at me from behind the palm trees, giggling. The girl's stern look silenced both of them.

"I recognize that dress," I said and took hold of the silk hem. I had seen that embroidery before. "Where did you get this?"

"Don't touch," the girl hissed and scratched the air between us with five very long, sharp nails.

I pulled my hand away. "My mother made that," I said defensively.

"Your mother?" she hissed and then laughed like a ghost. "Mothers! Mothers don't much interest us. Isn't that so, boys?"

"Except rich mothers," Moon said.

"Very rich," Ra echoed.

"We rob mothers," Moon explained.

"We rob fathers, as well," Ra added. "We are robbers."

"Shut up, you idiots," the girl hissed and kicked a palm pot. "We're not robbers. We're hunters, and this is a jungle." Then she turned to me and said calmly, "Mothers are make-believe."

The boys glanced at each other, looking worried, and shook their heads.

"Mew!" they whined like two kittens. "Mothers aren't make-believe, are they, Mew?"

The girl stiffened and pressed her hands on the boys' mouths.

"No names in the jungle," she whispered, agitated. "We're going now," she said and pulled India's sleeve. "You, too."

India glanced at me and waved good-bye.

I waved, too.

22.

I went home, and I knew right away from the atmosphere that Dad had heard about the punishment. He was standing in the kitchen holding a vegetable knife, chopping carrots and peppers into cubes like a relentless food processor.

"It wasn't my fault," I said, although I thought that maybe it was. I leaned against the doorframe, poking at the floor with my toe.

Maybe it was.

Dad probably thought so, too. He still didn't look at me but continued to chop. He had swapped the carrots for onions, and they made his eyes water. He sliced them until he caught his finger with the knife. That was strange. Dad was usually careful to the extreme. He never made a mistake with vegetables. He was clearly disappointed.

That was what Verity Poole said, as well. "You have betrayed your father and the family," she said and dragged me by the arm into my room. "Your father is grief-stricken," she continued. "And how do I know that? How do you think?" she said, lowering her voice into a whisper. "He has forgotten the recipe. He can't remember how to make goulash anymore."

Poole was already leaving the room when she suddenly turned

around and took me by the shoulders. "Where is it?" she asked and shook me. "Why don't I see it?"

"What?" I asked, and then Poole snatched my backpack and dug my filthy coat out of it. "This here. This is what I meant. Your coat and your badge. You must not go around without the badge."

"But it's dirty," I said stubbornly. "Mom says that—"

"This matter is decided by other people, not your mother. Your parents have not been strict enough with you. Your father regrets it. That's why you are in this situation. He has asked me—or actually demanded for me—to be hard on you, especially now that your mother has gone and left you."

I tensed up like a bow and started to shake. "What are you saying?" I said.

"She left you a message."

"Where is it?" I shot into the kitchen and started to pull Dad's arm. "Dad! Dad! Tell her to give me Mom's message."

Dad leaned closer to the sink and wouldn't look at me. Verity Poole laughed. "You are impatient," she said. "Didn't I just tell you about your father and what we have agreed? From now on I am calling the tune when it comes to your upbringing. Your father does not have the necessary strength of character. In matters of upbringing, he cannot reach the right note."

"Where is the message? It belongs to me."

My heart was pounding. I hoped that Poole was lying, but when I thought about it even a little, I immediately began to see the boxes in which Mom had packed the wedding dresses, and I knew that Poole was telling the truth. Mom was gone.

"You're lying!" I screamed anyway.

Verity Poole sneered. "Is that what you think, boy?" she said. "Why would I lie to you? Your mother's sewing business is in big trouble, as you know, and she fled from her creditors. That woman really does not understand finance. And you were a great expense for her. I don't think we will hear from her very soon."

"You're lying!" I shouted again, louder than before, more desperately. "I hate you!"

"Vladimir," Poole called in a shrill voice over her shoulder. "Come and tell Storm the news. The boy doesn't believe me."

"It's true," Dad said, setting down his knife.

"Mom didn't say anything to me," I said quietly.

"You know your mother hates good-byes."

"Did you talk to her?"

"She won't talk to me."

Then Poole took me to my room. Dad accompanied us, now holding a knife and an onion. They left, but I stayed put. I listened to their voices through the door. There was nothing else I could do in there. At some point in the evening, Dad asked cautiously whether or not he could take me a little supper. Just the thought of it made my mouth water. Dad can make some awesome suppers. I would eat them even if I wasn't hungry, which I was anyway. I was so hungry that I had already glanced at the fish food pots by the aquarium several times—and even at the fish themselves.

"Darling, you don't seem to understand yet," Verity Poole replied. "This softhearted slipping from discipline has turned Storm into a boy who has very few choices in life. The boy does not respect boundaries. You can only blame yourself. Fortunately I am here to take care of these things. Without me, we would soon be back where we started."

I heard some kind of mumbling. Dad evidently agreed.

I sat on my desk and stared at the darkening city between my Superman curtains. Because I didn't want to think about Mom, I started to think about the curtains and how intensely I hated them. If you saw them, you would know what I am talking about. You'd hate them, too. There is no way you'd ever want curtains like those in your window, and if you have nice parents—and I am sure you do—those curtains would be taken down right now and put in the trash or given to your neighbor to wrap her dead cat in for burying in the garden. A shroud would be the best use for those curtains. To be honest I must confess that I hate almost all other curtains, too. It doesn't matter if they have nice pictures on them. I don't like things that cover up the world outside. They give me claustrophobia. I can also easily start imagining that I am sitting in prison, serving a life sentence.

Then I drifted into staring at the factory behind the roofs. It was a bit like a ghost ship without lights floating on the dark ocean, disease-ridden and forgotten, yet full of possibilities. Maybe India was there even now. I wondered if she had gotten into trouble because of me and what exactly *trouble* meant on that side of the battlement. Or was it just a wall?

The mirror-image boy in the window pressed his palm against mine.

I looked at the tower. I looked at it for so long that it started to sway in the end, and then I fell asleep.

23.

Will is expected in the office," Rob Reed hollered from the classroom door the next day.

We had just had the morning inspection, and every student was standing a little stupidly in the corridor. The morning inspection consisted of the students emptying their bags, pockets, and the contents of their desks onto their desktops, and then we stood waiting in the corridor for the teacher, the headmaster, and Counselor Poole to go around the class and check to see if anyone had anything forbidden or "rebellious." If they found anything, it was taken to the glass case. The glass case was stuffed full at this point, because something was always found. Many things were classed as rebellious. You couldn't predict when inspection was going to happen, because it always varied.

When Will's name was mentioned, he straightened up, although his back was already straight. It was a mystery how anyone could stand so straight.

"Your report is awaited," Rob announced, and Will immediately touched his forehead with the edge of his hand.

"Yes," he said in a monotone.

I didn't have long to enjoy getting rid of one of my nuisances, because I was being targeted myself. "This concerns you, too, Storm," Rob said. "You are both going."

At first I almost swallowed my tongue. Then I glanced at the badge on my sleeve.

We didn't look at each other much on the way to the office. Will marched alongside me as rhythmically as a metronome. Looking at him, I started to think that if I scratched the surface, I'd find a machine underneath. I slouched. I was desperately trying to work out why I was being taken and what they wanted from me this time, but I couldn't find an answer to either question.

"Storm, walk properly. Don't drag your feet," Rob encouraged. It seemed that Rob was also a direct descendant of metronomes.

The headmaster was sitting in his office behind his large desk. He was bending his long, thin fingers into unnatural shapes. "This is what being marked means," he said. "We don't defend you anymore. We don't punish those who attack you. It gives you a kind of foretaste of being an outlaw, which will happen to you if you lose your chances. We want you to learn. Do you understand?"

I really didn't understand. I didn't understand anything.

"Is everybody just allowed to throw trash at me?" I asked.

"Sir," the headmaster said.

"What?"

"Say *sir* politely when you are talking to me, the headmaster. Good manners are the top and bottom of everything. Are we rabble, Storm? Certainly not. What did you want to know?"

"Is everybody just allowed to throw trash at me, sir?"

The headmaster bent his forefinger against the desktop before answering. The finger kept on bending endlessly. Anyone else would have broken a bone doing that.

"That is how it is, unfortunately," he said at last. "We do not interfere. As a marked person, you have lost your immunity. It is a sort of suspended sentence. However, you still have a chance to fight to get rid of the badge. It is difficult but possible."

After the headmaster had talked for a while, he turned to look at Will. I also looked at my official friend then. He stood to attention next to me, as if he were a bow someone had drawn tight but forgotten to release.

"Will, yesterday you had an assignment. How did it go? Tell us," the headmaster urged.

Will bowed and started to speak. "Yesterday we threw waste from the kitchen at him, sir. Today he is wearing the badge on his sleeve, so there has been no need to punish him again."

The headmaster speared a doughnut with his long finger and started to move it toward another doughnut by the edge of the box. It seemed to me as if he were playing a mysterious board game. Soon one of the doughnuts would destroy the other. The one with the pink icing would destroy the one with the brown. Rob stood behind our backs the whole time. He was like flypaper hung on a doorframe, trapping everything—the cockroaches, the flies, the innocent, and the guilty.

After Will had finished, the headmaster looked at me. "Do us a favor. Do it, above all, for yourself. Get rid of the badge. Many have given up. Don't you do the same."

I nodded.

"Whose voice was it? Who spoke on the loudspeaker?" I asked and quickly added, "Sir."

"That's of no importance. We generally only refer to it as the school spirit."

"Like the spirit of the lamp? Or a ghost?"

The headmaster shook his head.

"As you have perhaps already realized, we don't go in for fairy stories here, but facts," he said. "The voice belongs to this school, the spirit of this school. Here everyone pulls together—the students, as well as the teachers, and, of course, all the other staff. We look after each other. We reward, punish, serve. Everything is shared. Shared things. That's what it means. The spirit permeates everything. If you disobey us, you shouldn't trust anything anymore—not even the food you put in your mouth. At this school the parents of the students are also pledged to this."

I frowned.

"Oh, yes, that reminds me," the headmaster said, and I began to expect the worst. "You probably want to hear the news concerning your mother. She called us here at school, and we have informed her of your current position. She was very worried but understands the situation. As you perhaps know, your mother has had problems with her business and has had to leave the city. As we have asked her not to speak with you out of respect for the school spirit and principles, she will not contact you. We told your mother that it would not be a good thing to interfere with your life. You now need all your strength to get rid of the nastiness, all the wickedness that seems to cling to you more tightly than we imagined. Do you want to try?"

"I do."

"We will not, however, protect you from the peer pressure of your friends—not for the time being."

I nodded.

"Coach Reed has agreed to include you on the Possibilities' soccer team. That will give you a start. It's a shortcut."

I looked at the floor and thought about what I had heard. A long line of ants was bustling along where the wallpaper ended and the floor began. I raised my eyes back to the headmaster, who was just biting into a doughnut. Was there anything I could do? Was there anything *else* I could do?

"I'll try. I'll do my best," I said.

"That's what I like to hear," the headmaster said, and he reached out to shake my hand. He wrapped his fingers, sticky with sugar, around my hand.

Rob Reed also patted me on the shoulder. "It'll be all right. You'll learn quickly," he said with good humor. "The first training session is after school today."

24.

I started on the team that same evening.

I had some skill with the ball, which soon became obvious and surprised everyone, including me. I managed to keep up—and not *just* keep up, either. I was actually quite good, or at least you could see that I was going to be good. I had decided to succeed. That was the starting point. Then I just ran. I also shot, passed, attacked, defended, and feinted. I kept getting the ball, losing it, and then running even faster. I ran between two defenders toward the goal, hit the post but didn't give up, then tried again, and finally scored. I became a ball chaser and enjoyed it. At least I tried hard to enjoy it. I had decided not to miss "it"—not anymore. I would forget skating. The world is round like a ball, not flat like a skateboard. That was proved centuries ago, and it was time I accepted it. When you start to get better and better at soccer, the dreams change, and the boy changes with them. That's what happens when you become a soccer player. That is what would happen to me when I became a soccer player. I would stop seeing places for doing tricks everywhere and instead start noticing good locations to practice passing. Railings and stairs would stop being interesting, and they would be replaced by open spaces. My new dream city would be a level green, not a bumpy and hilly skater's paradise.

The one flaw in my new career was that I only got to play in training games. That became clear after a while. I was a substitute. My teammates kept their distance. They glanced suspiciously at my badge, but they still let me have a go. It was their duty. The marked student must be allowed to try to get rid of the badge. The team had no other obligation. They were allowed to abandon me outside in the rain to get changed and prevent me from drinking from the water fountain. A surly wall of backs and stiff necks formed a barricade in front of it, and it was impossible to get through.

But I was allowed to *try* to get rid of my badge, and I certainly did just that. If trying was rewarded with bags of money, I would have received a dozen of them. Of course all the time I thought that I would soon get rid of the badge, that Mom would again be allowed to contact me, and that Dad would no longer have to retreat into his restaurant kitchen to avoid having to speak to me. Things would return to normal, and I would again have my chance.

When I returned home after the first training session, a group was gathered around the kitchen table waiting for me. At first I imagined that an insect, a spider, or some other creature with lots of protuberances, tails, feelers, limbs, and other swaying parts was in the room, because that was what the shadow on the wall looked like. Then I stepped inside and saw that it was just the light from a reading lamp playing tricks and that Verity Poole, her daughter, and my official girlfriend were all sewing at the table. The shadows of the threads and the needles were like long fishing lines, a net that would trap me if I took a wrong step—or would trap me no matter what I was doing.

"Bring these to your room," Poole said, taking a pile of marked garments from the table and pushing them into my arms.

There were shirts, pants, long and short underpants, socks, and T-shirts in the pile. There were more clothes on the table in a jumbled heap. They were all mine. In a box next to the clothes and the reels of thread was a pile of very familiar badges. The sewing circle was attaching them to my clothes.

Everything was marked. It was almost too much to bear.

I carried the pile to my room and heard what I didn't want to hear. Bridget was running after me.

"I'll help you," she shouted from the door.

"No you won't," I said. I was about to shut the door in her face when I remembered all my sacred promises to be obedient—to do my best, that is—so I let her in. She turned her nose up at a pile of junk and went to stare at the fish.

"India was here!" Bridget suddenly cried out. "Why does it say so on the aquarium?"

I gulped. I didn't know about that.

"There's something else, too," Bridget said and bent closer to the glass. "There's a lollipop in the aquarium!" she shouted. "Two lollipops! And there's a third one."

Bridget looked at me, puzzled. "Why do you have lollipops in your aquarium?"

"Do I?" I yelled and shot across to look.

There really were lollipops in the aquarium. They stood in the sand between a couple of tufts of waterweed like a cluster of mushrooms that had gotten lost underwater. A snail was crawling on top of one of them.

At first I didn't know what to say, but then I did. "It's for the fish. I want to—I was trying to cheer them up."

"Fish don't eat candy," Bridget interrupted.

"Tell that to the fish," I said and spread my arms innocently. "I'm training them."

"Training?"

I nodded enthusiastically. "Haven't you heard that you use treats for training animals?"

Bridget snorted. "That's dog training," she said.

"These are Indian catfish," I said. "They want to feel like they are in India, in the Indian Ocean. I wrote *India* on the glass so that they wouldn't forget their roots."

"You're lying. As if fish could read."

I shook my head. "I just told you that I'm training them. It hasn't been proved that fish can't learn to read. Catfish are quite intelligent."

Bridget looked at me suspiciously. There was a limit even to her gullibility.

"Well, I just wrote it," I said. "For no reason. For fun."

Bridget had started to rummage around my room. It was really disturbing. She spoke without pausing for breath. She was everywhere and touched everything. It really made me feel sick. I almost wanted to push the girl into the aquarium to calm her down.

"I thought of asking to be excused from the position of girlfriend after your lapse," she said and looked at me with her hands on her hips, like adults do when they are angry. "That's what I thought, quite seriously, but then I realized that now you need me more than ever."

Then she forced her way into my closet and picked up the skateboard pieces. "What are these?" she asked.

I snatched the pieces from her and threw them back into the closet. I closed the door and leaned on it. "Maybe it would be best if you left now," I said.

Later I picked the lollipops out of the aquarium and washed India's writing off the glass.

What was she trying to tell me?

The factory is not far. I am there, watching. I see you all the time. I am a guard.

I pushed a wet lollipop into my mouth.

25.

My role on the Possibilities' team went like this: take part in training games, never in proper matches, run, run, and do your best, then clean the changing room and watch from the edge of the playing field while the others get to play real matches against real opponents.

The most miserable part of the hobby was just that—I didn't get to play for real. I would have liked to. You would have, too. It's frustrating to see a bad player lose the ball in a situation you know you would be able to control. I could have tried to get rid of the badge by playing better than anyone else. I would have done that and gotten my Mom back at the same time.

That was what I thought, but I didn't know everything about the School of Possibilities.

The hall, the shiny floors off which I had cleaned food waste on my second morning at school, became more than familiar to me. It was the same building where I had been sentenced and marked—the pride and the heart of the School of Possibilities. It was still new and shiny, and there was a lot of it to clean: long corridors, windows, benches, lockers, and underneath them all. They became really familiar to me as I, with the other marked ones, scrubbed everything. Sometimes the other players organized surprises for us. They were called Easter eggs. I might find a pile of dog droppings or a dead rabbit under a bench. All I could do in these situations was scoop the carcass onto a shovel and dump it into a trash bag.

Team shirts with school mottoes and ads were worn for matches. Because the city had financed the hall as a reward for the exemplary work the headmaster had done on the education of children who had strayed, the shirts bore the city's crests. Many wealthy city center businesses also sponsored the team. I had badges on all my clothes—even on my shoes. Marked girls washed and repaired the team's sports gear after matches. Girlfriends of the marked were also on the laundry team. Bridget was, too. She told me that she saw it as her duty.

When I asked Rob about league matches, he just tapped his protruding chin with the whistle. "Your time will come," he said. "We have a big tournament coming up in the spring. That's when we'll see who's who. That's when you'll have your opportunity."

"Not until spring?" I complained. "Do I have to sweep the changing rooms until then and watch worse players than me foul up on the playing field?"

"Tut-tut, boy," Rob said, again tapping his chin with the whistle. "If you have a badge, you can't play in matches. You must have the right attitude. You must get rid of the badge. You must get rid of the badge, boy," he said and blew the whistle.

The team ran from the playing field and gathered around him. Some of them glanced at me and snickered. Rob handed me a broom and ordered me into the changing room. A new surprise was awaiting me—a stinking, thawed-out chicken lay in the washbasin.

At the same time as my hobby was progressing, a new execution device was rising up in the punishment corner. It wasn't a gallows or a guillotine. It wasn't a pot for executioners to boil murderers alive in over a low fire. It looked a bit like a hut. You know, the shack in the children's song, built by the second-dumbest pig, which the wolf easily blew down. The structure looked innocent enough.

"Is it a bonfire?" Alexander asked.

The teacher shook her head.

"The punishment is inside it," she said and wouldn't say any more. "All will be revealed in time." She tapped the door of the shack she had drawn with her pointer. No one answered the door. I didn't know whether that was a good or bad thing. Sometimes during a lesson, I would stop and stare at the door of the hut. I thought about the punishment inside, it devoured bad deeds and kept on growing.

The next sentencing at the school was on Friday. During the first recess of the morning, there were whispers, and after lunch it became clear that the rumors were accurate. This time the broadcast was being followed on television in the classrooms. The boy brought in front of the sports hall court was Jack from the third grade. He looked small on the large field, but according to the voice coming from the loudspeaker, he deserved his punishment.

On the surface, the boy looked innocent, but the list of his misdeeds was as long as a spoiled child's list for Santa Claus. I looked at Jack sweating in the spotlight and knew that soon he would be cleaning up dirt and surprises in the sports hall corridors. For us other marked ones, the work would ease off. I was a little shocked when I realized what I had just been thinking.

I heard nothing from India.

I had thought about her, but because my days were full and my evenings even fuller, I finally forgot about her. I played soccer, and I cleaned. When I closed my eyes, I saw kicks: free kicks, penalty kicks, corner kicks, and goal kicks. I also saw swinging mops and miles of dirty corridors lit by electric lights. As the school year properly got underway, there was also a lot of homework, which meant dozens of pages and several hours a day. Finishing it usually took until late evening, when all the daylight had gone from the world. The School of Possibilities focused on language skills. English alone was not enough in this world. It was also good for every child to learn elementary Latin, Hebrew, and Sanskrit. In case you didn't know, soccer in Latin is *follis*, and a penalty kick is *iactus poenalis*.

With Dad's agreement, Miss Poole had also enrolled me in the Russian club.

"The boy can then work in the summer as a waiter in his father's restaurant," she had said to the headmaster, so I had another useful hobby to add to the list. The language I learned to speak was a mixture of all the languages. Russian, Hebrew, and Sanskrit words got mixed up with each other, and the sentences I uttered might have started in Russian and ended in Hebrew. Bridget came to my home every day after school, and we sat at the kitchen table doing our homework. She tested my vocabulary. At school there were random tests: vocabulary tests, oral tests, and cross-examinations. For good results you got flowers. For bad ones you received more lines on the gallows.

Then one evening Moon appeared in my room—or to be more precise, he descended into my room through the window. He was alone.

26.

When Moon peeked through the window into my room and woke me, I had already been asleep for a while, having loads of dreams, all of them featuring soccer balls and some including a broom. The balls were more like animals than objects. They had a will of their own, and I didn't know what they wanted. They didn't have eyes. Balls don't have eyes, even in dreams, but these were still able to run away from my feet and stop me from scoring. They looked quite like beetles, and I couldn't seem to catch them. I never touched a ball. I didn't score a single goal, although I flailed my foot around and sometimes wielded a broom. One of the balls was a chocolate egg, and it melted into liquid before crossing the goal line.

As I opened my eyes, the dream continued—sort of. Or that was what I imagined, because in the window, I saw Moon. And I don't mean the white heavenly body that orbits the Earth, but the small boy with sticky hair. It looked as if he was hanging in the air.

I sat up and rubbed my eyes.

Moon stayed where he was. He was swinging by a rope and trying to reach the windowsill with the tips of his shoes. When he had managed to attach himself, he pressed his hand against the glass and looked at the room from under his other arm. He pushed his nose flat against the glass.

He wanted to come inside.

I pushed my feet down onto the floor and ran to the window. I opened the latch, and a damp night wind swept into the room. The Superman curtains flapped in the breeze. Moon crawled between them onto the desk and knocked off the schoolbooks. He looked at me, crouching down like an alert animal.

"Moon! Where's Ra?" I asked.

Moon shook his head and looked out of the window. He had a rope around him.

"India has something to tell you," he said.

"Where is India? Why didn't she come herself?"

"She can't."

"Where's Ra?"

"A hostage," Moon answered.

"Hostage?"

"I have to go back soon, or Ra will be in the tower all alone. Ra gets scared in there. There are crackers. They crunch."

I nodded. Of course crackers crunched. That's what crackers did.

"What does India want to tell me?" I asked quickly.

"You have to come with me. She'll tell you herself."

"How can I come with you? I can't fly, and the door is locked." I ran to the door and pressed down the handle to prove it. The door remained firmly shut.

But Moon wasn't listening to me. He shoved his head out the window and whistled. I climbed beside him on the table and peered out of the window. Long blond hair and a piece of white lace train flowed over the edge of the roof.

"Is that Mew?" I asked.

Moon glanced at me and nodded. Then he whistled again, and Mew dropped a rope from the roof. The end of it swayed in front of us, exactly where Moon had come down a moment earlier. Moon snatched the rope and yanked. He then handed the rope to me.

"Tie it around yourself," he said.

I stared at the rope. I didn't take it.

"We have to hurry," Moon said impatiently and shook the end of the rope in front of me.

I could have gone. It would have been easy. I would have met India and then returned home. No one would have noticed a thing. I glanced at my soccer shoes on the floor and then at the School of Possibilities team shirt, which hung on a hanger on the closet door, washed and ironed by Miss Poole. There weren't any risks—or were there? Everything had been going well at school lately. I hadn't been caught doing anything wrong. I had gotten several flowers in the punishment corner, and even a couple of butterflies, which were far more difficult to get. I could soon be rid of the badge.

Was it worth sacrificing all that?

"I can't come," I said quietly.

"You can't?" Moon sighed in disbelief, and then he again shook the end of the rope. "Of course you can. You need to."

"No! I need to get rid of this," I said emphatically and yanked my pajama sleeve so that he could see the badge. "If I get caught escaping, I'll lose my chance."

Moon looked at my badge and quickly turned his head away.

"You will get rid of it," he said quietly. "But...it's horrible."

I looked at him, frowning. Moon avoided my eyes.

"What do you mean?" I asked. I pressed the shiny surface of the badge with my fingers. It felt a little different now. It stung my fingertips like disinfectant.

I grabbed his arm. "Will I get rid of this?"

Moon kept glancing at the window furtively. He nodded.

"In the basement," he whispered and pressed the edge of his hand against his throat, as if it were a sharp knife and not his small hand. "That's where the marked—" Moon then fell silent. He pushed the rope toward me.

I caught it. The damp asphalt shone below me. The windshields of the cars in the parking lot also shone. The leaves on the trees and the puddles of water glistened. The whole night glimmered. It was quite beautiful, really. I nearly started to cry—that's how weird I felt at that moment, and I felt unbelievably lonely, almost as if I had died. The factory tower was observing this situation, black among the gray clouds, housed in the middle of the darkness. It was familiar to me, like an old summer place from the past where everything was good and you were five or even younger—young enough not to have to make any decisions about right or wrong or anything at all.

I breathed in the cold drizzle deeply, as if I was gathering courage. Then I walked uncertainly, taking really small steps, toward the window. I looked down. The dark asphalt was waiting, and it didn't look like a very promising landing pad. I thought about the jump. If the rope didn't pull me up into the air, it would be almost like committing suicide or something as bad as that.

I closed my eyes and tied the rope around me.

Then the key to my door clicked, and the door opened.

I looked behind me.

Miss Poole was standing there with her hand on the doorframe. She was wearing a flowing nightgown, and she was staring at us. Although her eyes were only shadows in the dark, I saw that they were shining, that they were as deep as an abyss. She let out a shrill shriek. It sounded more like a bird than a human being, and it made my heart freeze.

Moon, crouching beside me, was also shaken. He squeezed my arm.

"The masks," he whispered, and his eyes had become as big as pools.

"What?" I cried out.

"Beware the masks," he whispered and stood up.

I moved next to him.

"It's about your mother..." Moon hissed. "India knows where she is." He stepped onto the windowsill, took a deep breath, and jumped.

"Grab him!" Poole shrieked behind me. "Grab that boy, Storm!"

I nearly closed my eyes but didn't, and I saw Moon disappear from the window.

"No!" I yelled and threw myself out after him.

I was hanging by my waist half in, half out of the room, like a rug about to be aired or shaken. I saw the asphalt below me—only the damp, shiny asphalt, not Moon. When I looked up, I saw the sky. It was gray and smooth like a wall. Moon had disappeared.

Poole yanked me back into the room and started to lean out the window. She was trying to see something. She was also looking at the ground and the sky. Then she got up and straightened her back. "It is dangerous to keep windows open at night," she said very calmly and closed the window. "Anything could come into the room. Now go to bed. You'll catch a chill." She swept out of the room and soon returned with the door of the crockery cupboard. She nailed it over my window. She had her mouth full of nails, which she immediately banged into the frame. "Now you are safe, dear child," she said and tucked me into bed. "We'll get some bars for the window soon."

The key clicked in the lock.

27.

It's about your mother.

I thought about Moon's words all day at school.

Beware the masks. And then: *In the basement.*

"What are you thinking about?" Bridget nagged.

"I'm not thinking about anything," I said and sank back into silence. It was like quicksand that made me sink deeper every time I moved. Outside, beyond the window, was the yard, and beyond the yard were the tracks and the trains. I had great difficulty in keeping my eyes off the factory beyond them.

It's about your mother.

What had Moon meant by that...or the masks?

India wanted to tell me something.

India has something to tell you. She knows about your mom.

I knew, too. I knew that Mom had left. She had closed down her sewing business and sold the wedding dresses. She had changed cities—maybe even countries—and wanted me to succeed at this school. She hadn't said good-bye to me, because she hated farewells. I knew that. When I moved from Mom's to Dad's on Fridays, Mom had barricaded herself in the bathroom and only emerged after I was gone.

Had Mom left her address with someone? Maybe she had given it to one of her former boyfriends? There had been a lot of them, but I knew hardly anything about them—only their names. One was Julius, another was Eric, and a third was Gunnar. There had been others. I didn't even know the names of some of them—only their hobbies or jobs. The tall man played basketball. The shorter one with the crew cut hacked hunchbacked human figures out of stone. The guy with the tan mended clocks. I didn't know where any of them lived. Besides, the men usually turned nasty when they stopped liking Mom. Mom would surely not have left her address with the dude who had thrown the contents of the milk carton at her during breakfast or the one who had written obscenities in black marker on a wedding dress she was working on.

After school I walked home with Bridget. I was desperately thinking how to defeat the locked doors so that I could visit the factory. When I went into my room, I took India's skateboard pieces from the closet and turned them around in my hands. I tried to find some communication in them—message, something, anything. I scratched the paint with my nail.

Suddenly I felt scared. I felt like I was somewhere high up, losing my grip. I tried to recall things I had thought important a couple of weeks or months ago. I could hardly remember. I strained my memory, frowning.

I had changed or was in the process of changing. Something had happened to me.

The School of Possibilities was the cause.

"Stooooormmm!" Bridget called from the kitchen. "Stooorrm! History awaits you."

I pushed the skateboard pieces under the covers and slouched into the kitchen.

Later that night I woke up with a feeling that someone was near me. I got up immediately and crept to the window. The Superman curtains swayed in front of the boarded-up windows. There were no bars—not yet. Poole had already ordered them. "As strong as possible. The best steel." That was what she had told the installer on the phone, with a torrent of explanations over the necessity for the bars and the urgency of the matter.

Suddenly I heard a sound behind the boards. It was scratching, or maybe it was rustling. Was Moon there...or India?

I pushed my fingers into the gaps between the boards, but I couldn't see anything. All the time I could hear Miss Poole moving about in the apartment behind my locked door. She might come in at any moment. Perhaps whoever was scratching also knew or sensed this, because he or she disappeared quite soon. I felt disappointed in a strange sort of way.

In the morning, as I ran across the parking lot to where Bridget waited for me every morning, I noticed that something was written on the window, that words had been sprayed on it. I stopped and shaded my eyes. BASEMENT, it said, and then several times, BEWARE. I squinted and saw: BEWARE! BEWARE! BEWARE!

28.

Then the posters appeared. They were stuck up everywhere. They were in the corridors, on the doors, on the fence. I also saw them in town. The students of the School of Possibilities had distributed them. Some students stood in the marketplace and handed out leaflets. The whole school took part.

This is what the posters said:

THE CARNIVAL OF POSSIBILITIES IS APPROACHING

FACTS ABOUT DISOBEDIENCE AND THE FIGHT AGAINST IT

HIGHLIGHT: SOCCER TOURNAMENT

IDEAS AND ENTHUSIASM

REMEMBER: BE WHERE IT'S HAPPENING

ENTERTAINMENT

FOOD AND MUSIC

THE MODEL STUDENTS' DANCE TROUPE PERFORMS: THE BIG WITCH HUNT

LIBERATION CEREMONY

The Liberation Ceremony?

It was the last item listed in the leaflet.

I wondered what it meant and immediately asked Bridget, who was examining the poster beside me. "What is this great Liberation Ceremony?"

"You will be liberated from your badge there," Will's voice answered from behind me. That boy was a real world champion at sneaking around. I turned around to look at his military-stern, waxy face.

"I will?"

"If you deserve it," he added. "It has to be earned."

"What happens after that?"

He looked at me seriously. "You will be allowed to play."

"Is that all?" I sighed, quite pleased. "That's good. I would like to play in the tournament. The team needs me." I smiled a little. Will didn't smile back.

The appearance of the posters kicked off the preparations for the fair. There was still some time until the event, but every teacher, student, mother, and father seemed to be bustling about, preparing for the fair or the big tournament. The students' parents sold raffle tickets and organized fund-raisers in the schoolyard on the weekends. Dad baked small pies for raffle prizes in his restaurant kitchen.

Nothing was heard of Mom or India. No more lollipops appeared in the aquarium. I felt as if I was waiting for something all the time.

29.

Then Dad disappeared, I made a discovery, and nothing was ever the same again—nor could it be.

"Dad," I called into the kitchen in the morning. "I need your signature on this exam paper."

Dad usually slept later than me and the other two occupants of the pad. The restaurant didn't open until evening, and it stayed open until midnight. After closing up, Dad always made sure that everything was ready for the next day. In the mornings he usually dragged himself into the hall to say good-bye to me as I put on my shoes and backpack. The other members of the family were always awake—or so it seemed. Mona left for school before me, and Miss Poole flitted about the corridors in her flapping coats at all hours of the day and night like some restless spirit in a ghost story.

"Dad!" I called again.

He didn't reply.

"He won't answer," Mona said.

"Won't answer? What do you mean, he won't answer?"

"He won't answer because he's not here," Mona said and stared at me with her head tilted back.

"So where is he?"

"How should I know? I'm just telling you what it said on the refrigerator door."

I pushed her aside and dashed into the kitchen.

There was a piece of paper held on the refrigerator door by a magnet. I read it through several times without believing a word.

I HAD TO LEAVE. I HOPE WE WILL SEE EACH OTHER AGAIN.

TAKE THESE PIES TO SCHOOL. THEY ARE FOR THE RAFFLE.

That was what it said. Next to it was a boxful of the pies Dad had baked.

"What the hell?" I shrieked. I was choking.

"What is that you've got there?" said Miss Poole, who had appeared in the kitchen and took the exam paper from my hand. "That's very good. I'll sign it now that your father's gone."

"Where is Dad?" I shouted. "I want Dad here immediately!"

Miss Poole shook her head sadly.

"Vladimir appears to have left us. Sometimes people do that. Leave without a trace. Unexplained disappearances. It is sad. I am terribly disappointed."

"Dad wouldn't do that. Never!" I shouted.

"My eardrums will burst," Mona complained. "Tell the prince to be quiet."

"We'll let him have his tantrum for a moment," Miss Poole said and captured me in some sort of a stranglehold resembling a hug. "The poor little thing is almost alone in the world. Everyone has abandoned him."

"Storm's a crybaby," Mona said. "Look at me, Storm. I get along quite well without a father. Fathers aren't necessary."

I pressed my fists into my eyes really hard and counted to ten in all the languages I knew. *Unus*, *duo*, *tres*, and so on. My fingers were becoming horribly clammy.

"I have a father," I said. "I have a father and a mother."

"Then tell us. Where are they, and why have they left you?" Verity Poole asked. "Maybe they had enough of you. Or got tired. That happens, too. Not all parents can cope. But don't worry, because you won't be alone. We will take care of you. Me and the School of Possibilities. We are all there for you."

Maybe this was a nightmare. Maybe this was an age-restricted movie that I was acting in, even though I wouldn't have been allowed to watch it on television.

"Let's sign that paper of yours so that you won't get a reprimand," Verity Poole said and let go of me. She spread the history exam out on the dish drainer, signed it at a stroke, and pushed the paper to me. I stared at it, dumbfounded.

"You can't sign it."

"Yes, I can," she said calmly. "It requires the guardian's signature. Do you see such a person around? I am responsible for you until your father comes back—if he comes back, which I doubt, for men seldom do once they've left. You can call me *Mom* if you like."

I stared at her, and I couldn't believe my ears. *Mom*? Then I turned around faster than a flutter of a bird's wing and dashed out the door. I slid down the banister and ran outside. My heart was beating madly.

There was a note on the door of Restaurant Vladimir. It said, CLOSED.

Closed? And no explanation? No dates or promises of return?

I sat on the step and squeezed my arms really tightly around my knees.

I closed my eyes, and instantly I saw a sunny playing field and Dad. Mom stood on the edge of the field under a tree with her arms wrapped around her. It looked like she was hugging herself. Mom often stood like that. It was her habit. She looked at us, and I waved. My hands were on the handlebars of a new bike. "Here we go, Storm," Dad said to me, and I got on the bike. Dad kept hold of the crossbar and ran alongside me. I pedaled furiously, and then Dad let go as I carried on pedaling. I was really good at it and rode fast. There was the birch tree and Mom. There was the goal. "Dad, I can do it!" I shouted and then rode into the goal and straight through it.

Now I was alone.

As I thought about it, fear closed in around me. It was like a large snake winding its heavy body around me. Every time I breathed out, the pressure increased. The rib cage protects a human being. A human being is not as easy prey as a deer or a gazelle, but even a human being loses the battle in the end. At some point comes the moment when the ribs snap. At some point even the strongest boy is suffocated.

"Shall we go?" Bridget asked, appearing beside me.

I wiped my eyes.

"What are you doing? Are you crying?"

30.

The next morning I got a call. "Your dad," Mona said at the kitchen door. She waved the phone handset next to her ear.

I lunged forward to snatch it from her hand.

"Dad!" I screamed. "Where are you?"

"I have to be brief," Dad said. "Everything is fine. I have just left."

"I know," I interrupted. "Why didn't you take me with you?"

There was silence on the line for a while. Or rather, it was the sort of humming you'd hear in outer space. "Where are you?" I whispered.

"I can't tell you. I don't even know the address of this place. You have to accept it and obey. Obey Verity."

"What? I don't want to. Come and take me away." I was close to tears at that point. "That hag claims that she's my guardian. I have to call her *Madam Mother*. I will never call that old bag *Mom*. Tell her to stop it."

"Don't be nasty. You won't get rid of the badge if you can't behave yourself. Verity is now your guardian," Dad said. "Behave yourself. Otherwise I can't come back."

"Why did you abandon the restaurant?"

"I have a new job in a hotel kitchen," Dad said. "Your mother is here, too. She looks after the linen and cleans the rooms. We are fine. You just try to get rid of the badge."

"Are you two together again?" I asked. I was surprised and also pleased.

The line went silent for a moment.

"We just happen to work in the same place," he said.

"Will you both come back?"

"I have to go now."

"Wait!" I shouted.

There was only humming on the line.

"Call me again, Dad," I whispered into the hum.

Mona stood at the kitchen door with her arms folded, waiting.

"Well?"

"Well what?"

"Did he tell you why he abandoned you?"

I pushed Mona aside and went into the kitchen.

"He has *not* abandoned me," I said emphatically. "He told me that he is working at a five-star hotel with my mother. They have Jacuzzis in the rooms. When I get rid of the badge, they will come and get me. Dad will leave your mother. He has already changed his name back to John. We are going to live in the hotel."

Mona raised her eyebrows.

"You are lying, you stupid boy," she said. "With those skills, you should become a writer. The better the liar, the better the writer. Do you think anyone can leave my mother? That just doesn't happen."

31.

Have you heard anything from my dad?" I asked every morning and evening from then on. "Has Dad called, Madam Mother?" I always said that with particular emphasis so that Poole would understand that I meant to get rid of the badge and that my parents would come and collect me after that. I also watched the mailbox and guarded the phone. I looked up hotels in the phone directory. There were dozens of them—hundreds if you counted hostels, youth hostels, and farm accommodations. It was impossible to guess in which one Dad was working. The place might be in a totally different city. A visit to the headmaster's office had also confirmed what I already knew: the spirit of the school demanded that children must be left alone to reform. Poole reinforced this by having bars nailed on my window. I had to get rid of the badge. It was the only solution. I stopped waiting but not hoping. I wrote on the aquarium—things like, "Tell Dad that I will turn you into dessert." I also wrote that Verity was going to turn the Russian restaurant into a hamburger joint unless Dad came back to defend his goulash. If there was one thing Dad couldn't stand, it was hamburgers.

The fair was getting closer all the time, and the whole school was mobilized. The enthusiasm was almost catching. I waited tensely to be told how to get rid of the badge. I planned surprises to welcome Mom and Dad back.

Then one day during a math lesson, something extraordinary happened. First the teacher received a call from the office and then sent Will to fetch some things from the storeroom. She ordered me to go with him, which surprised the whole class, as well as me. Going into the storeroom was the number-one assignment of trust. Only students beyond any suspicion got to go there. They had no lines on their punishment hills. They were faultless. I wasn't like that. I was marked, and although I had done quite well at school, I was still a risk.

I followed Will into the corridor. I didn't scrawl my name on the wall, didn't scribble it on the door or anywhere else. Of course it occurred to me, but I overcame the temptation. I had stopped doing bad things and was becoming quite successful. "You are making progress, Storm," Rob had said at the weekly meeting, and it was surely true. A sizable swarm of butterflies was already fluttering around the teacher's half-finished shack in the punishment corner.

On the door at the end of the corridor, where Will inserted the key, it said, STORE and NO ENTRY. From the door I could see a brightly lit, narrow corridor with a line of shelves and archive cabinets rising up on both walls. They rose up several yards, massive as mountains. Between them I began to feel like an ant or some similar insect. I also began to feel claustrophobic, because the shelves seemed to fall in on me, they were so tall and full of stuff. There were all sorts of unused items and other things biding their time. I read the labels on the sides of the boxes while Will looked at the map marked with red crosses indicating the spots we had to visit. We walked for a long time. Will counted the turns the whole time, creasing both his forehead and the map. Every now and then, he turned around to look at me.

"It's easy to get lost in here," he said. "Stay close, and you'll get out."

I did. I didn't even consider doing anything else. The place was like a labyrinth. No one would want to get lost in such a place.

Will walked on with his nose in the map, interpreting the markings carved on the ends of the stacks. After the sixth or seventh turn, he found the spot he had been looking for. He ordered me to climb up a ladder to the edge of the ceiling and bring down boxes 505XY and 601KB.

They weren't very heavy.

"What's in these?" I asked as we fastened the boxes to the cart.

"None of our business," Will replied.

As we continued on our way, something unexpected happened.

Will disappeared around a corner, and a short circuit—or who knew what—cut out the electricity. The lights went out. The ensuing darkness was total. It was astonishing in a place that was never dark. I wondered if the lights had gone out elsewhere in the school at the same time. I tried to feel my way in the same direction that I had seen Will disappear. I called him, and when I received no reply, I staggered forward. The darkness around me was the kind of total and ravenous darkness that ate up sound and that you never got used to. Darkness like that couldn't last forever—at least not in the School of Possibilities, which was always full of light. I continued onward between the stacks and was no longer sure whether I was going back or deeper into the bowels of the storeroom.

I called Will again.

"Will!" I yelled. He didn't reply, because he couldn't hear me. And I couldn't hear him. The shout was stifled among all those boxes. There was no echo. It was like yelling into velvet.

When I came to a corner, I turned. When I came to stairs, I climbed. When I encountered an obstacle, I went around it. Of course I knew that if you got lost—lost in a forest, for example—you first had to work out your location and only then go on. Otherwise a lost person could go around and around in circles and lose his strength vainly trying to find the way out. In spite of this, I carried on walking, because I also knew that you could die in the snow if you stopped and fell asleep.

Then the floor beneath me vanished, and I fell. Suddenly there was only an abyss and hard objects against which I crashed but couldn't see. When I finally came to a stop, I stayed down, motionless. At first I didn't dare move, and then when I did, I immediately felt all sorts of pains in various places. I was at least bruised and probably broken into several pieces.

I tried to work out where I was, and by feeling the floor, I found the stairs. Then I found the walls, and at last a doorway.

I listened to the darkness. It sounded like breathing.

I want you to remember what I just said. This was the first time I have talked about breathing. Breathing was my first thought, my first mental image. There was someone breathing down here. That was exactly what I thought. Only later, when the lights came back on, did I think of ventilation, air conditioning, and other obvious and mundane things. Breathing was not a mundane thing. It was a strange thought. It is the sort of thing you start to think about when you are standing in the dark, hurt and lost. You think that way because of the darkness, the same way that you start to believe there is someone under the bed or in the closet—someone waiting in the dark. Darkness turns familiar objects in the room into things you can't identify. It makes the world a colorless shadow. When the lights finally came back on, I realized it was just the air conditioning. That was when I stopped thinking about breathing.

Still wandering in the darkness, I had fallen into some kind of a large space. The room was as cold as a refrigerator, and right away my skin came up in goose bumps.

I called for Will again. The echo of my voice remained flickering in the darkness like an anxious shadow. I heard sounds like creaks or footsteps among the humming. At first I thought that Will might be down here, injured, that maybe he'd fallen down the same stairs and that the boxes he'd been pulling were lying on top of him. As he'd been walking in front of me, it was possible—even likely. Although I didn't like him, the thought of him lying injured somewhere nearby was frightening.

I felt the floor in front of me with my toes. Every move hurt.

"Will, are you here? Did you fall, too?"

Suddenly the lights came back on. They crackled for a moment and went out, but finally they lit the whole place. Everything changed at a stroke. If I had imagined that the fall in the dark had taken me to some kind of an underground dungeon, I was mistaken. The room wasn't dirty, nor did it look like a pit or a cave. It was a large hall and looked like the sterile operating theater I remembered from a class visit to the central hospital. White and blue tiles gleamed on the walls and the floor. The lights revealed every nook and cranny.

In the middle of the room was a bed—a kind of table covered with green sheets. Glass cases lined the walls.

I walked toward the cases carefully—the way you walk on thin ice or on glass that probably can't take your weight. I knew that something was there, waiting for me.

And so there was. Even so, the sight took me by surprise.

Behind the glass of one case was a face. There was a little boy who stared at me without blinking, like someone who had fallen asleep with his eyes open while playing. There was something in the boy's eyes that almost made me expect he'd immediately open his mouth and start to talk or sing.

I stepped up to a second glass case and then to a third. I gasped, but I went on to a fourth, fifth, and sixth case. There were dozens of them in the room, and behind them all, there were more faces, more children, and then—

My heart was pounding anxiously.

Inside the next glass case was a familiar boy. It was Will.

I cried out loud, and the floor began to sway beneath my feet. It was as if I were out at sea in a storm, and I was getting seasick. I could have vomited over the railing. In spite of this, I forced my-self to open my eyes and look at the boy more closely. He stared at me with startlingly live eyes. But after the first scare had subsided, I realized that he wasn't alive, that he was just a doll like all the others in the room. He was missing arms and legs. He only had a face.

I looked hard at the boy. His face was familiar and strange at the same time. There was something in it that I couldn't recognize.

"So you found them," a familiar voice said behind my back.

I whirled around.

"Will!" I called out. He was standing behind me. He was staring at the face in the glass case with an inscrutable expression in his eyes.

"What are these?" I whispered.

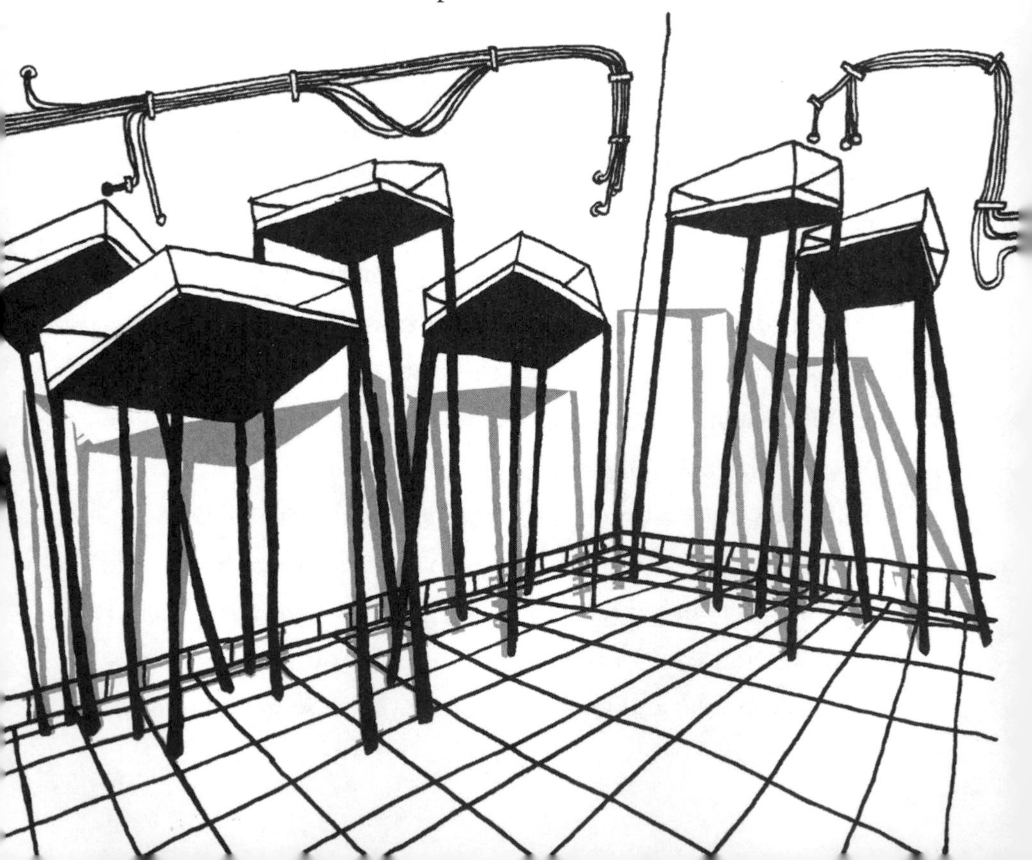

"They are death masks," Will said.

"Death masks," I said and tried to catch my breath.

"One is made of every student of the school. This is quite an impressive gallery."

I couldn't deny that.

"Why death masks? You're not—" I swallowed the word *dead*.

Will shook his head. "They are just portraits," he said. "This is a very old tradition. Did you know you can draw all sorts of conclusions from the shape of a head? You can tell if there are any criminal tendencies in a child or whether he is a genius or not. Come! I'll show you."

Will yanked my arm and pulled me along the rows of glass cases. I now recognized all the children looking at me from behind the sheets of glass. Some of them were in my own class.

"There's our team," Will said when we got to the back wall.

I peered into the cases, and true enough, there behind the sheets of glass was every player of the team. The whole squad was present—all except me and a couple of other marked ones.

"Should I have been allowed to see this?"

Will stared blankly at the goalkeeper's face.

"Maybe they wanted you to see them. Your turn is coming, too," he said. "See?"

Will pointed at a label on the lower edge of Alexander's case.

"What does it say?" he asked.

"'At the Liberation Ceremony on the fifteenth of April,'" I read from the label.

Will nodded.

"That was last year," he said. "You should have seen Alexander before then. The boy was hopeless. But now—"

I took a step back.

"I don't think I want to," I said.

"Don't you want to get rid of the badge?"

I stared at Alexander behind the glass. I wasn't so sure.

"Does it hurt?"

"Nah," Will huffed. "You don't feel a thing. It's like...like a dream. Otherwise you won't get rid of the badge, and you can't play on the team."

I went on looking at the face behind the glass and thought that it looked as if it were in water. Something in the faces made me wonder and also scared me. There was something more in them than in the live children around me...or something in the masks that was lacking in the children.

"This is the procedure," Will said and pointed at the pictures on the wall. They showed step-by-step instructions of how first a plaster cast was made of a child's face and then a mold, into which wax was poured. This was finished off and put into a glass case.

"Who does it?" I asked, no louder than a whisper.

32.

Hello, Storm," a voice said at the door. Verity Poole glowed in the bright lights of the room, as white as freshly fallen snow. Her clothes, like everything else in the hall, reminded me of a hospital.

"I've been expecting you. Your trusted friend seems to have shown you around already. He must surely have also told you about the idea of these masks. Thank you for that, Will."

Will nodded and took a step back.

I looked at him, astounded.

"You knew!" I said angrily. "You brought me here on purpose?"

Will wouldn't look at me.

"You wanted to get rid of the badge. It will take place here," Verity Poole said and took a green coat from a hook. She put it on.

"Now?" I cried.

"Oh, no, we are not usually hasty about these things."

"So you're not the counselor, after all?"

Miss Poole buttoned up her work coat. "You could call me that," she said and pushed her face closer to a mirror. Then she pursed her lips and smiled at her image. "I help children to cope. That is my task. I help students who have been given a last chance to start a new life. You, Storm, are naturally in a privileged position among them. You are, after all, almost my own son now that your father has left us."

"I am not your son, and Dad has not left me!"

I shouted this quite loudly, which did not faze Poole at all. She just carried on picking up jars from a closet, undisturbed, and piling them up on the table.

"You can go now," she said. "I'm about to start making the dough. You can take Storm back to the classroom, Will."

Will gestured for me to go with him. I followed, trying to swallow my anger.

When we were on the staircase leading to the storeroom and almost out of the hall, I noticed the posters on the wall. There was a long line of them. They looked like wanted posters. HAVE YOU SEEN THIS BOY? one of them even said.

"What are these?" I asked, pulling at the corner of a poster.

Will stopped and glanced over his shoulder at Miss Poole. She was just leaving by the back door.

"Escaped children," he said, lowering his voice.

I stepped closer.

"Have they escaped from the School of Possibilities?"

Strangely the matter had started to interest me. I moved on to the next picture.

Will looked at me with his head to one side.

"They are marked, or at least, they should be—every one of them," he said.

I stepped up to one of the pictures. Only now could I see it properly, and it made me gasp out loud. In the picture was a boy with his hair slicked smooth and freckles around his snub nose. In another poster next to it was the same boy wearing a different-colored top.

"I know him—or both of them," I whispered. I glanced at Will. He stared at me with a strange, hungry expression. Instantly, I realized that I had said too much.

"You know them? Is that what you said?" he asked.

I shook my head violently. "No, I don't, after all. I made a mistake."

Will raised his eyebrows. "They were at this school last year."

He walked on ahead of me and stopped in front of another picture.

"Look at this one," he said.

The girl in the poster looked right at the camera with her back straight, a severe look on her face. She had long blond hair in two tight braids. The look in her eyes could have meant anything. The girl was not wearing a ragged wedding dress, and her hair was not matted, but I recognized her anyway.

"She is one of the most dangerous children of all time," Will said. I could feel his suspicious, sharp look prickling against my skin.

"She looks dangerous," I said, trying to keep my voice normal. I moved closer to the poster and inspected the text on it. "They promise a reward for her capture," I said.

Will let out an odd hiss. "Seven thousand dollars," he said.

"That's a lot of money. What did she do?"

Will glanced over his shoulder. I did, too. Verity Poole was out of sight.

"She caused a death," Will whispered.

My eyes widened with amazement. "No!" I hissed. "What happened?"

"There was an explosion. A child died."

"And India?" The words came out. I looked for her picture on the wall.

Will's eyebrows rose then. "What about her?"

"She sat in my place. That's why I'm interested in her," I said quickly.

"She was also at this school a year ago," Will said. "Didn't you hear what the teacher said? There's no point in talking about her anymore." Will looked particularly sullen now.

"Is she dangerous, too?" I asked quietly.

Will didn't answer, because he was looking at the poster in front of him. His eyes glistened, and his laugh was vile.

"India was on the school team…" I tried again.

Will shook his head. "Not quite," he said. "She was marked like you. She showed promise with the ball. That's why I was annoyed when she disappeared from the scene. She would have been a positive strength on our team. You won't find anyone with a better eye for the game. But now…"

Will did something astonishing. He spat on the floor. "Now… she is nothing."

"What happens to them?" I asked. The children in the posters looked serious.

Will shrugged his shoulders. "They will lose…"

"Their chances?" I suggested.

"Their lives," Will said.

"Their lives?" I said, scared. "Are they going to be killed?"

Will shook his head. "Losing your life is not the same as death," he said calmly. "Some think that it's worse. I have heard that they will be exiled. When they are captured, they will be sent to...somewhere far away. I don't know where, exactly."

"To the School of the Lost," I suggested.

Will nodded. "So they say, but first they will be made harmless. At present the bounty hunters are hard on their heels."

"Oh?"

"If a School of Possibilities student sees any of the fugitives, it's his duty to inform the school staff or trusted students. If you know anything about the matter, you can—or rather, it's your duty to tell me."

"Are you still here?" Verity Poole said then. She had lowered her long-nailed hand onto Will's shoulder.

Will straightened his back and clicked his heels together. "I was just talking about the escapees and our duty to keep on the lookout for them."

Verity Poole nodded thoughtfully.

"Will is right," she said. "Sometimes children go missing. We must be alert. Take Storm away."

"Yes, Madam Counselor," Will said.

33.

The horror of the masks in the basement dissipated once I got back to my own classroom and desk. Now that I knew about them, that they existed, I wasn't so worried anymore. I repeated to myself that the masks were only a student archive and that they were an unusual but harmless way of keeping records of the students. A mask was a means of getting rid of the badge. My fear had been groundless. I had been frightened—but who wouldn't have been? The masks looked terrifying, even though they were just plaster and paint. The feeling of drowning was an illusion created by the lack of oxygen in the basement. A replica of my face would be made, and I would be free. Then Mom and Dad, crushed by my failure, would also return. The basement was oppressive, but that didn't matter. I wouldn't have to lie there. It would only be my face, only a mask, only an image.

At home I bent over to look at the fish that Dad had slipped into the aquarium. They glistened in the lamplight, probably imagining they were in a freshwater pond somewhere on the equator. They didn't know that they had been abandoned, that no one was interested in them, and that the vast ocean around them was just a mirror image reflected on the sides of the aquarium. One of the fish was floating belly-up on the surface. Maybe it had suffocated when it had realized this. I wrote some song lyrics on the glass of the aquarium, because I couldn't think of anything better to do. One of the songs was about greasy French fries being sold in the Russian restaurant downstairs.

Then I noticed the words.

BE AFRAID OF THE BASEMENT.

That was what it said on the aquarium glass. I squinted.

BE AFRAID OF THE BASEMENT. And then it continued: OPEN DOORS. DON'T CLOSE THEM. BREATHE AIR, NOT WATER.

I looked at the dead fish and read the words over and over again.

Was it a poem? If not a poem, then what? A warning?

Someone had walked in past all the locks to warn me. Was it India again? Or one of the boys? Mew—or someone else? I searched the aquarium for further messages. I searched for lollipops or candy wrappers, but there was nothing there.

OPEN DOORS. DON'T CLOSE THEM.

I wiped the glass clean and climbed onto the table. I peered at the factory through the bars. It stood alone in the dark. It was cold and drafty, but at the same time, it was a sanctuary where no one would find you—if you didn't want to be found, that is. I wondered if India was there now. No one seemed to know what had happened to her.

At some point a light came on in the tower.

On the spur of the moment, I placed India's skateboard up against the window.

Sometime later I fell asleep.

I dreamed of the masks.

I heard long, deep breaths in and out.

I awoke to a sound in the corridor. At first I thought that it was just Poole going to bed. Then the door rattled, and my heart began to hammer. Of course it could have been just the refrigerator coming on or the plumbing gurgling as someone next door flushed, but still, I was fully awake and alert.

Through the bars I saw a figure in the dimly lit yard.

It was crouching in the shelter of the hedge and waving its arms.

I pressed myself against the glass. The figure was signaling to me. There was no doubt about it. I then pressed my hand against the window—all five fingers spread out like a maple leaf. I tried to see whether the figure was Moon or Ra. Or was it India?

The light was still flickering in the factory tower.

I pushed my face against the glass.

If only it were possible to get to the yard and come back—or was it possible? I thought for a moment of what would happen if I was caught and I wasn't able to lose the badge. An indefinite sentence awaited anyone who had lost his last chance, and it would be served in the School of the Lost. That was a boarding school or a prison, and it meant being separated from your parents. Actually I was already separated from mine.

I looked at the skateboard hanging in the window for a moment. "If you need help, put a sign in the window, and I will come," India had said.

I went to the door and listened for sounds in the hall. There were none. I breathed deeply with my hand on the handle. I would have to go. It was important to ask about Mom. And now Dad, too, had disappeared. Maybe India knew about him, as well.

I pressed the handle down.

The door opened. I hadn't expected that.

I stood still for a moment with my hand on the handle. I listened to a new silence. Was it possible that Poole had forgotten to lock my room? I pushed the door ajar and peeked into the corridor. There was no one to be seen. Verity Poole wasn't floating along the corridor in her gauze nightgown. Mona wasn't shuffling restlessly from room to room. The living room was dark. The kitchen was dark. The refrigerator hummed, and the clock ticked. Apart from that it was quiet.

I stepped cautiously into the hall. Not one alarm rang out. Trip wires didn't spring.

I pulled on my shoes. I took my coat from the hook and unlocked the front door. I left a shoe wedged in the door so that it wouldn't close all the way.

I would go out quickly and return just as quickly.

Or that was what I thought.

"India!" I called in the yard very quietly, but there was no reply.

I ran to the factory and walked into the darkness.

"India!" I shouted.

I couldn't see anything.

"India!"

Suddenly I felt a hard blow. Then I fell over, and someone was pressing me onto the floor.

34.

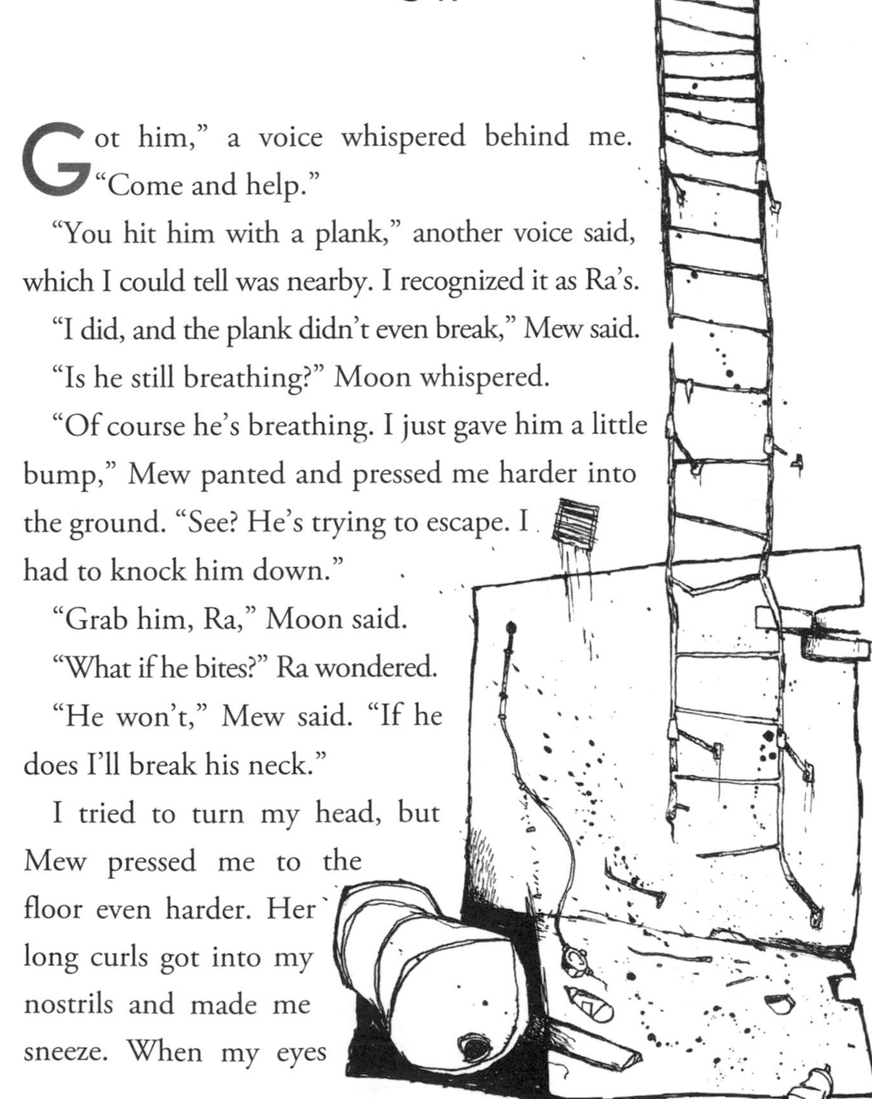

"Got him," a voice whispered behind me. "Come and help."

"You hit him with a plank," another voice said, which I could tell was nearby. I recognized it as Ra's.

"I did, and the plank didn't even break," Mew said.

"Is he still breathing?" Moon whispered.

"Of course he's breathing. I just gave him a little bump," Mew panted and pressed me harder into the ground. "See? He's trying to escape. I had to knock him down."

"Grab him, Ra," Moon said.

"What if he bites?" Ra wondered.

"He won't," Mew said. "If he does I'll break his neck."

I tried to turn my head, but Mew pressed me to the floor even harder. Her long curls got into my nostrils and made me sneeze. When my eyes eventually got used to the gloom, I saw dozens or even hundreds of spray paint cans and two pairs of dirty shoes. They stood in a puddle. Between one sneaker and a trouser leg, a hand was scratching an ankle.

"Where is India?" I groaned.

"He's talking," Ra squeaked.

Mew tugged my hair. "What are you doing here?" She pushed her face close to mine. She looked dirty and angry.

"India knows—" I mumbled with my chin against the floor. I tried to say something about Mom and the hotel, about Moon, who had been in my room, and about the messages on the aquarium; but I only got bits of dirty floor in my mouth, and the words were stifled.

"He's trying hard," Mew said severely and pushed me even harder into the floor.

"He's looking for India," Moon said.

Mew gave a hollow laugh. "Of course he's looking for India," she said. When Mew at last changed position, I was able to explain why I had come.

"I want to know where Mom and Dad are. I want to hear about the hotel where they work," I said.

"What's he talking about?" Mew asked, irritated.

"Should we help?" Ra said.

"It's almost a rule—" Moon agreed. "If someone marked needs help…"

"Rules," Mew snorted then. "As far as I'm concerned, they could have thrown him into the basement. Rather this boy than us."

"But—"

"You don't seem honest somehow, you snooper," Mew murmured into my ear, adjusting her position so that her knees were pressing into my back something nasty.

"India is my friend," I tried to say. "Moon and Ra, she is, isn't she?"

"Shut up," Mew snapped and rammed her knee into me again. "India has made mistakes before. She's sentimental, which is a problem. I wonder who she will entice here next. Maybe Will."

All three laughed.

A flood of swear words and the sound of ripping cloth followed the laugh. Then Mew blindfolded me, yanked my arms behind my back, and tied them up.

"I know what to do with him," she said.

"What should we do?" Moon and Ra said with one voice.

"We'll take him to the tower and throw him off. That's what you do with snoopers. It's a rule," Mew said.

"Is it?" the little boys yelled and sounded pleased.

"It's a rule I just invented, and now it's in force," Mew said.

"Take him! Take him!" Moon started to scream threateningly.

"Take him, and throw him off!" Ra joined in the excitement.

"You can't mean—I promise I won't tell anyone about you. I mean it," I whimpered, and I certainly did mean it. I feared for my life and was scared to death.

But Mew tugged me up and started to push me roughly in front of her. The cans clattered at our feet, and the dampness soaked through my sneakers.

"Tell me what you know about Mom and Dad. When I know, I'll go away and never come back," I said. "I won't mention India to anyone."

Suddenly they were all quiet, and Mew stopped prodding me forward.

"Have you told them about India?" Mew asked.

"Has he told them?" Moon asked, as well.

"Of course he has," Ra cried out. "What has he told them?"

"No, I haven't," I shouted. "I haven't said anything!"

Ra interrupted me. He started to babble with his hands over his ears, the way kids do when they don't want to hear what others are saying during an argument.

"We haven't done anything. Anything at all—at least, nothing bad," he chanted and wouldn't stop until Mew stamped her foot.

"You are a liar, and you definitely have told them about us," Mew said to me, tightening her grip. "But now we'll make sure that you stop blabbing."

I wrenched my arms wildly.

"Let me go. This is deprivation of my liberty and a crime."

Mew laughed again. "Did he say *crime*?" she asked. "Will he send us to jail if we don't obey?" More laughter followed these words. Then Mew moved me on again. "You see, we are already beyond all that," she said and pushed me in front of her. "We are outlaws and vagrants. There's a bunch of bounty hunters and school police and who knows what after us, and we don't care. We can throw you off the tower if we want to, and we damn well want to, don't we, boys?"

"We do," the boys shrieked, and then Mew untied my arms. She poked me in the back.

"There's the ladder. Climb!" she ordered.

I took hold of a rung and started to climb. The loosely tied rag fell away from my eyes, and I saw the rusty rungs.

"Don't drop me," I begged. "I'm on your side."

"Be quiet and climb," Mew said and poked me.

I climbed.

35.

The first thing I saw in the tower was India. She was sitting astride the railing, watching the city with the binoculars I had given her. "You found the snooper!" she exclaimed, lowering the binoculars to her lap. She wasn't smiling. She looked at me sharply. She looked at me as if I was some kind of intruder.

"I am not a snooper!" I shouted out in protest.

"He says he's your friend. Is it true?" Mew asked, climbing up next to me onto the tower platform.

India looked at me for a moment, tilting her head and then shaking it. "Isn't this the boy from the School of Possibilities? In that case I don't know him," she said, turning away. "You can do what you like with him."

From the darkness Moon and Ra appeared next to me.

"We are going to drop him," Moon said.

"Yes, we are," Ra said. "Storm has betrayed us. He has told them about you."

India spat over the railing and again looked at me.

"I haven't!" I shrieked. "I haven't betrayed you. I haven't! I haven't!"

Then India jumped down and walked in front of me. She bent over and pinched my chin between her thumb and forefinger. "I think we'll find out whether or not you are a snooper," she said. "We can squeeze the truth out of you like water from a sponge. We can use the school methods."

"School? What school?" I said, scared.

"The School of Possibilities, of course, stupid," Mew said.

"Let's try the thumbscrew," Ra suggested.

"Freezing," Moon added.

"Burning," Ra dreamed up.

Mew strode up and grabbed hold of me under my arms. "Oh, no, we'll drop him off the tower right now," she said, starting to drag me toward the rail. "Come and give me a hand!"

Moon and Ra came at me right away.

I made myself all floppy. I thrashed around and kicked. I called for help. "I don't want to die!" I shouted.

"Did you hear that?"

"He doesn't want to die."

"Doesn't he? Really?"

Suddenly they all started to laugh. India jumped back onto the rail and teetered recklessly. Mew slid down to sit against the cracked brick wall of the tower. They were both laughing. Moon and Ra were writhing around on the ground, giggling.

I stared at them all, confused, unable to understand what was happening.

"The fact is that we can't just damn well let him go now that he knows our names and that we are the most cunning gang of robbers in town," India said, lowering her voice and causing another burst of laughter.

Mew clambered next to me and gave my shoulder a shove.

"You probably thought we would really drop you," she said, stretching out to snatch Moon away from the ladder and stop him from falling.

"Did you think that?" Ra asked, interested.

I glanced at him and then at the other children. I nodded lamely.

"Aren't you going to, then?"

"Why the heck would we?" India sighed. "We want to save you, not bump you off." She looked at the city through the binoculars again.

"We also wanted to give you a bit of a reminder," Mew said. "You were, little by little, becoming just like the others there." She spat out the last part and then pulled a face.

India was pointing the binoculars at the School of Possibilities' yard.

"We keep an eye on that lot. We are on our guard all the time," she said. "These have been useful." India patted the binoculars.

"That's how you knew to come to the school, when they—" I said, at the same time making a throwing movement. "When I was marked."

India glanced at me and nodded.

"There are warrants out for you," I then said.

Now they all looked at me. "We know that," Mew said. "Some clever bounty hunter is trying to get a large amount of money out of finding us, don't you think, friends?"

"Loads of crisp notes for soccer shoes," Moon said.

"And plane tickets to the World Championships for the whole family," added Ra.

"Aren't you scared?"

"What is that?" Mew sighed. "We don't think about such things."

"We haven't got time," India said.

"We are dangerous kids," Moon explained.

"They want us," Ra added. "Our heads on stakes."

Both boys laughed. They shook their heads so that their hair flew around.

"The fooling around stops now, or you'll lose your heads before a single bounty hunter gets to the scene," Mew threatened, but she said it quite softly. Then she wiped the boys' snotty noses on an old newspaper she picked up off the floor. "We haven't had anything to eat for ages," she said. "Should we just take Storm to our place and put that right?"

The boys started to whoop.

"Let's check the traps."

"We want rat!"

"I want pigeon—"

"—and a bat."

"A couple of cockroach sandwiches."

36.

The factory was as big as a city. It was a maze with endless black corridors always leading to new corridors. It was packed full of rooms, stairs, dead ends, ladders into the gloom, and drops into the dark.

"Careful!" India shouted and grabbed my arm when I was about to fall down one of them.

"City of robbers, here we come!" shrieked Ra, banging the wall with a metal pipe.

When we came to a pile of iron bed frames that looked impenetrable, we threw ourselves among them like swimmers trying to dive into a sea of tubes. The air inside was stale and made me think of damp cookies, wet mattresses, and dead rats and cats. Here and there filing cabinets, wheelchairs, pipes, bottles, and other junk lay rotting.

"This used to be a hospital," Mew said as we descended through the floor. She was lighting the darkness with a flashlight. "There have been all sorts of diseases here, from yellow fever to whooping cough, and then later on, this was where bread and cookies were made."

I nodded in the dark and tried not to stumble. Bread and whooping cough didn't go well together, but I had heard of

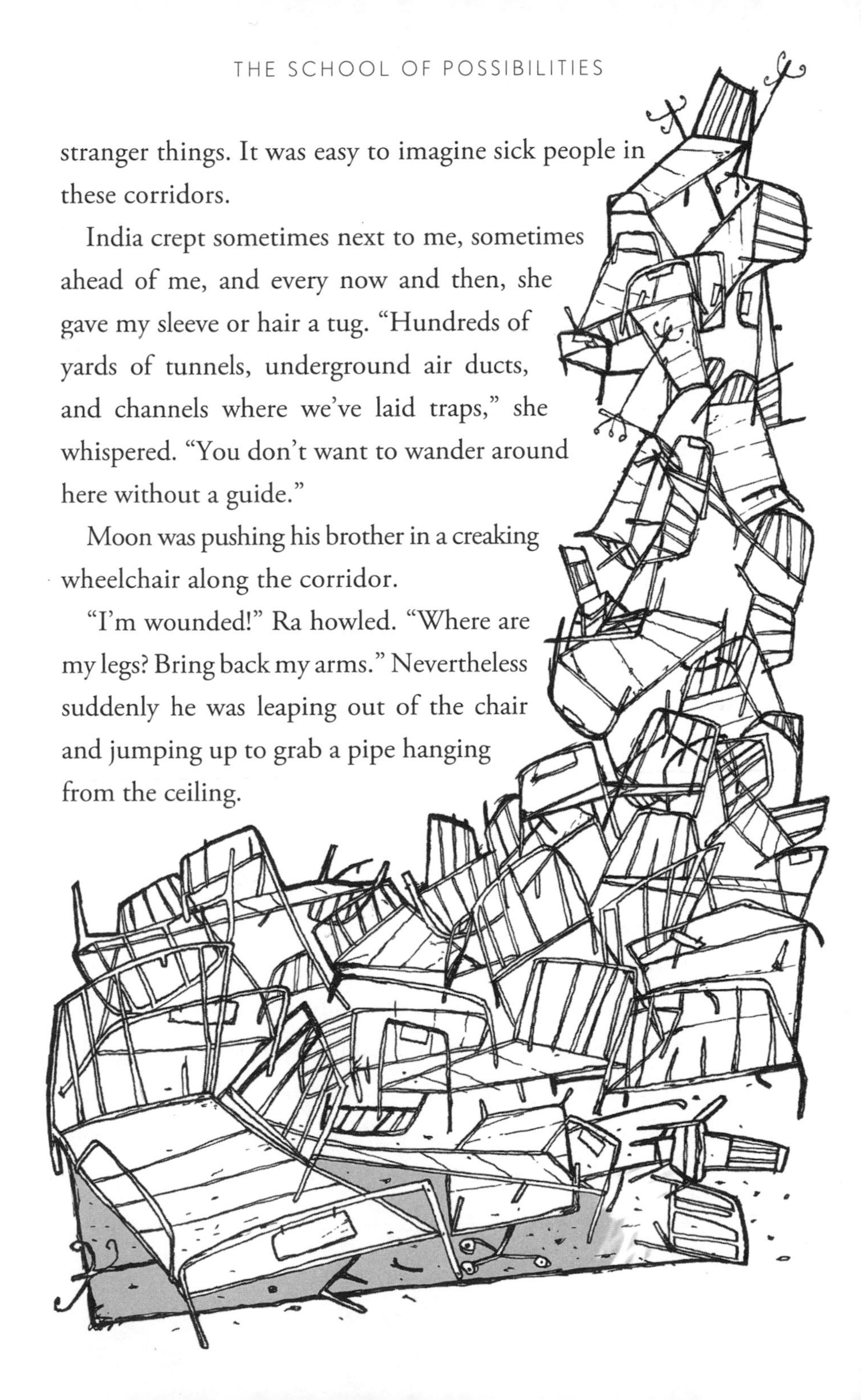

stranger things. It was easy to imagine sick people in these corridors.

India crept sometimes next to me, sometimes ahead of me, and every now and then, she gave my sleeve or hair a tug. "Hundreds of yards of tunnels, underground air ducts, and channels where we've laid traps," she whispered. "You don't want to wander around here without a guide."

Moon was pushing his brother in a creaking wheelchair along the corridor.

"I'm wounded!" Ra howled. "Where are my legs? Bring back my arms." Nevertheless suddenly he was leaping out of the chair and jumping up to grab a pipe hanging from the ceiling.

I looked around me, alert. The place made me think of a tangled thicket, a forest inside of a building. It made me think of a rhyme I had hated when I was little and still didn't like: "Caw, caw, come round the bend, and you shall meet a sticky end."

"Awesome," I sighed and crashed into a filing cabinet. It made a metallic boom. I had never come across anything like this before.

"We're proud of this place," India said. "We protect it, and it protects us."

"Protect? How?"

"We scare off intruders," Moon said.

"We haunt them," Ra said and snatched the light from Mew's hand. He lit up his face with it and howled, "Yooh-ooh," and didn't look at all like a ghost.

"Give it here, you little monkey," Mew said and seized the flashlight back. "Light is precious here, and you don't play with precious things."

She lit the corridor into which we turned next. It was covered in pieces of white paper. Loose wiring hung from the ceiling. A contraption for hanging bags of blood and liquid food used in hospitals was leaning against a door.

"We're here," Mew said, lifting the stand away from the door. India pushed the door open and waited on the doorstep.

I stared into the darkness.

"In there?"

I carefully stepped closer.

India sighed and gave me a nudge.

"Go on," she said. "Darkness awaits you."

I glanced at her, annoyed. It was easy to talk about the darkness as if it was your best friend if you were able to move around in it as easily as a bird in the sky.

All the factory children were able to do this.

"We're going to check the traps," shrieked Ra and took off somewhere with his brother close behind, helped by legs that knew the corridors and corners by heart.

"And do not play with the lighter," Mew called to them. "There is a lot of—"

"—combustible stuff," continued one of the twins. A small flame flared briefly in the darkness and disappeared just as quickly.

India swore, and I grinned.

As I stepped onto the doorstep, India caught hold of my wrist. "Remember that you are bound by a promise," she said. "You must tell no one about this. You must think of them."

India nodded toward the corridor down which the boys had disappeared, where Mew stood on the edge of gloom and darkness like a white ghost.

"Not think of you?" I asked.

"Me? Oh, no, I have no worries."

I nodded, not believing her, and stepped inside the room. Before I realized what was happening, India had snatched my wrist, scratched it, and pushed it into the doorframe. It left a patch of blood.

"Ouch! What are you doing?" I yelled and pushed my bleeding wrist into my mouth.

India tore a shred off the hem of Mew's dress and bandaged my wrist with it.

"It's the custom here," she said matter-of-factly. "That was an oath."

"I'd call it a wounding," I grunted.

India shrugged her shoulders. "It's a blood oath, and it's traditional."

Mew stepped closer. She lit up the room by pointing the flashlight over my shoulder. India twirled around the room, lighting candles here and there. The flames lit the room with a restless light. "The robbers' kingdom," she said and spread her arms.

The room had been cleared of most of the trash and furnished with things found in the corridors. It still looked like any other room in the factory.

"We change camp often. The place mustn't look too inhabited."

There was no fear of that, because it didn't look inhabited. The floor was a bit tidier, and there was a little less trash than in the other rooms; but there was still plenty of junk and debris. Postcards and newspaper cuttings had been stuck on the walls. There was a picture of a skater in one corner.

"My bed," India said and flung herself on her back onto a moldy mattress.

I nodded and sat down on the floor. Mew was gathering food in a pile on the table, which was also a bed.

"Where do you get washed?" I asked, curious.

They glanced at each other.

"What do you mean?" India asked sharply. "Are we dirty? Do we stink?"

"We don't stink..." Moon said at the door.

Both boys had just appeared in the room and were looking at us enthusiastically.

"We smell," Ra said. "We smell of a catch."

"Look!"

Moon lifted two long-tailed creatures above his head. Ra dangled a bird by its wing. Mew threw a dried-up piece of bread at them, and they each did a matching jump to one side.

"I didn't mean that you—that you stink," I said. "I was just interested to know how you take care of everything. Where do you wash your clothes, for example?"

"We don't wash them," Moon said.

"Or ourselves," added Ra.

"We like dirt."

"Dirt is warm."

They looked at each other, nodded, counted to five, and then simultaneously crammed a whole slice of bread into their mouths. Then India grabbed Moon by the neck and wiped the boy's face with quite a dirty rag.

"They're lying," she said. "We do get washed. We wash just the right amount and not too often. Skin dries up if you shower all the time. We wash in the public restrooms in the shopping mall."

"Don't forget the hamburger joints," Moon said.

"The Chinese restaurant and the station," Ra said.

"On trains and at the airport."

"The Russian restaurant."

"The Russian restaurant?" I interrupted.

The boys nodded.

"Restaurant Vladimir," they said together.

"It has a huge restroom."

"Big washbasins."

"We tested them and splashed around," Ra remembered, his head tilted to one side.

"That place belongs to my dad," I said. "What do you know about it?"

"Only that it's closed," Moon said. "Now we climb in from the backyard. We do a lot of that."

"Do what?"

"We have baths in places that are closed," India said. "When it's cold and we can't stay the night here, we sleep in stairways."

"We have memorized at least two hundred street door entry codes in this city," Ra said proudly.

"There are mattresses and bedcovers in basements and attics. Apartment blocks usually have communal saunas and showers. Sometimes they even have swimming pools. We can't heat the saunas, but the showers always work. When you get the street door code, you're already there."

"Like taking candy from a baby," Moon assured me.

I glanced at the ceiling and whistled. "Seems to work," I conceded.

"Works very well," India said. "It's still important to change stairways every so often. You can't use the same one several times in a row."

I stared at them. The scenario started to become clear.

"Should we fry the rats now?" Ra interrupted.

"The pigeon has to be plucked," Moon said.

They both waved their fingers in the air like cat claws and stared at Mew, pleading.

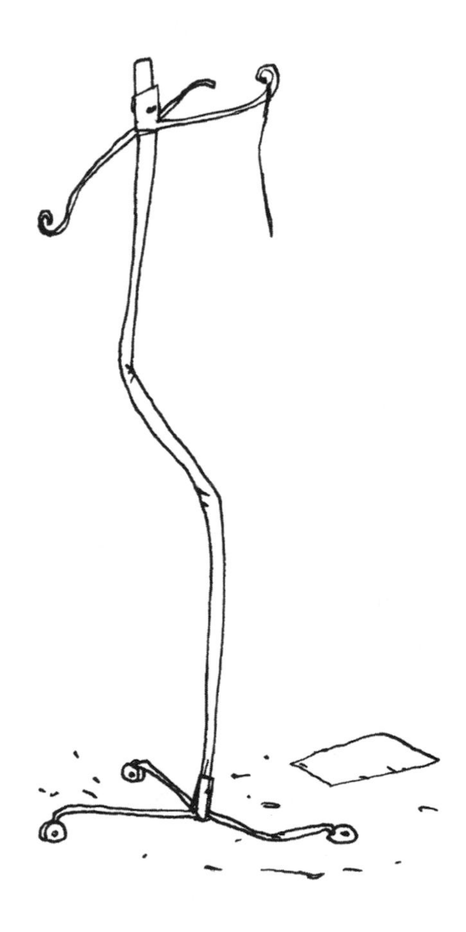

37.

There was no sleep that night.

Streetlights and a dim full moon lit the large hall. Passing cars cast moving shadows on the walls and the ceiling. The place was like a crazy palace which exuded cold but where you could keep warm if you kept moving.

"The one and only real Circus of the Lost meets and performs in this factory!" Ra proclaimed and snapped his fingers. It was a sign for Moon to climb onto a roof beam. He did it with the agility of a trained monkey. On the beam he performed a series of reckless cartwheels. Each movement was repeated by a shadow on the wall.

"I've been practicing this for almost a year," he yelled, out of breath.

When India tested the skating ramp, she proved to be as good as I remembered. I was worse than I remembered. It felt as if the old tricks I could do had seeped away, and my eye for jumps had disappeared.

"You'll learn," Ra said sympathetically.

I bit my lip and tried again. I tried again many times.

There were ropes hanging from the roof beams. We could get up onto the beams all the way along them. There were also some other structures good for climbing. We used them all. It was better than any official indoor climbing place. You just had to learn to place your feet and hands correctly. You mustn't hesitate. You mustn't be afraid of the dark. And you mustn't get lost in the shadows.

In the end we were all sitting high up like ravens in a tower.

"I have to go," I said.

"That's not a good idea," Moon said.

"That's true," Ra echoed. "Stay here."

"Why was I allowed to know about this?" I asked and made a circle in the air with my arm.

"It was India's wish," Mew said. "India wants you to join us. India doesn't want—"

I turned to look at India. "We don't want them to put you into the basement," she said.

I laughed cheerfully. "What do you mean—into the basement? You don't understand. I won't be put into the basement. They'll make an image of my face..."

India glanced at Mew and then at me. "You know about the masks," she said. "We don't want them to make one of you."

"If a mask is made of you, the game is lost," Mew said.

"Just a minute," I interrupted, surprised. "Do you mean those plaster casts? You don't understand. They're not dangerous. They're just portraits."

India and Mew glanced at each other again meaningfully.

"We don't believe they're just portraits," India said.

Mew shook her head. "No, we don't, and that's why we're here," she said, looking gloomier than ever before.

"They made a mask of her brother," Ra whispered into my ear.

I swallowed and said, "You have a brother?"

Mew nodded.

"I did—and parents," she said. "But that's enough of that. We believe that a mask is worse than death."

"Why do you think that?"

"You should, too," India said.

I closed my eyes tightly and immediately saw a load of faces molded in plaster, clay, or whatever material, and eyes looking at me from behind glass domes, as if they were alive. For a moment I almost heard them—something that I had thought was the air conditioning. The breathing—the long, heavy breaths in and out.

But no, it couldn't be.

I shook my head, determined.

"I don't know," I said. "I just want back all the things I have lost."

The children glanced at each other.

"You haven't lost this yet," India said, resting her hand on my chest, over my heart. I was naturally startled and was about to get palpitations, which are rare in a twelve-year-old. For a second, I thought about it, felt afraid, and hoped just a little that she might have something more in mind—that she would try to hug me, or worse still, kiss me. I already knew to be on my guard against such things, because I was always under attack now that I had an official girlfriend who wanted top marks in her school report and an honorary mention for being a girlfriend.

"Did you think that I'd stay here?" I asked and thought for a moment about life on the staircases as a possible way of going on now that Dad and Mom weren't there any longer and Poole was looking after my interests.

India shook her head. "We want you to investigate a couple of things for us," she said.

"We want to destroy the basement," Mew said. There was a fire burning in her eyes.

India raised her hand as if to calm things down. "But we are not going to be hasty," she said. "First we need to work out how the masks might be destroyed."

"And whether it can be done without harming the children," Mew continued.

"Sounds a bit odd," I said. "Sounds a lot like superstition."

"Everything that seems like magic is not," India said.

She was right, of course. My life had taken an extraordinary turn. It was like a fairy tale with child-eating witches. The world was not a simple place. That surprised me every day.

"You have to help us," India said, resting her hand on my shoulder. "Do you understand?"

Mew gave a tense laugh. "When it's done, we'll leave," she said.

Moon started to jump around wildly. "We're going to stow away on a ship," he screamed.

"Yes, we are," Ra joined in the laughter. "We'll move to a warm city where there are lots of mothers."

"No mothers," Moon snapped. "We are big now and can manage."

Ra's dance came to a halt. "There have to be at least two," he declared.

"None."

"One each."

I covered my ears with my hands.

"You're mad," I cried. "Warm cities can be even more dangerous than cold ones. But I'll try. I'll try to find out what's happening in the basement. I'll see you here when I know something."

"Leave a message in the window!"

"I'll do that."

The boys and India clapped. Mew did a thumbs-up and smiled a little.

As I climbed out through a crack in the wall, I took one more glance behind me. To tell the truth, it was easy to imagine the wailing of the dead here but impossible to imagine living here.

India walked me home.

"I know your street door code, as well," she said, waving her arm.

"I figured you did."

"Do your best," she said and disappeared.

Everything was as I had left it: the door ajar, the shoe wedged in the door, and the Pooles asleep in their rooms.

38.

The next day Will went into the basement again. I stared at him as he left the classroom. I put my hand up.

"I could go with him," I volunteered. "I could help Will."

The teacher looked up from her book at me for an unnecessarily long time.

"Not this time," she said and told us to open our books to page sixty-seven.

I decided to ask Bridget about the matter at recess. "What do you know about the masks?" I asked briskly.

Bridget looked at me, surprised. I usually only spoke to her when I had to.

"Have you seen them?" she asked.

I nodded. "I'd like to see them again," I whispered to her and smiled nicely. It's worth noting that I tried to be really charming.

Bridget, however, turned pale.

"There's nothing to say about them," she said, pushing her way out of the corridor into the yard. I followed.

"You must know something about them," I tried again. "You've been here for years. You must know."

Bridget shook her head.

"Why would I know about them? Walk me over to the girlfriends' meeting now, or I'll tell my father about you," Bridget said.

Now it was my turn to be astonished. "Why should I be scared of your father?"

"My father is the headmaster."

I whistled. "Your father's the headmaster? At this school?"

"That's what I just said," Bridget said.

I tugged at a thread on my cuff and thought. I had been made the boyfriend of the headmaster's child. Perhaps it shouldn't have been surprising, nor any wonder that the headmaster particularly trusted this girlfriend.

"Have they made a mask of you?"

Bridget shook her head fiercely and said, "I can be trusted without one."

Then she looked a bit frightened as she realized that she had said too much.

"What do you mean?" I asked.

"I mean—"

"Never mind," I said. "I'll take you to that meeting now."

In the afternoon I had an idea. The answer—and perhaps the key to the basement, as well—might be found at the headmaster's house.

"Could we do our homework at your place today?" I whispered to Bridget over my essay paper.

"You mean—?"

"I mean that I could come to your house. How does that sound?"

Bridget looked at me suspiciously at first, and then more enthusiastically.

"Do you really want to?" she asked.

I nodded as eagerly as a boy scout. "I do," I said as convincingly as marriage vows.

"Perhaps I should ask Father."

I gulped. "Do you have to?"

Bridget nodded.

"He's at some headmasters' conference and not in town right now."

"Well, that's that, then," I sighed, disappointed.

After the lesson had finished and I was putting my coat on in the corridor, Bridget caught me by the sleeve. "You can come after all," she whispered.

39.

The headmaster lived in a large apartment in a building in the middle of the city. It had a swimming pool and a roof terrace. Bridget let me peer into the rooms.

"This one is Mother and Father's," she announced.

There was a lot of brown and a large bed in the room. The bedspread was as smooth as autumn ice. Looking at it made me realize it had been stupid to imagine that a solution would be just hanging on a wall in the headmaster's home.

"Does your father have a study here?" I asked.

Bridget shook her head and said, "He doesn't bring his work home."

I swallowed my disappointment, even though it was big and made my stomach ache.

We went to do our homework in Bridget's room. I felt I was under continual observation there. There were dozens of pictures of horses on the walls. They all stared at me with their moist, horsey eyes. I could almost smell the revolting stench of manure and almost feel a kick on my backside. I hadn't been in a girl's room before, but I had always thought this was what it would look like.

Bridget, too, watched my every move, and quite soon I realized that my exploration would remain wishful thinking. But at one point, the phone rang, and she left the room. At the door she hesitated, and for a moment I was certain that she was going to lock me in. Fortunately she didn't.

I heard Bridget talking on the phone. She was chatting with her father.

"Yes, Storm is here," she said. "He is being very good. Mother knows about it, and so does Verity Poole. We are doing our homework."

And she continued with more of such nonsense.

Keeping low down I scampered into the headmaster's room.

My disappointment deepened when I found nothing there.

Now that I am thinking about it after the event, I can see that it would have been strange. Why would he have left anything incriminating at home, where anyone from the plumber to the electricity meter reader would be able to look at it—not to mention the daughter's curious boyfriend?

I returned quietly to Bridget's room.

She was still talking on the phone.

"No, we won't eat your doughnuts—honestly, Father," she said. "Just bread from the cupboard."

I sat on the floor under the accusing stares of the variously colored horses and opened my essay exercise book. The task was to write about islands. *What do you see when you stand on the deck of a boat? I see water*, I wrote, and pushed the pen into my mouth. *I see water, a couple of gulls, more water, and then just water, water, endless water.*

Maybe my head was rusty from all that water. I couldn't think of anything more to write. Actually I had loads of thoughts I could write about, but this teacher's homework stultified my imagination.

That was when I saw the lollipop in the window. The lollipop was swaying behind the glass. It was multicolored, like a rainbow. Of course it looked odd. A lollipop and a window went together as badly as penguins and a desert.

The lollipop moved up and down. I knew right away that it wasn't a winged piece of candy. The lollipop had no wings or anything else. There was treasure at the end of the rainbow. Someone was moving the lollipop, and I had already guessed who.

I got up on my knees onto the table and opened the window. The lollipop swayed in front of my nose like a worm on a hook. I took hold of it and gave it a yank. Both the lollipop and the line it was attached to stayed in my hand. I pushed my head out the window and peered up.

India was sitting astride the balcony above, waving. I waved back.

"What are you doing here?" I formed the words with my lips.

She pointed at the gateway to the yard. "Come with me," she whispered.

I made my decision in one second. When I turned into the room, Bridget was standing at the door with her hands on her hips. She stared at me.

"What are you doing there?" she asked.

"Getting a breath of oxygen," I answered. "I feel a bit weak. I need to go home. It could be my asthma."

"You have asthma?"

"Really it's just hay fever, but I call it asthma."

"Oh," Bridget said. "I'll take you."

"You don't need to," I said quickly and scooped my books into my bag.

"Yes, I do. I promised Counselor Poole. You were allowed to come on the condition that I make sure you get home without straying."

I bit my lip. Yes, of course.

Again it only took a moment to make my next decision. I just shot out of the apartment and relied on being faster than Bridget.

And I was.

India was waiting for me behind the trash cans in the yard. She dashed beside me through the gateway and out into the street.

"I followed you." She drew breath once we were safely away from Bridget.

"So you know the headmaster's street door code as well?"

India nodded and grinned.

"Not a particularly brilliant stairway, by the way. We've only slept there a couple of nights. The shower is hopeless, but the swimming pool is okay."

I laughed. "You're crazy," I said.

"As crazy as you?"

We gave high fives as a sort of victory sign and continued to run. Every now and then, India jumped high into the air, as if she were trying to reach a bird or an insect. She showed me how to camouflage oneself in the city and how to get food in fifteen minutes without anyone noticing. She also showed me how to be present and invisible at the same time.

"It's quite easy," she said and started to talk about nomads, people who lived in the desert, for instance. "Nomads are wanderers," she said enthusiastically. "They melt into the desert. They believe that everything in the desert has a spirit. Every stone, animal, tree, and flower has a soul. When someone dies in the desert, his spirit remains wandering there to finish all the jobs he didn't get done when he was alive. Some return to guard their treasures, some to care for people, and so on."

India looked around her eagerly and stretched out her arms.

"This is our desert," she said and started to whirl around with her arms out and her head thrown back.

I looked around me in a sort of daze, because I realized that for India, everything in the city was alive—there was something alive in every street, lane, magazine stall, and shop.

"Maybe dead people wander around here, too, protecting people and taking revenge," I suggested, and India began to laugh.

She laughed so that all her white teeth were showing.

Then we just ran about here and there and laughed a lot more. Hardly anyone took any notice of us. For instance, we slid between the fruit and the fish stalls, and no one was bothered. Every now and then, India picked something up and put it in her pocket: a fish, a coconut, or a bunch of bananas. No one noticed that, either.

Then India pushed a stalk of parsley behind my ear and let forth some kind of a melodic cry. "This is a hunting cry just right for the city. It's a sign to the other hunters," she said.

I nodded.

Suddenly India grabbed my arm. "Do you remember?"

"What?" I asked.

"I promised to tell you sometime when we were in the city where your mother and father are working."

I immediately got excited. "Of course I remember. So you really know where they are?"

"I know something," she said. "It's a hotel."

"I know it's a hotel. It's a five-star hotel."

India laughed. "I know something else," she said. "I know why they've gone."

"Do you?"

"They are in a labor camp, paying their debts to the school."

I chewed at a dreadlock.

"They are working for the school. They are working to pay your school fees and other expenses. Make no mistake—they are in trouble, because you are such a difficult child."

"Where is the hotel?" I asked fiercely.

"If I knew, I would've shown you already," India said. "What do you think about all this?"

I stared at a hole in the asphalt, frowning. "Children turn their parents into prisoners," I said quietly. "And adults think that hiding themselves away shows they love their children."

"It makes a boy or a girl obedient when they can't rely on a single thing in the world anymore and everything important disappears like snow in the spring. It's educational. That's what they think at the school, anyway," India said and picked up a stone. She threw it a long way, spinning it. I wouldn't have been surprised if it had broken a window, but it didn't. It fell into a trash can.

"Can they be freed?" I asked.

"Maybe we'll think of something," she said. "Find out about that basement. I'm serious."

She said good-bye to me on the corner of my home block.

"Come to the factory when you know something."

"I will," I said and turned away.

"Wait!" India shouted and circled around me. She pushed a flashlight into my hand. "You dropped this awhile back. I changed the battery."

I took the flashlight and flicked it on. I stayed on the spot, staring after her.

I don't really want to tell you about everything that happens next. But I'm the narrator of this story and can't stop now.

It's my duty to the story.

It's what I have to do.

40.

The door wasn't open that night or the next. It wasn't open again any night that week, but the following week it was.

That night there was a full moon. I was looking at it and how it lit the yard when I saw the children. Immediately I realized that they had come to get me. They had come to ask me about the masks. They wanted to know whether or not I had found anything out. They couldn't wait any longer, and that was why they were standing between the streetlight and a bush. There were two of them. One was wearing a black hoodie, the other one a white dress.

I felt a nasty stabbing pain inside me, because I had no new information. I had nothing to tell them. I had tried to do what they asked me, but the storeroom and the basement were guarded as closely as the English crown jewels were. Long story short, I had not succeeded yet. At one point I had even tried to get inside the headmaster's office, but I had been caught and given detention.

I waved to the children, and they waved back. They were gesturing to me, and it occurred to me that maybe it was the other way around. They had learned something that they now wanted to tell me.

Suddenly in the middle of all these thoughts, the key turned in the lock, and the door clicked. Someone had opened it—someone who could get into our stairway and inside the apartment, because she knew the door codes and could pick locks. I held my breath and waited, but as I heard nothing more, I peeked out the window. The figure in the white dress was still standing in the same spot in the shadows, but India had disappeared.

I dashed to the door. It was open. I peered into the corridor. It was dark.

This time I prepared more carefully than before. I fashioned a bundle that looked like a sleeping boy wrapped inside the covers and put it in the bed. I hoped that it would fool anyone who happened to peek in the door. I rummaged through the closet for my knife and pushed it into my pocket. I also took the flashlight and India's skateboard pieces with me.

All this time I felt weird, expectant, and for some reason, almost sad. I stood for a moment at the door to my room, already halfway through to the corridor, listening to the unbroken silence—the humming of the refrigerator, the air conditioning, and the plumbing.

I peered into the living room.

Verity Poole's legs trailed over the arm of the sofa. Her hair fell over the other arm like black seaweed. I wanted to run away immediately, but instead I crept nearer to make sure that the woman was asleep. Luckily she was. A trickle of spittle hung off the corner of her mouth, as often happens to people who are asleep or to poisonous frogs that drool venom.

The television was tuned into a shopping channel. A man was selling the exercise machine of the millennium. I stared at the screen for a moment, took deep breaths, and retreated into the hall as lightly as air or a bunch of feathers. I was ready.

No one stopped me at the door.

No one stopped me on the stairs.

No one was waiting for me in the yard.

The children were gone.

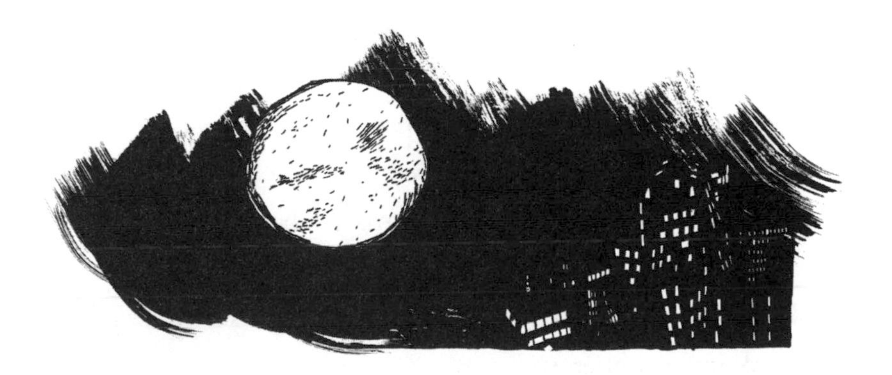

41.

The factory was in darkness.

I climbed inside and let out a long whistle. At first the only reply was the rustle of the wind and mice. Then a hand was pressed over my eyes.

"Where have you been?" India whispered.

I hadn't heard any steps, any breathing or clattering. She was just there suddenly, as if she had just materialized out of the wind and dust.

"We thought that you'd forgotten us and the task," she said.

I shook my head fiercely.

"Of course I haven't. I have tried—"

"Good," she interrupted, and then she whistled.

Almost at once two boys descended from the ceiling on ropes.

"You called us," Moon hollered.

"We came right away," Ra continued.

India put her hands on her hips and surveyed the boys sternly.

"You're dirty," she said.

"We've had troubles," Ra huffed, and Moon nodded.

"Bad troubles."

"And you still don't know the whistle signals," India said.

The boys lowered their heads.

"I suppose you realize that's dangerous. You could lose your life. Why did I whistle just now?"

"You…"

"…we…"

"…don't know."

"We thought that you were calling us."

India shook her head. "I was letting you know that the danger has passed," she said.

The boys nodded and looked pleased. Then they started to swing on the ropes.

"Why did you come, by the way?" India suddenly turned to ask me.

I looked at her, surprised. "You came to call for me. You were in the yard and—"

Suddenly Mew descended into the room, as well. "What has India done?" she asked.

"She…both of you," I looked from one girl to the other. "You came to our yard tonight. I saw you from my window."

India and Mew glanced at each other.

"What's he talking about?" Mew asked. She sounded quite threatening.

India shrugged her shoulders.

"India has been to my room," I said. "She's written messages on the aquarium. She's left lollipops."

Mew turned to look at India.

"Have you?"

India nodded.

"We've got Storm's entry code," she said and smiled a little. "I've been watching the situation. You know me. I keep guard."

I looked at India intensely.

"You left the door open for me," I said. "That's why I came here last time. That's why I'm here now."

India gave me a strange look. She shook her head slowly. Her face had altered now. Even in the gloom, I could see that she was pale and worried. She looked at me, and when she shook her head, the shadows of the lollipops swayed on the wall and resembled a dance of prehistoric creatures.

"No, Storm," she said slowly and stepped closer. "I have not left the door open for you. Not yet. I have only guarded you. I have visited you to remind you that I was near if you needed me. I have not left the door open. If you needed me, I would have come and let you out. But that's dangerous. You could have gotten into trouble over it, and you have a task. We have had to be careful. You are not invisible yet."

The room was in total silence. Everyone was waiting.

"I thought you opened the door," I said so quietly that it could scarcely be heard. "I've seen you in the yard before."

India took hold of my shoulders. "Oh, Storm, what have you done?" she said. "You brought them here!"

My heart froze. "No!" I cried when I finally understood.

Mew, who had been standing as tense as a bow beside India, sprang up now toward the boys swinging on the ropes. "Moon and Ra, quickly, out of here!" she shouted. "Storm has brought them here. They are here! Climb!" She almost screamed the last bit.

The boys swayed on the ropes, paralyzed, like two Christmas ornaments forgotten on a tree.

"Climb!" India yelled, too, taking two threatening steps toward the boys.

Then the boys started to clamber up the ropes up to the roof beam. India swung after them into the heights and disappeared.

Mew also prepared to climb. She managed to get hold of a rope and take off when we heard shouting at the door.

We both froze.

"The children are getting away!" screamed a voice I knew only too well. I would have recognized it anywhere. Verity Poole was in the factory. "We can't get them all now!" she shouted. "Turn on the floodlights!"

Right away a bright light was switched on, revealing everything in the room. I was almost surprised when I saw what a horribly miserable hovel it was and that Mew was just a messy child with black shadows underneath her eyes, like someone who last slept a hundred years ago. I covered my eyes with my hands. Everything looked jagged in this light, and I could hardly bear to think about what was going to happen next.

"Pull up the ropes and hide!" Mew shouted up into the heights. "I'll take care of this."

"Nooooo!" Ra's inconsolable cry was heard from above.

I stared at Mew, stunned.

"We're coming!" Moon shouted.

"And we'll bite!"

"If you come down, I will break your necks," Mew shouted.

"Go! Run! Quickly! Don't follow me." Then she looked at me and lowered her voice. "You lured us into a trap," she whispered through closed lips. "They made you the bait."

I shook my head, horrified.

"No, I didn't. I didn't. I don't understand anything," I said.

"Good evening," a new voice said then—a voice I recognized immediately. "Nice to have the family together again."

Will stood in front of us and stared at Mew. Mew stared back. For a moment I thought that they had both been sculpted from ice and that I would freeze there between them.

Behind Will stood a girl in a white wedding dress. It was Mona, a veil draped over her eyes. Her dark hair had escaped from underneath the veil, and the made-up slits of her eyes looked at me. She was silent. She didn't say anything—she just looked.

But Will wasn't silent. "Mew, Mew, Mew!" he said, stretching each syllable. "How's my sister?"

"Will, Will, Will, I'm not your sister anymore, and you know it," Mew said.

She didn't take her eyes off Will for a moment.

"Tie the girl up," Verity Poole said.

Mew didn't try to escape, which surprised me. She let them tie her hands up, and then they took her away.

42.

Mew was now a prisoner, and I had been the bait.

I was also the latest hero of the School of Possibilities. When I went to school the following day, there were banners everywhere that read: "Storm did it! Three cheers for the hero!"

It was nauseating.

Mew sat in a glass case in the lobby. It was a kind of room—but too small for a proper room, and too big for a closet.

"She is awaiting trial there," the teacher told us. "Our lost lamb has returned." On the class television, we followed a live broadcast of Mew sitting still on her bed, without moving, her knees pressed to her chin, drawing figures on her bedcover with her fingers. She didn't answer the interrogators' questions. She was in the case like the fish in the aquarium or the skateboard in the smaller glass case. She couldn't see us, but we could see her.

I thought she had shrunk somehow.

"That's armored glass," the janitor said and sprayed detergent on the window. She wiped the glass clean. "Nothing will break this. You can't crack it—not even with dynamite."

As I tried to stroke the glass, she swiped at me with a cloth.

"Don't mess it up with your fingerprints," she said. "No finger marks."

The worst thing about the events that night was that my status at school improved because of them. No one referred to my escaping from home anymore.

"You have displayed model behavior in the spirit of the school," the headmaster said, pinning a medal on my chest. "Once you get rid of the badge, as well—and that will happen soon—you will become a real model student of the school, worthy of our school and all its fine objectives."

"What will happen to Mew? What will her sentence be?" I asked.

"Don't you think about that," the headmaster said. "The girl is lost. She has lost her chances."

But I did think about it—constantly.

Lost her chances...

When I went back to my classroom, the teacher was scrubbing off my structure from the punishment corner chalkboard.

"What are you doing?" I cried, shocked.

"I am wiping away your bad deeds. They are now forgotten," the teacher said and washed her hands in the basin.

"Surely it's not that easy!" I said, confused.

"That's how easy it is," the teacher said and smiled at the class. "Storm has worked for the school. Note, children, that he has been given a medal, and he has brought honor to our class. He has used his good judgment to infiltrate the fugitives as their friend and organize an ambush for them."

"No!" I cried, upset. "It wasn't like that. Mew *is* my friend."

"And now you have done her the best possible favor. Once we catch the other children—it's only a matter of time."

When I left school in the afternoon, I slowed down by the glass case. I felt that Mew could maybe see me. She climbed down from her place on the bed and walked to the glass wall.

She wrote something in the air. She did it again and again, as if she was making sure.

Do not talk about India.

At least that was what her writing looked like to me.

"She can't see you," Will said from behind my back. "But to her you are the guilty one."

"I can't be. I haven't done anything."

"Haven't you? Are you sure?"

I looked at the girl behind the glass and shook my head.

"Rob Reed is waiting for you in his room," Will said. "I promised to come and get you. He's got something to say to you."

The subject was chilling.

"You have been a good boy," Rob said, "and therefore you can be let in on our secret. We have decided to include you in our bounty hunter training. As an exception you can join before the Liberation Ceremony."

I took a step back and bumped into Will. "I don't want to be a bounty hunter."

"There's time for you to change your mind yet," Rob said jovially. "And besides you don't have any alternative. The ceremony takes place soon. Once your mask has set and your loyalty to the school is sealed, you are a soldier, equal among us, and ready to be a bounty hunter."

43.

As I walked home with Will and Bridget, I couldn't describe how desperate I felt. The world didn't seem to be doing what I wanted at all.

Bridget looked unhappy, and she kept giving me sidelong glances. Will stared straight ahead. When we got to my home corner and I started to walk toward the stairway, he ran after me.

"I know what you're plotting," he whispered in my ear. "By saving her you will only get both of you into big trouble. I tipped off the school in your name. That's why you're the official informer. Mew also knows that you're the guilty one, and I'm sure all the other outlaws know, as well."

I stopped and turned around to look at him. "What did you say?"

"I gave the school the tip-off in your name."

"You made me the guilty one?" I repeated, unbelieving.

"Or a hero," Will said arrogantly. "You should be grateful. In any case Mew is my sister, and I have the right to punish her. She thinks she's above every rule. She's always been like that. She's never obeyed Mother or Father, and when she got into real trouble, she ran away. She hates me."

I stared at him, frozen into a pillar of salt. "You put the blame for her exposure on me."

"That's right," Will said. "It was a lot of money, but it was worth it. Now they will make my sister good, and that's the end of her reckless hobbies." Will then threw a stone in the air and smiled triumphantly. "Mother and Father don't love her anymore. She'll have a lot to do to atone for running away."

"You said that she's dangerous?"

Will nodded. "Now we're just waiting for her partners in crime to come and rescue her, and we'll pick them up."

"You are a worm," I growled. "I'm not involved in any of this. I'm going to expose you."

"You do that. Who is going to believe you? And it doesn't even matter. Most of the school probably thinks that you were only set up as a hero. In case you hadn't noticed, at this school the truth serves the spirit of the school and is adjusted according to what is good for the school. You will be a witness at Mew's secret trial, and regardless of what you say, she will fail. You won't necessarily do badly. You could become a top player if you play your cards right."

My shoulders drooped.

"You can only help my sister by staying away from her."

"You're not really evil," I said quietly, my voice full of defiance.

"What?"

"It's the mask!" I said, louder. "You're under a spell or a curse. They've made a mask of you."

Will grabbed me by my clothes and threw me on the ground.

His icy eyes flashed. Or that was how it seemed. "I am warning you," he said and spat in my face.

For a moment he reminded me of his sister. Then he turned around and ran off.

Of course I couldn't get to sleep that night. I thought about all this, about being tied up in a knot and short of oxygen, about my heart, which was beating for now but would soon stop.

The masks really were breathing—I knew that now. What I heard once in the basement—and later in my sleep—had not been the air conditioning, a vacuum cleaner, or any other humming gadget.

It was the breathing of children.

I understood that now.

If I wanted to save Mew, I had to start with the masks. I had to wake the children from their sleep. I had to give up my chance. In the night I made a decision that meant a new beginning for my story.

Let's start now.

THE PLAN

44.

How did I get out of a locked room? That was the first problem. The second problem was the packing. What did I take with me to go away for the rest of my life? What would I need on the street, in the factory, in a world where there were no radiators? When I thought about it—even a little bit—the task began to feel like a real challenge.

I decided to pack something quickly. It wouldn't do any good to think too much or too long now—no complicated thoughts. I would need all sorts of things to manage on the streets. The very first thing I needed, however, was a bag. I rummaged in the closet and selected the largest of the bags I could find. It was a backpack Dad had given me when he had stopped his fishing hobby. The backpack had lots of pockets, loops, and compartments for lures and other equipment. Dad's hobby had only lasted for one summer, and the bag was almost unused.

First of all I tied a sleeping bag on top of the backpack. I did it the way I had seen hikers do on television adventure programs. Then I pushed inside all the things I might need. I shoved in a couple of sweaters, underwear, socks, some extra pants, the flashlight, and of course, the knife. I thought a bit about a toothbrush. I imagined myself brushing my teeth somewhere in the factory, and the image was so funny that I nearly died laughing. On the other hand, it felt equally stupid not to take it. It was possible that the next few years would be spent in backyards, and I didn't want to be toothless by the time I was twenty. On the streets perhaps more than anywhere else, a child needed his teeth.

I also took some photographs with me. In one of them, I was seven and examining some mushrooms with Dad. The slimy fungi were huddled in front of us like huge snails. I was poking at them curiously with a really grimy finger, thinking they were ugly but interesting nonetheless. The mushrooms were full of all sorts of wormholes, but they grew well among the trees. We had picked them on a forest hike, during which we'd gotten lost twice and Dad had been stung by the last wasp of the fall. In the photo I could see that Dad's nose was already swelling up into a shapeless lump. In another picture Mom had a fishing hook caught in her hair.

After I'd packed the bag, I checked it and removed a pair of pajamas. I considered for a moment whether or not to take one stupid item. I noticed I had slipped in a white toy elephant with its trunk missing. I stared into its black button eyes for a moment and felt ashamed that it was there—I was twelve and too old for bedtime toys. I had owned the elephant since I was four. It held all sorts of memories. When I was little, I wouldn't go to sleep without it. Now I had slipped it into my backpack like some little kid. Still I let it fall back between the knife and the flashlight. Somehow it felt better that the elephant was with me, now that I had nothing else.

When everything was ready to go, I had my escape plan ready. I hauled the table into the middle of the room and lifted a chair onto it. I held a cigarette lighter under the fire alarm. This trick was as old as fire alarms themselves and had been used in numerous films I had seen. It always worked, just as it did now. Don't try it yourself, however—I don't recommend it, unless you're as desperate as I was.

When the alarm went off, Verity Poole and Mona dashed to open the door. I was behind it, waiting. I was ready—readier than I'd ever been before. I was holding a can of spray paint. The paint made mother and daughter bright red. Of course they screamed like wild animals. It only bothered me a little. I didn't believe they were in any pain for a second. Cleaning up would only take them a moment anyway, and I would use that moment to escape.

I dashed out of the room, the apartment, and the building. As I ran I thought of something I didn't dare think about while I was packing. I wouldn't be returning to the building. It was quite possible that I'd never see my parents again. Never was a long time.

None of these thoughts slowed me down. At some point the Pooles would be able to come after me, but I would already be at the factory, having made contact with the other runaways. They would either take me in with them or drop me off the tower. Or they might banish me. There weren't many alternatives. There was no return for me. That was clear. Tomorrow a new warrant would be pasted onto the wall of the School of Possibilities, and a bunch of child soldiers would come after me. By capturing me one of them could earn a large amount of money—or maybe just a small amount. I didn't know how dangerous they would classify me.

I felt oddly dizzy—almost happy. I was free at last. The weather outside was bright and sharp. The light from the streetlamps shimmered. Every time I saw someone, I withdrew into the shadows. Then a man and his dog jogged past me. The dog looked at me and wiggled his ears; however, the man didn't look. I wondered whether I was turning invisible or not. It was quite a startling thought.

When I reached the factory, I stuck two fingers into my mouth and whistled. I tried to make it sound like a summons—something like India's bird whistles. The next thing I knew, somebody tripped me up, and a sack was slipped over my head. I couldn't see anything or hear properly. I felt the grasp of several hands and was wrestled onto my feet. I was being taken somewhere—a place at the end of a long and grueling journey. Sometimes I had to crawl. Sometimes I climbed, went over, and fell down. My head became muddled, my legs and arms bruised. At last my escorts pushed me onto the floor.

"We got the traitor," Moon said. "He's stolen our whistle."

"He's stolen all sorts of things," India huffed. "Was anyone following him?"

"We don't think so."

"You don't think?"

"We're sure there wasn't anyone."

"Take the hood off."

The boys snatched the hood off my head. I was in a room lit by dozens of candles. India was sitting on a high pile of beds.

"Well, well," she said when she saw my face. "A criminal always returns to the scene of the crime. Isn't that some kind of saying? Was the lure of money too irresistible?"

I shook my head.

"Don't look so upset," India said. "A little bird told me you're going to be a bounty hunter. Is that right? Have you been given something already for our Mew?"

"I escaped," I said quietly. "I don't want to be a bounty hunter."

"Did you hear that?" India said, her voice full of scorn. "He doesn't want to be a bounty hunter. Should we believe him?"

"No, we shouldn't," Moon said emphatically. "He's lying."

"They will sentence Mew. Mew will be lost," Ra said in a shaky voice. You could hear that he was close to tears.

I also had a lump in my throat. How would I ever get the others to understand?

"I left home once and for all," I said. "Though, of course, it doesn't feel like home anymore, now that Dad doesn't live there. I've decided to join you."

"What's he raving about?" India laughed a low, harsh laugh. "Are we some kind of secret society? Can you join us like some women's cooking club? Oh, no, buddy. We are not a secret society or a cooking club," she said, standing on her rusty throne. "You can't join us, because we don't take unreliable types. I made a mistake. I was softhearted. I saw something worth saving in you.

That's what I'm like, and it sealed Mew's fate. I've been naïve, but not anymore. I won't protect you, and I can tell you that you'll soon be whistling through the air, off the top of the tower in the darkness of night. We'll be able to hoist your splattered body onto the School of Possibilities' gatepost as a victory sign."

"I have a suggestion," I realized I was saying out loud. After I'd said it, I couldn't stay silent any longer. At the same time, I realized I really did have something to say.

"Did you hear that, boys? He has a suggestion." India jumped off the pile of beds and stood in front of me, legs apart and chin raised. "Unbelievable tactics—to send the same infiltrator twice. Surprising they didn't send Mew's greedy brother while they were at it. That pathetic slug."

India spat on the ground.

"Or his girlfriend," Moon cried. "That horrible flesh-eater who hounded us in the shopping mall."

"Let's slit the spy's throat!" Ra demanded.

The boys were leaning against each other with their arms on each other's shoulders. They looked at me murderously. "Wonder what the suggestion is," they said in unison.

"Why don't you ask instead where the jail is he's leading us to?" India said and spat again.

"I can save Mew," I said forcefully.

No one said anything for a while. Here and there water was dripping, and something loose fell off the walls and the ceiling. India was the first to open her mouth, but she closed it immediately.

Ra climbed up onto the heap of beds. "Let Storm speak. Give

him a chance. We won't lose anything by it. We can drop him off the tower later."

India agreed.

So I told the others my plan. At first it had been just a thought, but it started to develop as I got going and became more enthusiastic. That's how it is sometimes. As I spoke I got more ideas, and most importantly, I started to believe in them. One thought gave birth to a second, and the second gave birth to a third.

"Quite interesting," Moon said.

"So crazy that it might just work," India said.

"We could try it," I said, encouraged by their comments. "We'll become guerrillas. We wouldn't just be a band of robbers."

"What's wrong with robbers?" India asked with one eyebrow raised. "We take from those who have so much that they don't even notice."

I shrugged my shoulders and continued to develop my idea. "This is a revolution without blood," I said.

"A bloodless revolution?" Moon suggested, and I nodded.

"Let's be bloodless revolutionaries then," suggested Ra. "Although I like blood."

India looked at each of us and then at me again. Her eyes flashed.

"We'll go with this," she said deliberately. "Could be...maybe we were wrong about you. But remember that I'm watching you. It's never too late to toss you off the tower."

"It's not, and it never will be," Ra promised, too. "We can still flatten you."

45.

The plan was simple. It went like this: make the enemy nervous. A nervous enemy sleeps badly and starts to make mistakes. A nervous enemy acts hastily. He is weak.

The attack would be bloodless. We would use words as weapons. You heard right. That's what I said. Words would be our only weapons.

Of course it was my idea, and it wasn't yet good enough for India. India wanted us to include pictures. We'd do all sorts of things. We'd paint and write. I'd be able to decide on the words, and India would do the pictures. The pictures and the words would go together. They would fit together—one on top of the other—on concrete. Everyone knew that was how it was done.

We met to polish up our plan in the murkiest depths of the factory. Because the enemy was searching for us harder than ever, we had to hide better. That was why we continued farther and lower into the dark, along unknown passageways into rooms filled with old trash—rooms where hardly anyone had been for decades. We only stopped when we found somewhere we were safe—or somewhere where we at least *felt* we were safe.

And that was a good thing. Through the binoculars, India had seen from the tower that the wanted posters had been taken from the basement to the schoolyard and fixed on the wall. On every old poster, a zero had been added to show that the amounts were worth the trouble.

There was also a new warrant among the posters. It was for a twelve-year-old boy who had last been seen at home, from where he'd escaped. He was dangerous, and a reward was offered for him. The sign read: WANTED DEAD OR ALIVE.

"How much is it?" I asked.

"It's fifteen thousand!" India replied. "Not bad for a runt like that."

I let out a long whistle, impressed.

"Wow!" Moon cried. "They're offering less for us."

"We're cut-rate," Ra giggled.

India slapped me on the back. "Welcome to the outlaws!" she said.

"Where's your poster? Why aren't you being hunted?" I asked suddenly. It was odd that India seemed to be the leader of the gang, yet there was no poster for her.

India glanced at the boys, and all three laughed.

"I'm too good at hiding," she said, and her smile made it clear that it wasn't a good idea to talk about it anymore.

When we got to the cellar and under some damp blankets, we spread out the papers in front of us in the candlelight.

"This doesn't sound like much of an attack now—not dangerous or convincing—but it will be," I whispered and tapped one of the papers with my pen. I had written a word on it.

"*Rilth*," Moon read. "It's a spelling mistake. Shouldn't it say *filth*?"

I shook my head. "The word doesn't mean anything," I said. "It's just a word. But imagine opening the refrigerator door in the morning, and the word is staring at you from the side of the milk carton. What do you do?"

"Let's not use milk cartons. There's no room to spray on them," India objected.

"We can use marker pens," I said, staring at the gang expectantly. "Well," I demanded, "what would you think then?"

"We'd be happy to see some milk and would check out the cupboard for cereal, as well. Then we'd pour the milk on the cereal and enjoy it," Ra replied enthusiastically. "I hope there are some honey crunchies."

I sighed. "We're not talking about street children now, but about people who look at milk every morning, noon, and night. Normally there is nothing extra written on the carton."

Moon scratched the floor with a stick, thoughtful. "Storm means that if we saw that carton, we'd wonder why something was written on it and why it said things that were wrong or things we didn't understand," he said. "Even if there were crunchies, we wouldn't dare pour the milk on them, so we'd leave for school hungry."

"That's exactly what you would do," I assured them. "You would also wonder who had written the word and what it meant. Maybe someone was threatening you."

"Or wanted to drop a hint that he knew my secret," India warmed up to the theme.

I nodded enthusiastically.

"When you find the same thing in the refrigerator the next day, as well—and the day after that—and when you start to find words in other parts of your home, you start to fear for your sanity. You think—"

"That I'm going crazy," India continued.

"Or that I'm being watched," Moon said.

"I would think it was Mom," Ra said and received a kick on his ankle from his brother.

"Moms are fairy-tale creatures," Moon said. "I've told you that a thousand times."

Ra crossed his arms and glared glumly at his brother from underneath his matted hair. "What if I'm fed up with this game and want to go home?" he asked.

"Then I'll make you see sense," Moon answered.

"This attack will be bloodless," I said. "Not a single stone will fly or head will roll. Let's at least start by not fighting among ourselves."

India gave a crooked smile.

"Psychological warfare," she said thoughtfully.

"What does that mean?" Ra asked, frowning.

"Exactly what Storm is talking about," India replied.

"If you get to spray, can we break dance? We do the helicopter really well. At least I do," Ra said and threw himself on the floor without being asked. His legs spun around like a ship's propeller.

"You can keep watch," India ordered. "Someone has to keep the rear secure."

"What? Watch? Can't we spray?" the boys shouted together, disappointed.

"Of course you can. But you can't make a mess," I said. "We don't make a mess. We produce quality. Do you understand?"

The boys nodded keenly, as far as that was possible considering the positions they were in, propped up on one shoulder and their hands with their legs straight up in the air.

"And when we are victorious," I said, "then you can do any kind of helicopter you want. We can promise you that."

The boys glanced at each other and at the same time leapt onto their feet.

"About keeping watch—what if someone attacks?" Moon asked.

"Or we're being shot at?" Ra added.

"Run away and find us."

During the hours that followed, we refined our plan some more. We would use words and sentences that we invented ourselves. At first they would mean nothing, but because they sounded like war cries, diseases, or the names of dangerous insects, they would bring to mind all sorts of things and would begin to mean something to the enemy, whose sleep we wanted to disturb. Imagine a word that reminds you of something serious that you'd already forgotten about painted on your door: a ghost you were afraid of when you were younger; a stream you could drown in; an accident you might become involved in; a typhoon that could lift your home up in the air and throw it into the sea; a forest you could get lost in and where you would walk around and around in circles without ever finding your way home. In the mind of the enemy, harmless words would become frightening. That was what we hoped.

We had ideas. Of course we didn't want to hurt anybody. Soon

Mew would be able to walk free. Of course we also wanted to examine the basement—or India did. I didn't think that far ahead. I was thinking of freeing Mew. I thought of the pictures on the walls. I concentrated on where we would strike. We selected a few people as targets who we thought were more important than others and who, therefore, had to be upset more. These people were the headmaster, Poole, Rob Reed, the arts and crafts teacher, my own teacher, and a few others. They knew what was happening within the school. They had the keys. They knew about the basement.

"Who says we'll be defeated by the grown-ups? They are experienced, but they are slow. They don't believe that anything out of the ordinary can happen," I finished.

Moon and Ra glanced at each other.

"Storm is right," Moon agreed. "The teachers are older than us and worn out."

Ra nodded in agreement. "Rusty," he said. "A few screws might have come loose or fallen off altogether."

India jumped up and nimbly climbed onto the junk heap.

"So let's do it," she said, pulling a dirty blanket over herself. "But for now, sleep. We need some now."

"Let's have a pillow fight first," Ra said and climbed on the heap of beds after India.

"Without pillows?" I questioned.

"That's the whole point," Ra said and pulled something off India—something like an invisible cover. India ripped the cover back, but because Ra didn't stop, she jumped up and pushed him. A wild battle began. We leapt from bed to bed, up and down.

We beat each other with invisible pillows. There were millions of feathers in each pillow, as white as snow or ice cream. They flew around as we thumped each other. The whole factory became completely white.

When we got tired, we sank down where we were and slept for hours. I dreamed about words that didn't mean anything yet, but they would soon begin to signify all sorts of things. The words would save Mew and all of us—eventually.

46.

During the days that followed, we spread out around the city, each with a can of spray paint and a bunch of marker pens in a backpack. India even had marker pens in her hair. As we looked messy, we melted into the landscape as naturally as trash or the birds that flocked in the sky above the square that everyone ignored. We were just a group of children, dirtier than normal, on our way somewhere. No one noticed us. No one cared about us. As India had said, "To be invisible isn't magic."

We stole the equipment we needed for the attacks from all-night gas stations. It worked like this: Moon and Ra arranged a commotion in the foreground of the selected station, while India and I picked paint cans off the shelves. Then all we had to do was run off as fast as our legs would carry us. That was a skill I had, and one I had developed more on the School of Possibilities' soccer team. Now I really needed everything I had learned on the playing field: feinting, weaving, and attacking. When we met with danger on our expeditions, we warned the others by whistling and drumming rhythmically on a lamppost with a metal pipe. We made robbing trips to a few gas stations. We didn't take more than we needed. India always dropped lollipops after her. They remained floating in puddles of oil, looking quite pathetic.

When everything was ready and all the materials had been acquired, we split up all over the city. Then we started. We began to spread words and pictures at selected targets. At first, it was all a mess, and things didn't go well. I made all sorts of mistakes. I wasn't invisible enough, and once India had to rescue me from a security guard's clutches. "Always look out for security guards," she taught me. "Be more careful with them than the police. The police are child's play compared to guards. Guards are individuals who at some point have applied to police college but haven't been accepted because they're too trigger-happy and their kicking reflex is too strong."

The others fouled up, too. Moon set off the arts and crafts teacher's burglar alarm, and Ra nearly forgot to take his foot out of the teeth of the cook's dog. He had terrible teeth marks on his pants. "A wolf took a bite out of me," he boasted in the evening, showing off his marks of victory.

So what exactly did we do in town?

We drew signs on gateways, staircases, and elevators, on the whitewash, concrete, stone, and tiles of passages. We painted and wrote. We drew pictures on surfaces like shower curtains, windows, pillowcases, and refrigerator doors. The pictures were good, and as we refined our methods, we developed into faster, quieter, and infinitely better painters and writers. We also became dirtier and couldn't be distinguished from concrete walls.

Observe and punish—that was the motto of our campaign. We had lifted it from a School of Possibilities advertising poster on the school fence and made it our own. We used a certain martial arts technique in our battle: we turned the stronger attacker's power against himself. If you've ever had a session on a tatami mat, you'll know what I'm talking about. You didn't need violence. You needed the right technique.

Here are some examples of the pictures we painted:

Things ranging from icy mountains to falling stars on the headmaster's door.

A sad face on the arts and crafts teacher's bathroom mirror.

And in Rob's elevator, we painted my nightmares. We painted bursting balls above a soccer field and a ball made of chocolate melting on the goal line.

It was easy to enter staircases and apartments, because India not only knew the codes but also how to pick locks. She taught me all sorts of important things. We couldn't know the effects of the attacks, because we weren't there to see them, but we hoped that there would be some. We hoped that sleepless nights and worrying about the school would make our enemies careless and that their attention would be diverted, because we would soon march through the gate to rescue our friend. We only bothered teachers, and when we returned to the factory in the evenings, we always altered our routines. We didn't use the main entrances anymore. Sometimes the boys stood guard at the factory. From the tower they kept an eye on events at the school and also in other places: the railroad tracks and wherever the binoculars could reach.

And if anything out of the ordinary happened, one of them would run to us with the warning so that we could be prepared. The flags they hoisted on the tower also served as signals. Red meant danger at school, blue some other danger.

I said a moment ago that we only bothered teachers and that we didn't interfere with the students. That wasn't strictly true. There was one student we hassled, and he got graffiti in his room. The picture was so good that he really didn't deserve it.

47.

I have kept this for a special occasion," India said, shaking a can of spray paint in a garden that the two of us had just entered. In the picture on the wall, she had painted a crippled soccer ball limping, leaning on crutches, going who knew where. It was sobbing, too.

"Why is it crying?" I asked.

India shrugged her shoulders. "That doesn't matter. You yourself said that the picture's meaning is in the mind of the enemy."

I curled up with laughter. "You don't like soccer, though."

"I do, and so does a boy I don't like."

"Let me guess," I said.

"You guessed right," India said before I could make a suggestion. "Will the Wily—or should I say, 'Weirdo'—the captain of the School of Possibilities' soccer team, lives in this house."

I whistled, and then I had an idea. "What if we painted on the School of Possibilities' team soccer ball?" I suggested.

Because the captain kept the ball at home, it had to be in Will's room. India clapped her hands at the idea; it was a good one.

We broke into Will's home. We found the ball in his room. It was in a cupboard where there were also photographs and a few trophies.

"Not a difficult one to pick," India said and unlocked the cupboard easily.

I looked around the room curiously—it was very tidy and didn't look like the room of a twelve-year-old—more like a hotel room or a dentist's waiting room. It was completely impersonal. Nothing was strewn about anywhere. Everything was in its place.

"There's no sign of the sister," I said and picked up a picture off the shelf—a picture in which a wedding couple was standing underneath a painted scene of a tree; a picture that looked as if it came from a period at least a hundred years ago. In another picture was Will, years younger than now.

India bounced the ball on the floor. "Are they interesting?" she asked.

"I don't know. There's no picture of Mew."

"You hit the nail on the head," India said and sat down on the floor. She pulled a marker from her hair and, with an expression of concentration, started to draw a smile on the ball. It was like the smile from the grinning cat in that story where the grin remained long after the cat had disappeared.

"He doesn't look cheerful," I said.

India carefully held the ball up with her five fingers, as if it were a tray. "No, he's not," she said. "How would you like being kicked in the head by idiots day after day? Get your act together, ball. Scram! That's what I would do."

India glanced at me slyly. We both laughed.

"Not the ball, India," I said. "I'm talking about Will. Will doesn't look happy in this picture."

India pressed the ball against her chest.

"I'll tell you something," she said. "And this is a secret. Will always used to bully his sister, and he was a real pain."

"That doesn't surprise me. He still is a pain."

India rolled her eyes and nodded. "He's that sort. Now he's fanatical about school. Before he used to run around after his sister. Will adored her. He tried to be like Mew in everything—just as brave. Mew played in the factory with me. At that time a lot of other children came, as well. The factory was a forbidden place, but children liked it there. I did, too. Mew escaped there to get away from Will. She hid in the factory when Will was looking for her. We saw Will and heard him calling, but we didn't reply. He never dared come inside. Will snitched on us to his parents and at school. That's how it was."

India threw the ball at the wall. "Once there was an accident at the factory," she said.

I was startled.

"I've heard about that," I said. "Will told me."

India bounced the ball, preoccupied.

"I was also there at the time," she said. "But then again I'm always everywhere whenever something happens."

"Tell me about it," I said.

"Just one small flame and then a big *bang!*—a huge explosion. That factory really was full of all sorts of flammable things, and it still is. After that no one went there except me and a couple of others. You don't need me to tell you that I'm not scared of small bangs. I bet the School of Possibilities people were really pleased about that explosion, because afterward the children at last started to get scared. I wouldn't be surprised if it was the adults who had hauled barrels of explosives into the factory."

India sat down again on the floor, holding the ball. She picked a new marker pen out of her hair and gave the ball green fangs dripping with pus.

"After the explosion Will became even more of a nuisance. When those who had been playing at the factory were sentenced, he was the key witness. For a while Will the Weirdo was the focus of everyone's attention, and he was so pleased about that. That's what he's like. Just so slimy."

I didn't find that hard to believe. "What happened in the accident? Was anyone injured?"

India aimed the ball at me. "Don't confuse me. I'm trying to remember," she snapped.

I protected myself with the photograph of Will's relatives, probably dead by now.

"After the accident there were a few express trials. They were held in the sports hall and shown on school TV."

I nodded keenly. Of course I knew those shows. I had myself starred in a few. The accused was allowed to say something, but mostly he just looked defeated. Very few said anything at all. Hardly anyone cried. Just the thought of the trials could make someone's heart beat faster or even explode with anger.

"Will was really helpful and gushing about the events before the accident and why he'd been hanging around in the banned factory yard. Every kid who had been playing in the factory was sentenced for being rebellious. Mew and a couple of others escaped before the sentence was carried out. Will, however, came out of it well. Quite soon he became the class leader and the captain of the soccer team."

"Where were you?" I asked. "Were you given a sentence?"

"Of course I wasn't caught. I'm invisible," she said and aimed the ball at me again. "Catch!" she shouted and threw it. It thumped straight onto my lap and broke the picture frame.

"Now look what you've done!" I shouted.

"Oh, help! Did I break the family heirloom? How can I ever make it up?" India mocked.

We bent over to look at the picture among the shards. There were two of them. Underneath the picture of Will, another one was hidden. I moved the splinters of glass to one side. In the new picture were India and Mew, both wearing ballet shoes on their feet and holding on to a bar.

I glanced at India and burst out laughing. "You've done ballet dancing? Nice outfit," I said and leaned closer. "I would have thought that ballet was too soft for a young lady like you!"

India grimaced and banged her fist on her palm. "Everyone has a past, and there's nothing soft about dancing. It's hard work," she said irritably. "And if you look carefully, you'll see others you know in the picture."

I leaned closer and whistled. "Will's here, too?"

"Wherever his sister was," India said.

I took the other picture and started to remove it from the frame.

"There might be more pictures of your hobbies here," I said, grinning. "Maybe belly-dancing classes."

"You know what? You're starting to get on my nerves," India said and yanked the picture out of my hand. She pushed it back on the shelf. "We don't have time for this. Come on."

48.

In the evening I saw Dad. He wasn't cooking at a five-star hotel but tipping a trash can into a garbage truck in a gloomy lane. Dad was wearing gloves and coveralls with CLEANING DEPARTMENT written on the back. He looked a bit odd. He had a beard and longer hair, but he was still Dad.

"Dad!" I shouted and ran toward the lane. "Dad! Da-ad!"

Dad turned around and looked me in the eye for a moment. He was still far away, but I saw immediately that he looked like an animal that was frightened by large objects.

I raised my arms and started to wave.

"Dad!" I yelled. "Dad, it's me, Storm!"

A warm sun and other things that made me feel safe bubbled up inside me.

Sometimes when you have lost something, you only realize you are missing it when you see it again. This was just like that. But at that point, Dad lowered his eyes and climbed into his truck. He reversed the truck out of the lane and ran over the trash can. It died, spewing trash out of its mouth.

I waved my arms even more frantically and yelled, "Dad, wait!"

Dad didn't turn around to look. The truck was making the sort of bleeping noise made by reversing garbage trucks. The next moment it had reached the street. I ran faster, but the truck was already too far away, crawling toward a corner around which it would soon disappear. I picked up a stone and threw it. It hit a bus stop trash can that displayed an advertisement for some margarine.

The garbage truck was grinding back and forth on my rib cage. That was what it felt like at that moment. Why did Dad do this to me? I was just about to toss another stone when India's hand caught my wrist.

"He's not allowed to talk to you."

I glanced at India.

"He said he was working in a kitchen. I imagined…I thought that…"

I swallowed when I realized that I had made myself believe in a five-star hotel, Jacuzzis, and beds with tall posts and drapes that I could jump up and down on quite childishly while Dad and Mom looked on approvingly, standing by the door hand in hand. The reality was, of course, something completely different.

Then India hugged me. "I know how you feel," she said.

I glanced at her and shook my head. No one could know that. But India nodded her head, and for a moment, she looked just like the boy I had seen that first night at the factory.

"I do know," she said and pushed something behind my ear. I pulled out a lollipop. It was salty licorice flavor. "It will all work out," India said. "Do you believe me? We will win."

I didn't believe it and called all the cleaning firms and garbage dumps in the city—every single one—but I still couldn't find Dad or Mom.

49.

But we weren't happy just painting pictures on the teachers' stuffy stairways or their even fuggier kitchens, on refrigerator doors and shower tiles—not for long, at least. We changed our plan. We moved outdoors. We went back on the streets and started to tell our story to everyone there—to anyone who wanted to listen, and even to those who didn't want to listen. We painted pictures of children with no chances.

I didn't know where the idea had come from. Maybe it had been maturing in our heads for a long time. Maybe the cause was Dad, who carried trash cans around and didn't listen to me. Maybe it was me. I wanted to leave a message. I wanted to shout out loud, to have a different opinion about everything. We also thought about Mew. It was impossible not to think about her.

In the streets we could communicate everything through graffiti. We told about our life in the factory and in the backyards of shopping malls, restaurants, and movie theater complexes. We told them about invisibility. We drew strip cartoons about the School of Possibilities and how impossible it was to be so obedient. We drew our messages all over town. That was how it went. We spread them on walls, and they were a bit like messages in a bottle, thrown into the water by someone shipwrecked, hoping that anyone would pick it up and come to rescue him in a lifeboat. Maybe Mom or Dad would come. Maybe friends from my previous school. Maybe the stationmaster at the station—or perhaps just someone I didn't even know.

"If we don't communicate all this, we could easily disappear as if we'd never existed," I said fiercely.

Then India looked at me really seriously. "That would be giving up invisibility," she said. "It's a different solution. It might be good. It might be the best, but it's not right for everybody—not for me."

"I want to wake up the world," I insisted, and India shook her head.

Above us the streetlamps were lit as we stood there facing each other, staring. The light fluttered and flickered. Then, India took me by the hand. Immediately I saw that she wanted to say something. She didn't say it, but I knew that if she had opened her mouth, she would have said that she wouldn't grab a life vest thrown from a ship by some adult. She was already saved. We were on opposite sides of some kind of boundary.

This made me really sad. "I haven't breathed in enough water yet," I said quietly, and somehow, I realized that was it.

India, of course, remembered the story. She had told it to me in town some months ago. "Once you breathe in water, you can't go back," she said, as she had said once before.

And then the moment had passed. We didn't talk about it anymore. We carried on painting.

The time for meaningless words was over. That, too, happened almost by accident. All four of us were downtown. I had just written something on a wall—or rather, I had sprayed it, because I was using spray paint, azure blue and pure orange—when Moon said it out loud. He said it first to say something. Actually he sang it. He rapped a sentence I'd written, and we all realized that what I had produced wasn't just any old thing but a song. It was words for a song that showed children living in the streets and looking after each other.

This idea encouraged me a lot, and suddenly I just knew what it was I wanted to do. I started to write more songs on walls. Moon and Ra sang them, and they had good voices. They were bright and childish like angels' voices, but they still sounded good. In the songs, I described what it is like to be hopeless in a world that is even more hopeless. I wrote about train journeys, Mom's wedding dresses, Dad, Russian food. I wrote about life in an aquarium. India's work changed, too. It became more colorful, fiercer, more hypnotic. She drew beautiful things, but also more gallows and guillotines.

It's not difficult to imagine this scenario in the city during those days:

Someone, anyone, walking the city streets during the night hears singing around the corner, so he either runs away, or he comes to have a look. If he comes to look, he will see darkness in front of him—only darkness—but when he strains his eyes, he will see a wall and a picture. Not children, not angels or demons, but only a

picture painted by me and India, only Moon and Ra's handprints on the concrete.

As we moved around the streets, I began to understand that communicating things takes courage. You have to have courage to do what you want to do. Writing also takes courage—and singing, too. It takes courage to tell people everything.

One of the pictures we painted was of a girl sitting in a glass cage. India did it on a hamburger joint's window. The girl could have been a Native American chief, because she had feathers growing from her head and skin. But she could have also been a bird or some long-extinct human species that by chance had survived on Earth among the other species. The girl was sailing along a stream in her glass cage. The glass of the cage was made of sugar and melted in the water. I sprayed on the concrete the names of all the rivers I knew. I wrote Missouri and Amazon, and immediately the words made you feel that nothing stood still, because rivers like that flowed through jungles and took with them boats, water creatures, trees torn off their roots, earth, and thoughts. They pushed everything into motion.

There were other pictures, too. In one of them, young soldiers were pointing their rifles at blindfolded children standing against a wall. Execution is *carnificina* in Latin. Just ask me, because I've studied languages. In Russian it is *otsecheniye golovy*. That was what I wrote on the picture. A person can be executed, but other things like hope and dreams and free thought can also be executed.

There were dozens of these pictures. There may have been hundreds. We did them all when it was quiet at night, when the streets were empty. We did them in the shopping mall, on the tiles in the ice cream parlor restroom, on steps, on the walls of parking lots, on telephone poles, on a pirate captain's gnashing teeth in a film poster, and on some car windshields.

We painted pictures in every place in the city where they could easily be seen.

50.

The twins watched the school and its surroundings whenever they weren't painting in town. They looked out of the tower with the binoculars. They followed teachers and signaled with their flashlights. They crept in the bushes surrounding the sports field and the school fence and left each other signs: broken skis, empty candy bags, and cigarette packs. They hung them on tree branches and dropped them on paths. They squeezed themselves into tiny holes that no one else could enter. When we saw them at the factory after these trips, we heard about the things that had happened and what they had found out. Usually they had something new to report.

The boys told us that the School of Possibilities had tightened its grip, that it was still preparing for a great gala and now for a trial, which was going to be a big event. At the end of it, the marked would be imprisoned in the basement, and Mew would be sentenced. "They won't wait anymore," Moon had said seriously.

The boys also told us that Mew was still awaiting trial in her transparent prison. She was accused of crimes more serious than had ever been known in the school. They were crimes against chances: neglect of chances, rebelliousness, and escape. Mew had given up her future. She had thrown it to the winds, as the saying went. We, of course, understood that these accusations were serious and that anything could happen as a consequence.

We still couldn't imagine what that "anything" would be.

What would they do to Mew?

"Something will happen to Mew," Moon whispered, pale.

Ra nodded at his brother's side and responded, "Something awful. Really awful."

When we looked at the schoolyard through the binoculars, we saw that barbed wire had been laid on top of the fence—and not just any old barbed wire, but the sort with razor blades sticking out of it. We also saw that a watchtower had been erected and that some kind of a bright beam of light swept the yard, revealing everything both in it and inside the school. The tower was continuously manned. Nothing could remain hidden for long. And nothing could get over the fence without burning. The fence was now electrified.

We watched all this from our observation point in our tower. We could see everything from there. We could see Rob training his troops. We could see every changing of the guard, and we could almost hear the tense electric buzz of the fence.

The school looked like a fortress. It was as simple as that.

But we didn't despair. When we looked at the School of Possibilities preparing for battle, we knew that what we had been doing was beginning to produce results. The teachers believed that we were up to something, and because they were so different from us and thought about things either really simply or in complicated ways, they couldn't understand what we were doing. Children had escaped from the School of Possibilities before. The teachers knew that they were being observed and that we were watching them. And they couldn't imagine how.

"They don't know what we want," India said, satisfied, and ruffled my already untidy hair.

Then came a turning point.

Ra met Mew two weeks after she had been captured and a week after we had started our graffiti war. The rest of us were in our hiding place in the cellar, preparing for our night's round, when he sped down with bones rattling around his neck.

"I saw Mew!" he shouted, distraught.

We immediately got up and started shaking the boy for more information.

"The we-e-e-d-d-d-ding dress—" he hiccupped.

"The wedding dress? What do you mean?" we whispered, alarmed.

"It's gone!" Ra cried. "She has...has...has some kind of coverall."

We looked at each other.

"What's happened?" I asked.

"What's happened?" India asked.

"They've started!" Ra howled.

"Started what?" we asked, distressed.

"Messing up and rushing things," Ra cried. "Something is happening. Mew said so, and that it's good. I saw Mew behind the fence."

"Did you speak to Mew?" I asked.

"Tell us!" Moon commanded.

"Let him speak," India ordered and lifted Moon to one side.

Ra glanced at his brother triumphantly. He straightened his back. "Mew was exercising around the schoolyard. There were two guards and some more people in the tower. We didn't speak, of course. Not aloud. We talked with our hands. We signed."

"Yes, of course," Moon said and nodded at India. "So Mew talked to you in sign language. Tell us what she said."

"She did this and walked away." Ra signaled something in the air, touched his eyes, and let his head flop forward. "She pointed toward the basement—she wanted to say something about the basement."

"The basement?" I said, frowning. "Is that where we have to go?"

"That's how I read the signs, and I'm the best at our sign language," Ra said.

India threw herself onto her back on the floor. She stared at the ceiling in concentration. "We can't wait anymore," she said after a while. "We are going in."

"Going in where? Are we going into the School of Possibilities?" Ra squeaked, his voice bright with excitement.

My heart had also started to beat quickly, as if the pace was being set by music with a pounding rhythm. "Maybe Mew will appear again, but if not…" I whispered.

India dug in her pockets and pulled out some paper.

"I have some ideas," she said and drew a horse on the paper. The horse had a hole in its stomach. "Look at this," she said.

We looked.

"Why is there a hole in the horse?" Moon asked. "Did someone shoot it?"

"I am not going to shoot horses," Ra said forcefully.

India shook her head. "It's not just any old horse. It's a Trojan horse," India replied.

I whistled.

"In an old Greek tale, soldiers besiege a city called Troy," India said. "The siege lasts for years, and the Greeks can't get into the city…until they think of a plan. One morning a huge wooden horse appears at the gates of the besieged city. It's really enticing, and after thinking about it a little, the townspeople pull it into the city. But the horse is full of Greek soldiers. They attack… and Troy is defeated. We learned this in history when I was still at school."

"It's in comics, too," I enthused.

"Where do we get a horse from?" Moon asked.

"We don't need a horse," India said and drew tires on the horse. "We'll use a garbage truck. It goes through the gate twice a week."

"Is a garbage truck enticing?" Moon asked.

India nodded.

"No one wants to be covered in trash—except us, perhaps. I got this idea from Storm's dad—Storm's dad's truck. Garbage trucks have access to everywhere. The drivers are never asked anything. One visits the School of Possibilities on Mondays and Thursdays." India started to draw something on the paper. I bent over to look. Two maps depicting the school area were taking shape. Two buildings—the school and the sports hall—and the fence emerged. "The trash cans are here," she said, tapping on the corner of the sports hall. "Then just across the yard and in…"

Ra took the pen from India. He drew a cross on the spot where he had seen Mew and two guns where he had seen the guards.

Then we just waited for Thursday and the garbage truck.

Soon we would trick the driver and climb into the truck.

Soon we would see Mew.

But the encounter in the schoolyard would change everything. It would make us realize that we were too slow, that we didn't have much time.

We would have to hurry.

51.

When we went to ambush the garbage truck, we took flashlights, which we didn't end up using all that much, and the kind of knives you need in the jungle for cutting overhanging branches and snakes. We took the binoculars but kept our heads down. We walked in single file along the roadside in silence except for the crackling and rustling, and when thorns pierced our clothes, we just ducked farther down and pushed forward, no matter what confronted us. There were thorns, prickles, and broken branches everywhere trying to tear our clothes and puncture us like balloons.

We stopped to wait for the truck in the yard of an apartment block behind the trash can shelter. The shelter was the last stop before the school gate. It was early morning, and our fingers were stiff from the cold. Then the truck arrived. The heavy drone of its engine could be heard a long way off. Of course I was excited just in case I'd see Dad again soon. All for nothing, though, because the driver was a stranger and bigger than two Dads put together. As he rolled out of the truck and grabbed a trash can, India and I climbed aboard and hid. The boys stayed in the yard. "See you soon," they whispered as we left. "We'll wait behind the fence. We'll watch what's happening. We'll be careful."

When the truck set off after what seemed like an eternity, we didn't dare breathe. India wrapped her arms around me—maybe because there was no room or because she didn't believe that I would be invisible enough on my own. Maybe she also liked me. That didn't seem too bad an idea. Or that was what I secretly wished. "Now nobody will ever snatch you," she whispered.

Then the truck stopped. The driver lowered the window and talked to someone in the schoolyard. We were at the gate. I knew that, because the inside of the cab was filled with so much piercing light from the floodlights that the electricity almost melted me on the spot. I knew about electricity—how it sounded. If you've ever been at some remote place with high-voltage power lines overhead, you know, too. The sound of electricity was a high-pitched hum. It was like thousands of microscopic insects. It was a lonely sound—the buzzing of thousands of creatures.

The gate opened, and the truck started to move again. The driver drove across the schoolyard and parked at the corner of the sports hall. When he got down, we did, too. When he moved, he puffed and panted. His face shone with sweat. He didn't notice us. Maybe his eyes were full of sweat. That was what I thought, but it might have been India's doing. I wondered if India had thought about getting back out again. We hadn't said anything about escaping. There wasn't much time for seeing Mew, and precious minutes were ticking away. The driver was slow, but even so, it wouldn't take him long to empty a dozen trash cans. The horse would drive out of the schoolyard and the unarmed soldiers would be left behind in Troy. But we wanted to see Mew. I reminded myself that it was why we were here and how important it was. We wanted to check that Mew was alive and that everything was okay—or at least that was the general idea.

In the schoolyard, I could see close up all the posters that we were in. They were really big—like sheets, which was quite frightening. In the pictures we were larger than life. We were giant children. This looked odd. When I saw a picture of a boy who was thirteen feet tall and had my face, I froze on the spot. I almost started to believe that the boy in the picture was dangerous and had to be caught. That was what happened to me. I couldn't move. Then India tugged at my wrist to get me to go with her.

There weren't many hiding places in the schoolyard. Behind the trash cans, we were at least slightly hidden. There was a neat and foul-smelling row of them by the side of the sports hall. From behind them we could see the whole schoolyard. We could see the

School of Possibilities and the watchtower and the guards standing in it. There were two of them.

"Where's Mew?" India asked, and I pointed at the main door.

That was where the lobby and Mew's glass cage were. There—somewhere—was Mew. I couldn't see her yet. It was too far away. It was too far to run across the schoolyard to the school windows. At this distance we'd get caught a hundred times over. We'd be noticed and picked up, and we'd be no help to anyone anymore. Or maybe we wouldn't get caught…

"I can't get you there," India replied, as if she had guessed what I was thinking. "You're too real," she said.

I wondered what she meant. Perhaps she thought I hadn't breathed in enough water like the boy in the story. I hadn't been on the streets long enough. I was too real. Or perhaps I was just different from India in every way. I existed too much. I was wondering what this meant when things started to happen.

"Look!" India hissed. She grabbed my shoulder and pushed the binoculars into my hand. They were hanging around her neck. Soon we wouldn't have them any longer. We would lose them. I would drop them, running for my life.

Now I was looking at the school through them. I saw a crowd of children that was congregating in the school lobby. They gathered around Mew's glass case, standing at attention like pieces on a chessboard. When Will arrived, they made way for him as he marched to the door of the cage. He opened it and marched inside. Two soldiers followed on his heels. They dived into the farthest corner of the cage and fished out Mew. Then they dragged her out. They dangled her between them like a piece of clothing or a corpse.

Now I understood why I hadn't noticed Mew earlier. She didn't radiate light anymore. She didn't glow white like a celestial body. She was really small and colorless—not the angry star I knew. She was wearing some kind of coveralls—not the wedding dress, no white hems—just as Ra had told us. Mew looked like a prisoner.

"Morning exercise!" shouted one of the guards from the watchtower into a megaphone.

Then the school's double doors opened, and the group standing in the lobby marched out in order. Mew was in the middle.

I could hardly breathe. I almost forgot to jump to hide behind another trash can when the garbage truck's iron pincers grabbed the can in front of us and picked it up into the air. At that moment I hated the school so much that I clenched India's hand too hard. She didn't say anything. She was very quiet.

Suddenly, Mew stopped. She raked her fingers through her long hair.

"It's a sign," India whispered. She put her hand to her hair and raked it, imitating Mew's gesture, which, of course, was difficult, as the bones and lollipops got stuck in her fingers.

"What does it mean?" I whispered.

"It means, 'Stay still. Don't move. Someone's nearby and looking at me and maybe looking at you too.' We've used it in the city, looking for prey. It's one of the five most important signs and means mid-level danger."

I glanced at India, frowning. If this was mid-level danger, what was the highest level like?

"Mew knows we are here," India whispered.

"How does she know? It's not possible, is it?" I whispered back.

But at that very moment, Mew looked at us. She looked straight at us in our hiding place behind the trash cans. Then I believed it. I felt shadows flickering inside me, as they sometimes did when I knew something was going to happen.

Mew's lips were moving. She drew a quick series of figures in the air, and for a moment, it looked like a star performer who had moved out of the spotlight. There was no sound. Only her fingers and lips moved.

"Is that your sign language?" I whispered.

India nodded and lifted her finger to her lips.

Mew seemed to be thinking about something. She glanced around her. She looked at the fence. She looked at the guards marching by her sides. She looked at the watchtower and then at the garbage truck just as the driver was grabbing a can in its jaws. Mew gave us a nod, or that was what I thought. And suddenly without warning, she started to run. She ran toward the fence. At first I was frightened. I thought that in her desperation, Mew would try and fry herself on the electric fence. But she changed direction and headed toward the gate. It was open. It was open for now.

"Come on. Let's go," India hissed. "We'll never get a better chance."

That was true. The truck was idling in front of us. It didn't take many fractions of a second for me to realize what India had in mind.

We ran from behind the trash cans toward the truck and climbed in through its open door. India sat behind the steering wheel. I clambered up next to her. Everything happened so quickly, and there almost wasn't time to see everything else going on around us at that moment.

India stared at the steering wheel in concentration. She went through all the levers of the truck and gripped the handbrake.

"Are you going to—?" I whispered, worried. "Do you know how?"

India glanced at me and at the schoolyard in front of us. At the back of it was the fence, buzzing with electricity, and the open gate. She released the handbrake, and the truck immediately lurched into motion.

"There isn't always time to learn," she said, and all the while, the truck was drifting toward the fence.

I was overwhelmed by a wild feeling. Here we were, driving a garbage truck out of the gate or into the fence. I should have been scared, but instead I was yelling out of the window.

"Good-bye, Troy! The horse is escaping!"

I shouted it really loudly.

It was windy sitting by the window, and I could see just about everything in the schoolyard. The truck had a trash can in its pincers, and when, at some point during our escape, it turned upside down, all sorts of foul-smelling garbage started to pour out behind us. It was wild. Although we were in a tight spot, I nearly burst out laughing. On our heels were dozens of child soldiers, some wading through the trash. But more soldiers started to crowd into the schoolyard through the doors of the school and sports hall. I wasn't laughing anymore. All the time the loudspeakers were letting out the kind of screech often used during a war to warn of the enemy approaching. Listening to it I thought at the very least that the ground must have been cracking open or a formation of bombers was flying toward the school in the dark, their sole intention to destroy us.

Mew was also running toward the gate. She had gotten a good head start, but now she seemed tired. She was still faster than the soldiers. She was naturally fast anyway, but it also helped that she wasn't wearing the soldiers' heavy clothing.

"Are you ready? We're going through soon," India said. She stared hard at the fence.

I did a thumbs-up and then pushed myself halfway out the window. I held out my hand so that Mew could take hold of it and climb into the truck or stay on the running board. Then we'd just drive out of the gate into the road, go to the harbor, board a ship, and go away forever. I don't know exactly what I was thinking, but it was something like that.

Mew was close now—so close that I could almost hear her breathing. She stretched her arm up toward me. She sped up, and I could see from her face that she couldn't run any faster.

"Catch her," the children in the schoolyard shouted, and someone blew a horn.

I pushed myself really far out. My fingers were flying toward Mew's outstretched hand. It was like one of those scenes in a film, and I was in a starring role.

Then Mew was hit. Will had thrown a stone at her, not an orange, and it flew straight at her like it was a bullet. Mew dropped to her knees. Then she fell flat on her face. She raised her head, and her blood-soaked hair hid her eyes. Then I heard something, or thought I did.

"Don't listen to me!" Mew shouted. "Whatever happens, don't listen to me!"

That was how it happened.

That was it.

I was shaking.

India drove toward the gate, which was closing in front of us. I started to yell at the top of my lungs and covered my eyes.

India glanced at me and pressed the accelerator. We drove through the fence. We didn't get electrocuted. We weren't crushed. I didn't know if the fence would have restrained us if the gate had closed in time. The gate was sheared off its hinges, and we were thrown forward. Everything was going around and around, and branches were smashing into the windows.

I thought I was going to die then.

When I opened my eyes, I saw India bending over me. Then everything went black. When I came around the next time, India was carrying me in a forest. Shadowy trees dropped light snow onto my face, and the sky was really black. I disappeared back into my own world. I didn't know where I was. I saw nightmarish images of us being chased by dogs and other animals.

Perhaps we were being chased. What actually happened was even worse.

Moon and Ra had been caught. They had been watching what was happening from outside the school fence. I imagine they had been frozen with fear and terror. Maybe Ra had cried. They had held each other's hands. "She's pretending to have an asthma attack," Ra probably whispered when he saw Mew on the ground. "It's trick number eleven. In a tight spot, act out an asthma attack. Number twelve is choking. Number thirteen, death."

We crawled toward the factory with our knives still in our belts.

We were wet, saturated by the ground and the air. We didn't dare think about what had just happened. We didn't dare think about what would happen next. We didn't close our eyes.

In the factory we silently withdrew into its farthest depths. We didn't want to talk about what had happened at first, but in the end we did. There were only the two of us now, and a biting wind, which was getting colder all the time, was howling outside.

52.

After our visit to the school, everything became gloomier. Although Moon and Ra were sometimes irritating, I missed them. An icy wind blew through the factory, and snow flew in through the cracks in the walls. The factory was as cold as a glacier, but it protected us. It hid us. We passed the time in its hiding places and ate birds that India trapped. That was the only food we had. We fried the birds on a cooker rigged up from a tin can. The bird meat was dry. It was almost like chewing coat sleeves or eating a shoe sole. We couldn't leave the factory. India maybe could have, I thought, but she didn't want to. "I'm not leaving you," she said, and I was pleased about that.

When we woke up in the mornings, the yard was covered in an icy crust. I was wearing two padded coats and a couple of pairs of pants. India had taken the clothes from the attic stores of apartment blocks and goodness knows where else. There were a lot of them. There were enough to clothe a large family—all of India's gang of robbers. I would have put on a third padded layer, but it would have made me too clumsy. I wouldn't have been able to climb, run away, or anything else. When you lived as a fugitive, you had to keep on the move, and that wasn't possible if you were as fat as a snowman. The nights were also cold. I slept curled up in a hole I had dug in a mountain of clothes. I also had my sleeping bag there. I asked India to come in beside me.

"You can come inside the bag if you want or if you're cold," I said. But India just laughed and said that she kept guard at night. That she wandered around and didn't want to wake me. Sometimes at night I woke up at these times. Then I saw India. She sat on a pile of beds in a pose like a statue.

We thought about the other robbers. We thought about them all the time. The two of us were the last ones left, and it wasn't clear how things would work out. It wasn't worth thinking about too much. Instead it was better to think about a plan. We talked about it all the time. We hadn't yet come up with anything decent, and time was passing. The gate had been repaired, and no garbage trucks or any other vehicles were allowed to go through it without an inspection. The school now had three important prisoners. No risks were taken. It was difficult to keep up with events now that we had lost the binoculars. I had dropped them in the garbage truck or somewhere.

We sat barricaded around the cooker. It had been five days since the boys had been caught. We hadn't left the factory for five days. I squinted at the cooker and imagined that it was a huge stove. With eyes screwed up, you could imagine anything to be something else. A flame became a blaze, but it still didn't warm our limbs.

I threw a bone over my shoulder.

"I prefer fried rat," I said to India.

India shrugged her shoulders.

"We haven't caught any rats in the traps lately," she said and pointed at the ceiling with a bird bone. "It's like we're cursed."

I made a sort of defying gesture, and India grabbed the bone with her teeth. She gnawed it neatly, wiped it on her pants leg, and pushed it into her hair. There were several bones sticking out of it already like trees in a forest. There were bird and rat bones. There was a mummified small bird with multicolored wings.

"Could Mew have been mortally wounded?" I asked.

India shook her head. Suddenly she flinched. "Did you hear that?" she hissed.

I froze and listened. The sound she was talking about was a sort of scratching. It was followed by a whistle.

We looked at each other, frightened.

India jumped to her feet. "Action stations!" she hissed and picked up a large stick.

I seized a metal pipe. Then we both sprang into action. The bone garlands around our necks rattled. We didn't make any noise, except what could be heard from our shoes and trinkets. Apart from that the night was full of all sorts of din. Trucks thundered on their way to and from the harbor. Ships blew their foghorns. Ambulances wailed. Fire engine sirens pierced the air. Somewhere a dog howled, and another one answered. I couldn't make out my own heartbeat.

We ran, dodged, and climbed. Soon we were in the biggest hall—the one the boys had called the street, because they practiced break-dancing there; the one I had called the skate hall, because I had been on my board there every evening. A girl was crouching in a corner. I could only just make her out, because she was so deep in the shadows. She was bent over with her chin on her knees. The only light came from the moon in the sky, the streetlights on the road that ran past the factory, and the cars driving along it.

I crept closer, but I already knew. I knew as soon as I saw her, but at first I wasn't absolutely certain. I had been mistaken before.

"It's Mew," I whispered.

India watched next to me. She was crouching, alert. She listened. "You can't know that," she said.

I stepped closer. "It is Mew," I whispered.

India shook her head slowly. "Not necessarily," she said. She lowered her hand on my shoulder and squeezed. "Let's not go yet. I don't have a good feeling about this."

Then the figure in the corner moved. "Help," she said, or maybe she said, "Help me." The voice was clearly Mew's.

"Is that India?" she asked. "Storm? Is that you, Storm?"

"We are here," I whispered, agitated, and India's grip on my shoulder tightened.

"It doesn't feel right," she whispered. "Something is wrong."

"Wrong?" I said and almost lost my temper. "Look! Mew is injured. It feels wrong if we don't help her."

Mew really was shivering in the corner, looking wounded.

"I'm going closer," I said and tore myself away from India's grip. I went to the corner where Mew was crouching. "What happened?" I asked.

At first Mew didn't answer. She was whistling quietly, but I couldn't quite make out what the tune was. It was like shallow breathing. For a while there were only the sounds of a deserted factory, sounds from outside—from the street, the city, and the harbor—and the whistle that sounded like a dying breath. The whistle was a bit like the whistle we robbers used to call each other—but only a bit.

"I escaped," the girl said at last.

Only now did I notice that her coveralls were dirty. They were muddy, as though she had crawled in them. They were torn, as though she had climbed in them. They were bloody, as though she had been wounded in them.

Mew didn't look at us. She looked at her hands, which were lying in her lap like a couple of abandoned objects.

"Tell us—" I started, and then India kicked my ankle.

"We mustn't listen to you," she said, and her voice was very clear. I was astonished at just how clear it was.

Mew raised her shoulders. She looked like a starved cat. "I came to get you," she whispered.

"To get us? Why?"

"I know about the basement," she replied.

I almost forgot to breathe. I leaned closer.

"I've been there, Mew. Don't you remember? I've seen the basement."

"Oh, no, you don't know. You really don't," she said, and then she gave a hollow laugh.

"What is it?" I asked.

India looked at me and rolled her eyes.

Mew took my hand and pulled at it like a water monster. "I have to get back soon," she croaked. "The boys are in there. The school was empty when I left. Everybody was away somewhere. I don't know…and I don't understand. But I have to go back. Moon and Ra need me. And all the other children—the children under the glass domes. I have seen them. They are behind the glass just like they are in crystal balls, and there are pipes on the walls and they make a noise like…"

Then Mew pressed her head into her knees. She started to tell us what had happened. She talked hesitantly, forgetting things. From these fragments we pieced together the story.

Mew had escaped. She had used the air-conditioning duct, some sort of a narrow tube which smelled of metal. The duct had led out of the basement.

"I jumped onto the roof and tried to leap into those branches behind the fence. I almost made it. I flew over the fence and fell on the ground. There was no one around anywhere. That's what I don't understand."

Confused, she kept repeating that there was no one there.

"Why were you in the basement?" I interrupted her.

"I woke up there," Mew answered. She looked like she was trying to remember. She raked her hair. It was dirty and sticky.

"I don't remember," she cried out. "I had hurt myself somehow. There was blood on the floor."

"Will threw a stone at you," I told her.

"And a couple of other vermin soldiers threw bigger stones," India said.

Mew pressed her knees tighter to her chin.

"The only thing I can remember from the yard is that truck," she said. "And there was also a wailing sound coming from the loudspeakers, and then...something hit me. I thought that I had died—that you had died on the electric fence or in the crash. Everything was really confused, and then suddenly someone started to scream behind the fence, and I saw Moon and Ra rush forward. When I woke up, I was in the basement. The boys were there, too. I saw Will's soldiers take them into that room. That ugly hag was there. 'No chances left,' she said and rubber-stamped them both on the forehead."

I glanced at India. Now we more or less knew what had happened in the yard. Moon had been caught because Ra had been caught, and Ra had been caught when a stone had hit Mew on the head.

"I could strangle those brats," Mew said, crying and refusing to say anymore.

When we tried to question her about the basement, she couldn't answer. She was scared of something in there. She tried to talk about it, but something held her back. She couldn't say what she meant, mixing up her words and saying something else instead.

"The air conditioning scared me the most," she said. "It sounded... it sounded like this."

The air behind Mew's narrow rib cage rasped. She breathed deeply and heavily.

"Like breathing?" I whispered tensely.

Mew nodded. "It sounded like someone breathing."

I knew now what she was talking about. Sometimes in the middle of the night, I woke to that sound. It was like a thousand children breathing in an endless sleep.

"We need to go there," Mew whispered desperately. "We need to go into the basement and save the boys. All the children. We need to free them. Something evil is about to happen. I feel—we need to destroy the basement."

"Who's going?" India asked.

"We all are," Mew said. "We're all needed."

53.

Then we went, although it wasn't quite that simple. First we had to make preparations. We agreed on signals. We decided what we would do if something happened—if we were caught.

We also made some crazy preparations, like tying more bones and feathers on the ribbons around our necks and painting stripes on our faces. We used pigeon blood for that. We used other blood, too. I gouged a scratch on my hand with my knife and another on India's. I did it with my eyes almost closed. "At these times your own blood is the strongest," India said. "You can trust it."

I looked at myself in a broken piece of mirror. I looked ferocious. I looked a lot like a primitive person prowling in the jungle—a cannibal who tears out his enemies' hearts and cooks them in a stew.

"Looking really good," India said and pulled a face at her own image over my shoulder. Then she ruffled her hair. "It's the lollipops, birds, and bones in the hair that make a warrior immortal," India said. She pushed something into my hair. "It can protect you, too. A rhino could stand up in that mess."

I picked the mummified bird out of my head and scowled.

Mew watched us from a windowsill. Her hair hung over her face. There was something ghostlike about her. She drummed her knees nervously, maybe because she was just cold. As I realized this, I took off my outermost coat and took it over to her. Mew put the coat on quickly.

"Did you notice, India, that we have a gentleman here?" she said and gave me a crooked smile. It was a familiar smile. I had seen it a thousand times.

I was just starting to pull off my outer padded pants. Just a coat wouldn't keep anyone warm. "What are you doing now?" Mew asked.

"I thought—"

Mew spluttered. "Why do boys have to get undressed as soon as there are girls around? Why don't you take all the rest off while you're at it?"

I threw the pants at Mew. "I only wanted to…help. Uh."

"What did he want?" Mew asked India and raised her eyebrows meaningfully.

India started to giggle. "Storm is like an onion," she said. "He can be peeled away endlessly."

I went red, or that was how I felt. Of course both girls thought it was hilarious. They giggled—almost like any normal girls in a similar situation. This sort of thing was not easy for a boy. In the end I was amused, as well, and for a while we forgot about all the horrible things and just laughed. Perhaps we didn't laugh our heads off, but it was almost cheerful anyhow. It was really great to see Mew smile.

It was one of those moments, full of anticipation.

Before we left India sprayed a farewell on the wall. She painted a picture of a girl on a raft. The girl was surrounded by water everywhere. It was rippling on the streets. It flooded in through the windows.

Mew was circling around. She was impatient.

"We need to go," she said, and her long hair hung over her face, covering her eyes. "We need to go before they notice that I've escaped."

"Haven't they noticed?"

Mew shook her head.

"There was no one there. That's what was so strange."

54.

This was what happened on the way to the school. I heard a noise behind my back—a noise I knew well. I turned around. A skateboard was rolling down the road. It was like seeing a ghost. I stopped in my tracks. Mew didn't notice anything, and neither did India. They were walking ahead of me toward the school. I was going to shout and ask them to wait, but I didn't.

I ran to catch the board and picked it up.

It was mine. It felt like mine.

My heart was pounding like crazy.

The board felt the same as before. I could identify my own board anywhere—whether in complete darkness or in searing light. Nothing else was quite like it. I had done all sorts of things with it, but then it had been put into the glass case. Now it was wandering about on its own in the dark. Was I dead, or was I seeing things? What was this all about?

Suddenly I saw a figure in the bushes.

Yes, of course.

There was something suspicious about this. It had to be a trap.

I clenched my hands into fists. I stepped closer.

Bridget was crouching under a bush.

"Bridget?" I cried.

Bridget said nothing. She gestured for me to come to her.

I went even closer. Bridget was alone, or at least it seemed like it.

"What do you want?" I snarled. "Why are you following me?"

The others were just disappearing into the shrubbery surrounding the school fence. I stepped back on the road in order to catch up with them.

"Don't go," Bridget whispered.

I frowned. What was this?

"What now?"

"Don't go to the school!" Bridget said frantically.

"Ugh," I huffed.

Then Bridget took hold of my arm. "I brought you the skateboard so that you'd listen to me."

I raised my eyebrows in a meaningful sort of way. We were getting to the point. "You mean that your father gave it to you so you could entice me into a trap? You must be trying to get that pretty big reward that's being offered for my capture. Admit it. What's a girl like you going to do with so much money?"

Bridget started to cry. Tears ran down her pale cheeks. I thought then, *You are making a girl cry in the bushes, Storm. How low are you going to sink?*

"How did you get this?" I asked, more gently. Bridget was the only child from the School of Possibilities that I had ever seen crying.

"I took the key from my father," she said.

"You mean you stole it?"

Bridget shook her head. "I didn't think it was stealing."

I spluttered. “If he didn’t give you the key, it’s stealing.”

I was nasty and couldn’t help myself. I said everything without thinking. Bridget fiddled with a branch and was thinking hard. Then she blew her nose on her handkerchief and raised her eyes.

“It’s not stealing,” she said quite loudly. “The skateboard belongs to you. I returned it. And there are other things.”

When my anger faded, confusion or something similar replaced it.

“You asked about the basement…” Bridget whispered. “I wanted to tell you that I have been investigating things. I found out something about it.”

“About the basement?” I said, raising my voice.

“The girl has been there.”

“I know. I have been in the basement, too.”

I peered after the others. They were no longer within sight.

“You don’t understand,” Bridget said.

I was sure she would start to bawl again, and I was already irritated.

“The girl is taking you to them,” she said.

A cold wind blew in my veins. It blew and wiped away all the warmth.

“I don’t believe you,” I said slowly.

“You must,” Bridget said. “I like you. I wouldn’t want anything to happen to you.”

I scowled, frustrated.

“Tell me quickly. I’m in a hurry. We plan to save the children.”

“The girl is taking you to them. Why do you think she was able to escape from the basement?”

“What do you mean?”

"In the School of Possibilities, all the children are puppets controlled by adults. The adults pull the strings. The children do what the adults want them to do."

"What are you, then?" I asked, although I wanted to shout. "Why aren't you like that?"

Bridget shrugged her shoulders with uncertainty. "I have always been good. Father knows that I will obey."

"Are you claiming that Mew is deceiving me?"

Bridget shook her head. "I am claiming that they are deceiving her. But it could also be that they have already made a mask of her. And then..."

Things began to fall into place, and I was frightened.

Sometime around then, I decided to believe Bridget and asked, "Do you still have your father's key?"

55.

When I heard the whistle, I knew who was waiting for me.

I started to jump back on the road.

"I have to go," I said. "They're waiting for me."

Bridget grabbed my hand.

"Don't!" she shouted.

Girls seemed to say that to me all the time. They also got hold of my arms. I pulled myself free. "Wait here. I'll be back soon," I said, and then I hurried onto the road. All the time I was really careful. No boy anywhere on Earth moved about so silently.

At first I didn't see India, and when I did, I was startled. She looked so strange. She was almost blue. It was because of something like the light or the lack of it. She stood by the roadside out of sight, staring at the empty road as if looking for something important she had lost. And she had—me.

For some reason India made me remember something distant.

When I was little, maybe five, and afraid of the dark, of being left alone, of fires, and of other things, Mom said that if anything happened to her or Dad—and of course, nothing would—she would send someone to take care of things. "Mothers always send someone," she said and tried to tuck me into bed. "Send someone with claws," I demanded, and Mom swore—crossed her heart and hoped to die—that she would send someone with long claws and fangs. Someone angry who would protect her black-eyed boy. Then I sprang out of bed and went to get my drawing materials. I drew a picture of my guardian on paper. I did it just to make sure. When the picture was finished, I showed it to Mom. "What do you see in the picture?" I asked, and Mom examined it carefully. "I see a monster that has someone's thigh bone in its teeth, a forked, venomous tongue, and laser eyes," she said. "Am I wrong, or is this monster my son's guardian angel?"

Of course she was right. When I was little, I didn't want to be followed around by some creature in a white gown with thin tissue-paper wings and toes that would be scratched as soon as we went into the sorts of thickets I was always wandering into; I still didn't. I needed a guardian with strong pads on its feet, thick lizard skin, and several hands who could survive for an hour underwater without breathing. My guardian angel was scruffy and looked like an animal.

My drawing hung on my bedside wall for a long time. I was now thinking about it while looking at India, and although India wasn't ugly and didn't have fangs or pads on her feet, she looked a bit like the creature in the drawing.

The road behind India was deserted. She had come back, and she was alone.

I pushed a couple of fingers into my mouth and whistled.

India stood still for a moment, as if she was listening. Then she ran to me. She ran straight to me, although I was standing hidden among the bushes.

"You won't believe this!" she breathed. "When we got to the school, the gate opened. Then Mew noticed that you weren't with us anymore. Of course I'd done my best to keep her from noticing."

"Was she deceiving us?" I asked, frightened, because I remembered then what Bridget had said about puppets.

India thought for a moment. "I don't think so," she said. "I think she wants to save the boys. I think they deceived her. They do a lot of deceiving."

Suddenly she fell silent. She had now noticed Bridget, who was crouching farther away in the ditch, looking up at the sky frantically. India's eyes narrowed, and her hands clenched into fists. "What does she want?" she hissed.

"Bridget gave me this," I said and held up the skateboard.

India gave a nasty laugh. "What a creep!" she said.

"Bridget also gave me these," I said and showed her the keys. They flashed under the streetlight. "We can get into the school with these and anywhere inside."

India grabbed the keys and twirled them around in front of her for a moment. I felt ridiculous. India would hardly understand why I thought I could trust Bridget. I didn't understand it myself. To my surprise she just stared angrily at her.

"You're right," she said and threw the keys to me. "The girl isn't tricking us. She's just dead boring."

"I think Bridget means well," I said.

"But I don't trust strangers, and never good girls. I only trust bones and lollipops and what is flowing in these veins." India flexed her thin arms then. "Keep the girl far away from me, or I'll shove a pile of bones down her throat."

India's eyes narrowed. "Listen to this," she said. "When Mew got into the yard, the gate closed behind her. She stood there for a while, looking frantic and whistling for you. She wasn't her usual self—not in my opinion, anyway, but I already knew that in the factory. And I'm usually right. Of course I turned around before I got to the gate and ran to look for you."

Just at that moment, I liked India quite a lot. Actually I think I might have ruffled her hair, and I think she might have smiled at me, although it could have been a scowl.

"What do you think that little squid would do if she was caught in a child criminal's company?" India then asked.

"Don't you mean two criminals?"

India shook her head so that a lollipop fell on the road.

"But I won't get caught. I'm only worried about you."

I shrugged my shoulders. "Why don't you ask her?" I said.

"I'm not talking to her," India said.

I sighed and returned to Bridget. I asked her if she was planning to sell us out and told her to be honest. I also gave her a push—not so that she fell down or anything, but a small one anyway.

She wiped her muddy face, trying to be brave. "I don't want to be good anymore," she sniffed. "I won't make that mistake again. I won't tell on you. Not anymore."

"Say that again. I didn't quite get that," I pressed her.

Bridget's nose was runny, and she looked a lot better with her snotty nose and dirty clothes. "Perhaps I could run away, too," she said as we started off toward the school. "I've been in the Scouts and can cook food on a campfire. I'm sure I would manage. I could also tidy up."

I glanced at India and grinned. India didn't feel like laughing. She kicked a couple of stones from the roadside, and they fell to the ground somewhere far off.

"Never," she whispered in my ear. "Over my dead body, and all the bones and birds that are in this hair. Period. Tell her."

I didn't, because I got the feeling that India was jealous—and not just a little, either.

"I like you, too," I said instead and grinned slyly. Then I sprang away like a stoat as, of course, she tried to punch me. However, it was easy to dodge that sort of a swipe.

"Damned kid," she hissed and turned toward the school. "Let's go. We've wasted loads of time on nothing."

We set off toward the school. It was fantastic now that I had my own skateboard beneath me. You can always borrow someone else's board, but it's never the same—not even close. I did all sorts of tricks. Every so often I jumped against benches and curbs, because there was no way I could ignore them since I hadn't been on my board for months. When I was in the air, I fleetingly forgot that there was no reason to be cheerful. I was untouchable on my board.

Bridget followed. She walked in the ditch and didn't notice India zigzagging through the woods, quite close. It was a bit odd, but then, I was starting to believe that India really could be invisible to those she didn't like or particularly care for.

Then the gate stood before us. Soon we would encounter things that would frighten anyone to death.

56.

At the school gate, we thought about what we should do first.

"I have an idea," Bridget said, and we weren't expecting that.

"What idea?" I asked. I wanted to hear it, although I didn't quite believe yet that it would be anything very promising. But Bridget took us by surprise.

"We have to turn the school off," she said.

Of course it was a strange idea, and I didn't quite understand what she meant. I glanced at India. I wondered what India thought about it. But she had run a long way off and was just peering at the fence top decorated with razor blades. The fence they called the "guard dog" looked like a porcupine or some even more pathetic creature.

"What do you mean?" I asked, although I really wanted to run to India.

"If I can get into father's study, I might be able to find out where the center of the school's electricity supply is."

I still didn't understand. "What do we need to know that for?" I asked. "We're supposed to find the boys and save the children—all the children whose free will sleeps under the glass."

"There's a place here that the teachers call the heart of the school."

I spat on the ground, a bit like India always did.

"Only someone with a heart can have a heart attack. Buildings don't have one, and neither do schools," I said.

Bridget shook her head. "But this school does. And we can disconnect it. That's what I was thinking of."

We looked at each other.

"So that everything is turned off?" I asked.

Bridget nodded. "The power will go off. Televisions will go blank. Radiators will cool down. Electricity will stop flowing. The whole school will come to a stop."

"But—" I started. I had already begun to anticipate what was coming.

India walked along the fence where light and dark met. She watched the yard, her hand on her forehead, and listened.

"It means that the children—there are risks, aren't there?" I asked.

Bridget nodded. "The air conditioning in the basement will go off, too," she said. "The masks—I don't know what will happen to them. Something, for sure."

"We don't quite know what they are," I said. "We know that they breathe, but what happens when the breathing machine is disconnected…?"

"The breathing stops, and the children will either wake up or—"

"They'll suffocate?" I whispered, turning pale as I realized that that could happen.

"There is that risk," Bridget admitted. "But because they could also wake up, we should—or what do you think?"

I looked at the blades on top of the fence. It was difficult to know beforehand.

"There are two alternatives," I whispered. "We could lose everything."

"Or win," Bridget said seriously. "I can't think of what else we could do. And life as a prisoner of the School of Possibilities is not worth much. Or do you think it is? We can turn the school off. They won't be expecting that."

"It's our last chance," India said at that point. She was standing next to me again. "Your friend is right. There is no other way. We have to do it."

I turned to look at India. There were snowflakes in her hair among all those bones. India pushed her hand into mine. I felt how cold it was, and how my own hand shook and my heart pounded, and how our blood flowed restlessly under our skin.

We could lose everything. Or win.

All three of us stared through the fence at the school, which glowed nakedly in the bright light. When I closed my eyes, I saw Moon and Ra's faces behind the glass, and I became scared. I almost couldn't move. Then I quickly opened my eyes and decided that I wouldn't close them again until it was all over and the story had come to an end.

57.

The School of Possibilities was lit up, and when I say *lit up*, you won't yet get the full picture. The school was so brightly lit that it was like a luxurious cruise liner in the middle of a dark sea. On one side of the yard, the sports hall stood like a smaller sister of the mother ship. Between them was the watchtower. I had only seen it in daytime before, through murky gray fall, and once very early in the morning. I had never stood in the yard in the middle of the night.

All the windows of every school building were lit in a sharp, dazzling light. Seeing them in front of me made me believe that nothing inside could stay hidden. Anyone running along the corridors on any floor of the school or anyone scoring goals behind the sports hall's glassy walls would be visible from the yard. There is no hiding place in an aquarium. It is like a stage. If you think about things this way, you won't be far from the truth. On stage everything is acted out—and yet the playwright is somewhere there. He is always hidden, but he is there.

The school had a secret that lay deep within it. It was darker than any secret I had ever known before in my life. It was the only darkness left in so much light. It was here in the middle of the cruise ship's sea of light. That was what I thought as I looked at the school.

But there was something different about the place today. There was no one there—not anywhere. No one stopped us at the gate. No one stopped us as we walked across the yard toward the main building. The school corridors remained empty. The tower was quiet. The loudspeakers were silent.

India held my hand. Although she was really thin and quite blue, I felt strength flowing from her. It went straight to my legs and heart—such power.

"You'd better not get caught," I whispered.

India clutched my hand tighter. "I'm never caught," she said. "I just vanish into thin air. You know that."

I didn't know that.

Together we walked closer to the school.

The largest screen of the school was showing a live broadcast. A trial was underway—yet another trial. A student was walking in front of the court, supported by the official defender appointed by

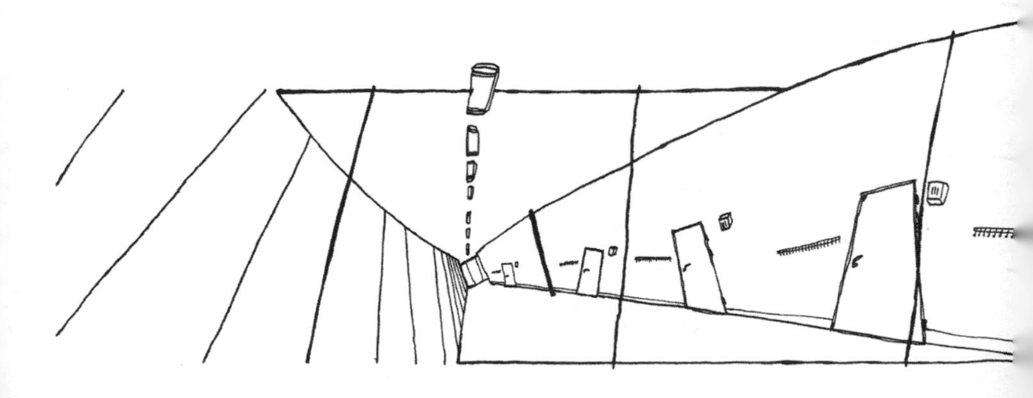

the school. This man was the school's own lawyer, and he stood next to the accused and spoke for him. I couldn't hear the words, but I knew that the longer he continued, the slimmer the student's chances became. At the end the sentence would be announced.

I stared at the screen, frozen to the spot as if something on it had hypnotized me. I couldn't take my eyes off of the accused. He would come to a sticky end, and I could see in his eyes that he knew it, too.

"Don't look at it," Bridget said and tugged my arm.

India let go of my hand.

"We don't have time," Bridget said. "We have to find the school's power center. If we don't find it, we've lost the game."

"But you said you knew where it was."

Bridget shook her head. "I said I might be able to find it."

I unlocked the door and stepped into the lobby. The girls came in after me. Not a single alarm rang out. Not a single bell began to chime. Only the electric buzz could be heard around us. It went through the wires and cables like blood in the veins of the building, keeping the

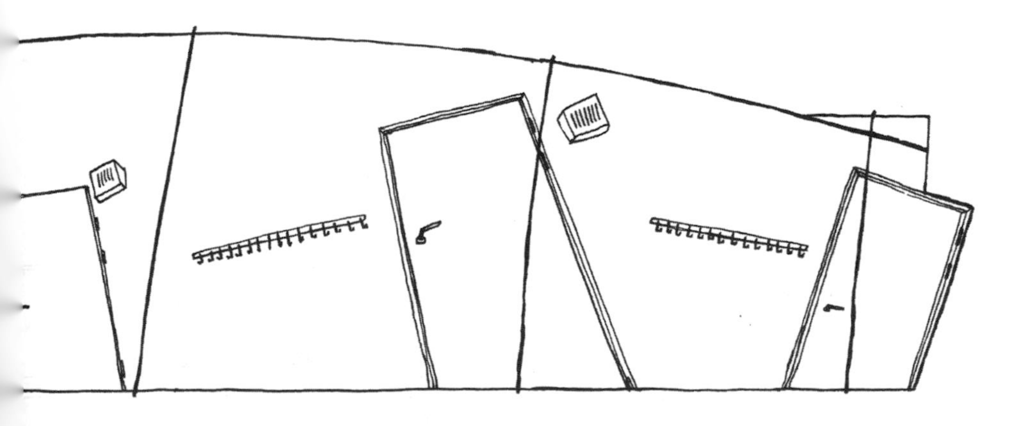

lights burning and the television screens alive. The screens flashed without any sound. The mouths moved, but nothing came out of them. The hum of the electricity was the only sound in the school.

Something else was different about the place now. There was something extra in it. Pamphlets were pinned to the walls, explaining why Eric, Josh, Sandy, or Ida had been sentenced, what they had done, what they had been accused of, why their class had to be ashamed, and finally what the sentence was.

"After your escape, the school tightened its procedures," Bridget explained. "We have security checks in the mornings. There are new items on the banned list, and some subjects advocating rebellion have been axed. They don't want us to know. They've told us to use stricter methods in the boyfriend and girlfriend training, too. Everything must be reported. 'You watch, we punish' is the name of that procedure."

India adjusted the bones in her hair.

I looked at her and saw how the corridor behind her was like a frame in which she stood, but it didn't suit her. She was a girl without a background, an exceptional girl, the oddest thing that had ever existed, and she certainly didn't belong here. I felt a bit miserable when I realized that India was wrong, after all. She wouldn't vanish into thin air. If she were caught, the consequences would be worse for her than for anyone else.

I dropped my skateboard on the floor. I stepped onto it and did a thumbs-up to India in order to wish her good luck and to encourage her. Then I took off and performed probably the first jump ever done in this school.

Bridget had run ahead of us and was already standing behind the staff room doorway at the end of the corridor. India followed me. She moved cautiously in the corridor with silent steps, as if it were a secret ice rink. She looked up and around her, and she was quiet and alert.

Still no one was seen, but they were all somewhere.

Were they in the basement?

They certainly weren't in the corridors or inside the classrooms. We would have seen that from the yard. From there you could see anyone's movements in the building, and if something was lurking, you would know much sooner in the yard than here inside the glass walls of the school.

Anyone in the yard would see us now.

But no one came.

We opened the staff room door. No one was there. We walked across the room to the headmaster's door and stepped inside. Still we saw no one. It began to feel spooky. It felt wrong. It was ominous.

The headmaster's office was a bit too familiar. I would rather not have gone inside. To be honest I would have rather not thought about the place at all. In that office I had signed a paper that bound me to the School of Possibilities. *I, Storm Steele, choose the future.* I had been there for a telling-off once or twice. These were not good memories—not at all.

There was a map of the school on the wall. It showed the whole yard. It showed the school and the sports hall. The tower had been drawn in afterward. The power center was not marked, although almost everything else was—but not that, or the basement.

"I don't understand," I said, and I really didn't. "The basement isn't marked."

All the floors of the school were shown. Even the desks were marked. Only the basement was missing. Bridget glanced at me, looking serious. Terror showed in her eyes.

"That man has had a lot of praise for his methods," India interrupted me. She was examining a framed diploma on the wall. "*The School of Possibilities works for the future.* That's what it says. *The school and its headmaster are doing good work for the sake of saving children who are all but lost.*" India tapped the glass with a bird bone. "Believe it if you want," she said. Then she turned around quickly and tossed the bone onto a rug on the other side of the room.

"Look there," she said.

"Under the rug?"

"Yes, there," India said. She rummaged in her hair again and snatched another bone out of it. She pushed it into a flowerpot.

I rolled up the rug.

"What are you doing?" Bridget asked.

"Rolling up the rug. What does it look like?"

There was a metal door under the rug.

I whistled, surprised.

"Why does anyone bother to hide a safe under a rug? Everyone always looks behind paintings and under rugs first."

"You found a door under there?" Bridget cried out, astonished. She came closer and bent over next to me to take a closer look at the discovery.

"It was India," I said and knocked on the metal door, impressed.

"Oh, India!" Bridget sniffed. "Yes, of course."

She started to examine the lock. It had some kind of a number combination with a hundred thousand possibilities. Bridget was not put off by it. "I can open it," she said. "I need fifteen minutes."

"No more than that?" I cried out in surprise.

Bridget shook her head. "Father has no imagination in these sorts of things," she said. Then she started to press numbers on the lock. She tried, turned, and twisted. And after about fifteen minutes, the safe opened.

"My birthday, Mother and Father's wedding anniversary, the date our dog Apostle died," Bridget said proudly.

I peered into the safe over Bridget's shoulder. There was nothing special in it—just a pile of papers. "There's nothing in it," I said to India.

India was hanging lollipops on the branches of a plastic houseplant, as if she were decorating a Christmas tree. "Look closer," she said.

And I did. Bridget had started to rifle through the pile of papers she had picked out of the safe. "Read this," she said and pushed a paper into my hand. I looked it over, frowning.

"Looks like a contract."

I read the paper. It was a debt certificate.

"Read on," Bridget ordered.

"*Everything has its price*. That's what it says," I whispered to India.

Of course it was something I already knew, but here it was now in black and white. India glided lightly around the room. Every so often she pressed her hand against the windowpane and looked out into the yard.

"Somebody called Gus owes the School of Possibilities...an absurd amount of money," I read from the paper. "All his actions are listed, and every one of them has a price. Almost everything is forbidden or criminal."

Debt certificates of people known and unknown to me passed through my fingers. The crimes were any old thing, such as wrong words in the wrong place, the wrong sort of way to move—anything, anything would do. The amounts that had built up were impossibly large.

"This one is yours," Bridget said and handed me a paper.

I read my name on it and the date I had entered the School of Possibilities. From then on it was downhill all the way. That was how it seemed.

India came up beside me and peered at the list over my shoulder.

"You sure are something," she said and whistled.

So I was. I was a child badly in debt.

India pulled a piece of paper out of Bridget's pile and folded it into a paper plane. She threw it into the air, where it glided around for a time and landed on the headmaster's desk. "These should be torched," she said. "They would look better with flame under their tails."

I took the rest of Bridget's debt certificates and dropped them on the floor.

"What do you think about it?" I asked.

"It's turned me to ice," she said quietly.

India had taken a marker pen out of her hair and was writing her name on the wall. She wrote it in really big letters. I got carried away, as well, because I flung the diplomas off the wall to give me more space to draw.

"Now it's this school's turn to be punished," I said. "The first line is for the headmaster who takes away our freedom, and the second one is because my skateboard has been rotting away in the glass case for months, stopping me from practicing and making me rusty. This long line is because you can't do or think what you want in this damned place."

Although I was laughing raucously while I was drawing, I wasn't happy at all. This could have been the last day of my life and my last rebellion. Tomorrow I might not exist like I did now. I was almost madly delighted when I thought about all our actions being recorded on the security camera tapes. When I had finished, I climbed on the headmaster's desk and looked at the gallows I had created.

"I think we have killed our final chance," I said, blowing my fingers.

Bridget looked at me from the computer.

"Why are you tearing around so much?" she asked. She had switched on the computer. "Come and take a look. I've found something," she said.

Sometimes when everything is confused, you move into a different time zone and situation. You forget you are in trouble and think of something else—anything else: perhaps a warm day in the park, green grass, a rug on the grass, and your parents pouring you juice into a brightly colored beaker, giving you a coin, and sending you off to buy a balloon from the seller by the ice cream stand. And you don't buy just one ball of air. No, you buy two—except you don't buy a ball filled with air but balls of ice cream instead, a yellow one and a white one flecked with chocolate. As you are eating the yellow ball, the white one begins to melt. It drips onto your fingers, and you lick them to stop the ants and all the other insects from tracking you down.

Sometimes when everything is confused, you think of things that don't occur to you outside in the sunshine. At those times you realize that the best guardian angels have fangs. I have to tell you something else about India. Maybe you have already noticed. Maybe you already know. Sometimes when I turned around quickly, I didn't immediately see India. It was easy to look straight past her. Sometimes I grabbed hold of her shoulder just to make sure that she really was there—that she really was flesh and blood. Sometimes I only saw her because I knew she was standing there. India herself would laugh about this and say that was what it was like when you could make yourself invisible. But I thought about it. And soon I would be thinking about it again.

"The heart of the school," Bridget said suddenly and pointed at a dot on the sports hall plan on the computer screen.

We looked at the screen and then, almost at the same time, out the window.

"So it's in the sports hall?" I cried.

Bridget nodded.

"It's the heart of the school," she said.

"Are you sure?" I asked—although if I thought about it even a little, I realized that the heart had to be there, that it couldn't really be anywhere else.

"Absolutely certain," Bridget said.

Then we sprang up and ran out of the office. But a surprise was waiting for us. The main door was locked and wouldn't open with the key. I wasn't worried—not at first. Locked doors couldn't deter India, and they never had. I turned around to look at her.

India was gone. She had disappeared.

"India!" I shouted.

But there was no answer.

I was really scared now. I tried to remember when I had last seen her. Was it before or after I had drawn the gallows on the wall? Hadn't she been looking out the window when Bridget and I were looking at the computer?

I pulled at the door, angry. I punched it. Then I kicked it.

Bridget looked at me a little strangely.

"Why are you in a rage all the time? You won't be able to open it," she said. "We've been locked in. So that's why it was all too easy for us."

I knelt on the floor. I pressed my hand on the glass door and looked out into the yard. It looked a bit like pictures on the news—pictures of an antiquated prison camp on the other side of Europe. I shouldn't really have been affected by it.

"The basement," I whispered.

"What about it?" Bridget asked.

"We'll go to the basement," I said.

58.

India had left me on my own just when I needed her, and I couldn't understand why. I was damned angry.

"Are we really going to the basement?" Bridget asked.

"That's where the boys are," I said. "Mew is there. And I think that India is there, too. We need to go."

Bridget grabbed my elbow.

"Won't it just be a total dead end?" she asked.

I turned to look at her. "Did you forget? Did you forget why we were going to the power center?"

"Because we want to turn the school off," Bridget answered timidly.

"Because we want to destroy the masks," I spelled out.

"To free the children," Bridget whispered.

"To free the children," I repeated. I looked out into the yard for the last time. It was black like deepest space. "I want to see them," I said. "I want to see the masks."

Bridget let go of my arm. "Do you really mean that?"

"I do," I said.

Then Bridget lowered her eyes.

"I want to see them, too," she said a little tearfully. "I may be frightened of enclosed places and of Father finding me and a lot of other things, but I want to see those masks."

We still had the key. It would let us into the storeroom. It would let us in anywhere we liked. In the storeroom we might get lost, but then again we might find our way. But we had to hurry. I noticed that I had taken Bridget's hand as we hurried to leave. I snatched it away immediately. I didn't want her to get any stupid ideas into her head, like I was scared or falling for her.

Then we set off.

"You talk about India all the time. Why?" Bridget asked.

"India is that girl from our class—the one we're not supposed to talk about," I said. And then I said something else. "I think I like India. Or maybe I love her."

I shrugged my shoulders rather nonchalantly, although nothing could alter what I had just said. In any other situation, I would have felt stupid to say anything like that out loud, but now it didn't seem to matter. Now it felt right.

Bridget looked at me for a really long time.

We were at the door leading to the basement. We were close.

59.

Our presence in the storeroom was expected.

Will and a bunch of bounty hunters were standing between the shelves. We were no longer alone in an empty building.

"Welcome, dear lady and gentleman," Will said as we shot out from behind the shelves. "I had already started to wonder what was holding you up and why you weren't coming to save your buddies. Tut-tut, and you, too." He turned away from me to look at Bridget. "I wonder what your father will say about this. Is that pathetic weakling really so charming that it's worth throwing everything away?"

The soldiers behind Will laughed.

Next we were frisked.

"Against the wall!" Will ordered sharply.

We turned around and pressed our hands against the shelves. I left the skateboard leaning against my leg.

"I'm taking this," Will said and picked it up.

Before I had time to do or say anything, he had dropped it and jumped on it so hard that it broke in two. I didn't see it. I only heard it.

"Don't!" I shrieked.

"Too late," Will said. "You won't be needing it anymore."

Then two other soldiers searched us. They had bludgeons on their belts like the police. They also had some sort of firearms. I wondered if they were real.

"Found this," one said and handed my knife to Will.

The knife clicked and clacked as Will snapped it open and shut.

"How pathetic," he said.

That wasn't true, of course. Dad had given me that knife, and although Dad was no hunter, he did understand about knives, having chopped pork and onions his whole life. He knew that a good blade cuts without leaving a mark, and that was the kind of knife he had bought for me. Even Will could see that the knife was excellent, and that was why he shoved it into his pocket.

"They have no other weapons," the other soldier said.

"Of course not. Rabble," Will sniffed and gestured for us to go with him.

We went. It was the only thing we could do. Bridget took my hand, and I didn't shrug her off anymore. Behind us marched a line

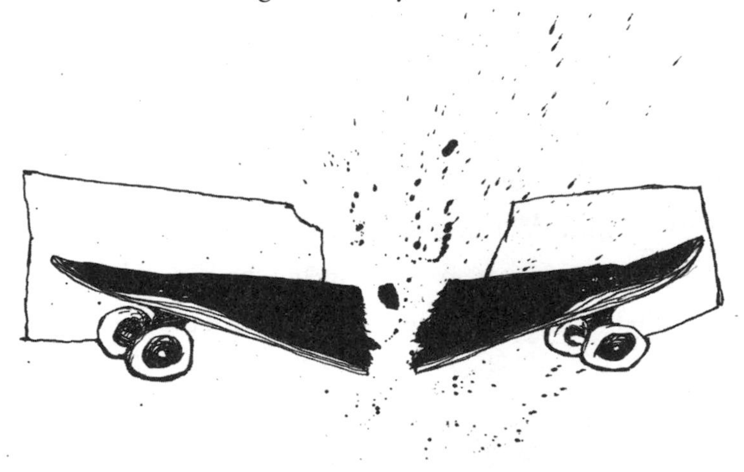

of Will's soldiers—boys and girls from the same class or the soccer team. They were all bounty hunters earning money for their future.

The place was familiar.

We were in the mask gallery.

A bright, greenish light was burning in the room, and the air conditioning hummed. The air smelled sickeningly of chemicals—a bit like a hospital or a laboratory. It made me dizzy, and the dizziness triggered all sorts of thoughts. I started to think that the room was a bit like a jar filled with strange liquid into which a collector put his butterflies before sticking pins through them.

The soldiers froze by the wall of the room, standing at attention. They clutched their bludgeons like little children clutching their bedtime toys. They were scared of the basement. Will was scared, too. He looked around, but when he saw no one, he plucked up courage and pulled me along with him. Bridget followed. In the middle of the room was a table that looked a lot like an operating table. It was covered by a green cloth, and next to it was a stand with instruments, a bowl, dishes—the job was obviously left unfinished. Someone had just been there and would be coming back soon. That was how it looked.

We went up to the table.

"What is it?" I asked.

Will glanced at me and frowned. He clearly didn't know.

"Are you going to look at it?" we heard Alexander ask weakly, standing by the wall at the back of the room. "We were only supposed to—"

"I know, soldier," Will interrupted. "We were only supposed to catch them. But now we'll do something else, as well," he said and snatched the cloth off the table.

I screamed out loud.

Will screamed.

Bridget screamed.

We all screamed, for we saw a body lying on the table. It was a child's body—a dead boy. Ra or Moon.

"Ra?" I whispered. "Moon?" It was impossible to say which one it was lying on the table. He looked so lifeless. It could have been either of them. I sniffed. "We're too late."

I felt paralyzed. Or perhaps I was just in very deep water—or maybe frozen stiff.

I wiped my eyes and looked around me. There were two other tables in the room. They were lined up against the wall as if waiting for their turn. There was a bump on each table. Will went to snatch away the sheets and uncovered the bodies of Mew and another boy. They were both lying there, completely still. Will's lower lip began to quiver. He pushed his sharp nose close to his sister's face. For a while his long fingers moved above her as if he were going to touch her, push her hair away from her face, or something. But then at the last moment, he pulled his hand away and straightened his back.

"They don't look like masks," he said stiffly.

"They look dead," Alexander, who had crept closer, whispered.

"This is a new thing for me, too," Will said, uneasy.

I had started to shake. I wanted to close my eyes, but I didn't.

I would only close them when it was all over. That was what I'd decided as I stepped into the schoolyard. Maybe you can remember, or maybe you can't. I would only close my eyes when it was all over—whenever that was.

"Are they dolls? Or are they dead?" Alexander asked.

Will straightened his back. He turned to signal to his soldiers. "Come closer!" he shouted. "Come and look at the criminals! You won't be able to keep from laughing. Counselor Poole has moved on from faces to whole statues."

The soldiers crept up to the tables like greedy insects. First they laughed uncertainly. Then they grew bolder. It looked as if they were sniffing the children. In any case it was disgusting.

"They look real," one of them said.

"They look like totally repulsive criminals," another hissed.

Bridget squeezed my hand. "What shall we do?" she whispered. "Do they seem dead to you?"

I didn't know, but something was bothering me. There was something disturbing about all this. The children were covered by sheets from the neck down. The sheets went up and down, as if the three chests were moving beneath them.

Breathing?

"No," I whispered. "They are not dead—or dolls. Look at them!"

Bridget hung on to my arm. "They're breathing," she hissed.

And then...one of the boys flickered his eyelashes. The group of noisy soldiers didn't notice it, though. Alexander had just picked up a syringe and was holding it above the boy.

"If they are dolls, you could stick this through them, eh?" he hollered. "Let's try it! Real people bleed. We'll soon see whether they are dolls or not."

Will grabbed the boy's wrist and twisted it so that the syringe fell to the floor. "Don't touch anything!" he ordered. "Just about everything here is electrified. You can never tell. Maybe the dolls are connected. Look! There are leads hanging off them."

There really were leads attached to all three of them. They were some sort of tubes like rubber pipes stuck into their necks.

"How long do we have to wait?" Alexander asked grumpily.

"Where is Counselor Poole?" a girl asked. Her name was Minerva or something, if I remembered correctly.

"When is she coming?" one of the troops asked.

"Captain Poole will appear," Will said. "She told us to wait. She left us on guard and gave us a task. We executed it. Hooray, we've captured the repulsive criminals and runaways, and now we will wait for her to come and reward us. Be patient, brave soldiers. This task will bring a lot of extra cash into our accounts and earn us bravery medals on our chests at the great festival for the marked."

I looked at them. They all disgusted me. "If those are dolls, where are the real children?" I asked and pointed at the boy on the table. "Where are Moon and Ra? Where is Mew?"

"We don't need to worry about them anymore," Will said, covering the boys up with the sheets. His hands were twitching. "They are not dangerous now, and in the morning, they will be taken to the wall. They will go to the School of the Lost. You will go there soon, too."

"Blindfolded and up against the wall," Alexander said and mimed shooting a series of bullets at the wall.

The others laughed excitedly.

"Has anyone ever been taken to the wall?" I then asked. It almost seemed like the most important question I had ever asked.

The soldiers glanced at each other.

"Some have," Alexander said.

"One has," Minerva said.

"I hate you," Bridget interrupted. Naturally she was sobbing. "If you take Storm to the wall—if Father sends Storm away, I will run away from home and never come back. I'd rather die than be good any longer."

The soldiers whistled and laughed.

"You can run away, crybaby," Will said. "You'll have no chance. It will take precisely ten minutes to catch a scrap like you. You'll go to the wall at the same time as your stupid boyfriend, who doesn't even care about you."

Suddenly it happened. All the waiting was at an end.

The loudspeaker crackled, and then a voice could be heard.

"Attention! Can you hear me, basement?" the voice said. "Attention! Attention!"

The voice belonged to Verity Poole.

Everyone was glued to the spot.

60.

This is where the story starts to get a bit weird. Look around you before the final act begins. Look at the soldiers, at all the children standing by the wall, frozen to the spot like dolls. They don't move without someone activating them, pulling a string, pressing a button, programming, ordering and commanding, forbidding and rewarding.

They are scared. They are scared of adults.

Of course you need to be scared of adults. A lot of them are like fifteen-foot-tall three-year-olds, holding a spade the size of a snow shovel in a sandpit. "Don't be a bad cake. Be a good cake," they say and hit every sand cake on the head with the spade. "Don't be a bad boy. Be a good boy." If you are caught up in that sort of thing, you could cnd up getting thumped. Believe it or not, you could come to a sticky end.

"*Attention! Attention!*" announced the loudspeaker into the basement.

Naturally it was Verity Poole's voice.

"The spirit of the school!" the soldiers cried in unison, trying to stand up straight.

"Dear Possibilities troops and pioneers of the future," Poole's voice said. "First of all I am proud of you. You have done your duty and captured the runaways. Absolutely great work. You have respected the school spirit, and soon you will be rewarded for that. A state of emergency has been declared at the school due to the events of recent days. Together with the school management, we have decided to hold an express trial and sentence the runaways without delay. A state of war requires wartime decisions—speed and thoroughness. Bring the prisoners to the yard."

"Er, what?" Will spluttered, astonished.

"Storm Steele," Poole said, "no one can stay on the run forever. Why should you be able to escape when no one else has?"

I scowled hard.

"Action!" Poole's voice ordered, and the soldiers started to poke us with their bludgeons. They pushed us in front of them. We were carried along with them out of the basement. In the yard the beams from the security lights swept over us. It was really cold and dazzlingly light. Snow was falling onto the asphalt. We could have been in outer space on a bright star.

This was the sight waiting for us.

The yard between the school and the sports hall was full of students. Not all the students had arrived yet, but all the time, more children were marching through the open school gate. They looked around them. They waited.

Bridget drew a breath.

"A public express trial," she whispered. "This has never happened before. The whole school has been invited."

I nodded grimly. The soldiers, too, seemed rather surprised. They were glancing at the children anxiously, and every now and then at Will, who usually knew which way the wind was blowing. They were also looking for Poole, the headmaster, and Rob—for any adult, really.

But no one could be seen.

Will seemed quiet. The winds were gone. There were no compass bearings or ocean currents, either—he didn't know what was happening. But he turned to his soldiers and started to speak. "The trial will be in the sports hall," he said and pointed at the hall behind him. It was bathed in full light, as was everything in the schoolyard. It looked empty. There was no one in the stands. In the middle of it, the playing field shone bright green, deserted. "That's where we'll get our medals, and all this chaos will end. That's where we'll take the runaways," Will said, and the children looked at him dumbly and gratefully.

Everyone followed Will obediently, much like the children followed the Pied Piper in the story. In that tale a musician promised to save a city overrun by rats and to take them away with him, and that was what he did. But when he demanded his reward and wasn't paid, he took his revenge by making all the children of the city dance off a cliff.

The school clock above the main door showed midnight, and the scene felt a bit like a ghost story. The students resembled the ghosts.

Soon we were all standing at the sports hall door. But it was locked. Will tried to open it. First he pulled it calmly, and then forcefully. Nothing he tried worked. The door remained firmly shut. It remained shut even when Will got the soldiers to help him. It didn't open in spite of his violence.

"Ah, it won't open," he snarled at Alexander.

And then in the midst of all this confusion, the loudspeaker rasped again. "Dear students of the School of Possibilities, esteemed pupils, girls and boys of our troops fighting in the name of the future," Verity Poole's voice said. "I want to speak to you now. I am your Possibilities Counselor, Verity Poole, and the good spirit of this school."

The students froze to listen.

"I detest children," Poole said. "I detest children more than anything. You are now all here, which is good, because I have all kinds of things to tell you."

The students' mouths had sprung open.

"What the hell?" Will yelped and rolled his eyes at Alexander.

Alexander shrugged his shoulders, confused. "Maybe no medals after all," he said, and Will gestured for him to be silent.

All the while, Poole's voice continued to speak. "I have the mask of almost every child at this school. You may not know this, but from the shape of the face, one can conclude all kinds of things, like whether or not a person has criminal tendencies or if he is a genius. From your faces I can foretell the future for each and every one of you. Ordinary clairvoyants read palms. I read faces. Faces don't lie so much. I have read from the shapes of your heads that not one of you has a future. No hope."

The crowd of children started to move restlessly.

"The most disgusting of all the children, however, is the hooligan who was admitted to this school in the fall," Poole continued. "Even without a mask, one can tell that Storm Steele is just a pile of trash. He is among you in the yard now. Send him to the sports hall for sentencing by express field court-martial."

The hands holding me tightened their grip. That was pointless—I wasn't about to escape. It wouldn't be possible now—unless I had been able to fly. But my wings were broken, and the pieces of my smashed skateboard were lying who knew where.

The voice continued speaking.

"I also want the recently captured little brats and Minna Somers. Bring your sister here, Will. Bring Mew here. After you've done all that, you can go home and wait for tomorrow."

"But—where?" Will began.

"The children are in the basement. Bring them here."

Will turned to look at me, confused. "The dolls?" he asked. At first it seemed as if he was asking me, and then in the same breath, he shouted it out loud. "There are only dolls in there. Are we supposed to bring the dolls?"

"Yes, the dolls, you blind boy! Those dolls!" the loudspeaker screamed in reply. "Now get on with it!"

Will stood to military attention and organized his troops. He sent six of his boys back into the basement. When they returned, they were dragging Mew and the rather floppy twins between them. As they flung their loads onto the ground, one of the bodies squeaked.

The children were not dolls. They were not made of wax or any other substance.

My heart began to pound.

"Wake them up!" Will screamed.

The soldiers attempted to slap some kind of life into the children, and when it didn't succeed, Will threw some water over them. Then all three revived—at least a little. They looked around them and couldn't understand anything.

"What happened?" Mew asked dopily, getting to her knees.

"Who am I?" Moon wondered, holding on to his brother.

"I am you," Ra replied, equally muddled. "Where are we? Storm? Mew? Mom?"

Will pressed his hands over his ears. "Take them into the building! Go!" he shouted at me. He was in a real rage—or frightened. It was difficult to say which.

I immediately bent over and took hold of one of the boys under his arms. The boy stood up unsteadily. Then Mew grabbed my shoulder, and we started toward the double doors of the sports hall. We were all staggering.

"Go!" Will ordered and hit me with his bludgeon.

We marched toward the door. At some point I happened to look at the sports hall window. It made my heart leap into my throat like crazy.

A sun was painted on the window. It said, KRAP TNEMESUMA, which, of course, meant "amusement park." The picture had been painted on the inside, and that was why the letters were back to front. In the picture, the sun, the stars, and the moon were hanging in space above a peculiar planet. Strange plants grew on the planet, and it had such a glow about it that it was almost difficult to look at directly. There was also some kind of a wall in the picture with children on it. They were dancing on top of it—or perhaps not dancing but running or doing some other activity. It was such a beautiful and awesome place that surely everyone would be safe there.

"Look," I whispered to Mew.

Something dawned on me at that moment.

Mew's eyes widened. She smiled. "It's India," she whispered. "Go, Storm. Quick. Go."

Suddenly someone on the steps blew a whistle.

Rob Reed was there, wearing a head lamp. Verity Poole was next to him.

"What is happening here?" Poole bawled. Well, actually it was more of a screech. It reminded me of a flock of vultures flying over a desert. It was not a pretty thing to hear. "What are you kids doing here?"

"I am telling the students about my project in the basement," the loudspeaker answered.

It was completely crazy. The children looked from Poole to the loudspeaker, dumbfounded. Everyone shook like leaves. I wasn't surprised anymore, because I knew who was holding the microphone in the sports hall.

Then the door opened, and all four of us started striding toward it as fast as our heavy load would allow. The boys and Mew staggered beside me.

The door was open a little, and we threw ourselves over the doorstep.

"Don't let them go!" Poole was shouting behind us. "A revolution! A revolution has broken out here!" she yelled. She also swore like a trooper, but because her voice shrank into a pathetic tweeting against the loudspeaker, no one could make anything out.

When we got into the hall, the door slammed shut behind us.

"Welcome back," a voice said above me. It was India's voice. It was India.

"India, is that you?" I asked and turned to look.

"India! India! India!" the half-asleep boys said, collapsing into a heap.

"You should be given a good shaking for thinking they'd beat me," India said, laughing into the microphone in a masculine, gruff kind of way. "Go home, kids. The soccer training is canceled." It was Rob Reed's voice. "We won't be winning the soccer championship this year. You are not the right material. I'm sorry. I'm too weary to go on. You are just too hopeless. You are too well-behaved to play decent soccer."

Then India covered the mic with her hand and laughed.

"Why do you torment my mother, little prince?" she said to me between laughs. This time she was speaking in Mona's voice.

Then I, too, burst out laughing, and I couldn't remember ever having laughed so hard.

61.

Situations can suddenly turn upside down. Winds can change direction. Storms can rise up or die down. Waves can grow as high as rainforests or cities and then shrink back to nothing in a moment. Sometimes everything you have can sink in a storm as easily as a ship and then come back one day when you least expect it. Then life is calm again. When that happens, you have to rethink everything in a moment and act accordingly.

I should have been used to surprises.

But I wasn't yet. I wasn't used to them at all.

We were in the sports hall, and we were surrounded by the enemy. Mew, Moon, and Ra were on the floor waking up. They were all cold, because they were wet. I got them dry clothes from the lockers. There were all sorts of dismal outfits that had been used in Christmas shows and other plays. There were also sports shirts there, as well as socks, shorts, and running shoes. The basement prisoners were confused and looked pathetic in their sports shirts and elf pants.

"What happened?" Mew asked, shaking. "They fooled me. I thought we were going to save the boys."

I nodded seriously. "They know how to fool you, all right." They really did. I had learned that.

"What happens now?" Mew asked, and then we all looked out the window. We saw ourselves as if in a vast mirror.

"They can see us," Mew said.

I nodded. They could. We couldn't see them, but they could see us. That is what it's like in an aquarium: you are not always aware when someone is looking at you. The walls of an aquarium are glass, but when it is dark outside, windows become mirrors. Inside it's easy to imagine that the world goes on into infinity. In reality you can't see out into the world—you only see reflections. And all the time, someone is watching—or maybe not. The thing is, you never know. But now we did know. We were being watched. Every inmate of the School of Possibilities was keeping a sharp eye on us and waiting for our next move.

"They won't stay outside for long now that they know what's going on," I said. "What are we going to do? What should we do now?"

"You will finish the task," India said. "You will go into the basement and destroy the masks. I'll hold them off."

"How do we get there?" Mew hesitated. "They can see us. When we leave here, they'll snatch us right away."

India shook her head. "Haven't I taught you?" she said with her hand over the mike. "People see what they want to see. They'll see you if you let them. They'll see you if I allow it. I have many more tricks up my sleeve to confuse them. I will protect you. Leave by the back door while I entertain them. They won't see you going back into the school."

"But we don't want to leave you," I said and looked at the others expectantly.

They kicked at the green playing field and nodded.

"It would be easiest if we just vanished—all five of us," I went on, and for a moment, I thought of all sorts of ways we could stay together. I thought of trains and planes, ships and spacecraft, desert islands and cities where we could easily disappear. I thought of our future in some other kind of place.

Then India interrupted me. "We have to destroy the masks," she said. "Our task is incomplete. Think of the children. If we don't stop these adults, no one will, and in the School of Possibilities, they'll be talking about another lot of children who were taken to the wall. It's our duty."

I cast my eyes down at the floor and nodded. India was right. We had to end the reign of terror. I looked at the others. They all nodded. Our task was to destroy the masks, and that was what we would damn well do.

"Let's destroy the whole school while we're at it," Ra said defiantly, fist raised. "Let's torch the shack."

We left the hall by the back door. India stayed in the hall. She ran around on the artificial turf. She cartwheeled and vaulted. She was a bit like a flying acrobat.

When we got to the door, India switched on the mic and tapped it.

"Can you hear me, School of Possibilities?" she asked, and screaming could be heard from the yard. "Can you hear me, Mother?" India spoke into the mic. "Your darling Mona is here.

The prince is holding me hostage. Agree to all demands, or something bad will happen to me."

Then she sobbed. But she was smiling at the same time. She waved to us.

I didn't feel like smiling.

Standing by the door, I looked at India before stepping out.

"Good luck!" India called after us.

62.

We walked across the yard. We walked past the crowd of children. Everyone was looking through the sports hall windows. No one looked at me. No one noticed us.

They saw India. They saw her for a moment. That's what I believe now. It was an optical illusion: one of the tricks she was so proud of—as proud as she was of the lollipops she dropped and all the other junk anyone had to pick up from wherever she had been. India revealed herself so that we could stay hidden. She did amazing vaults and cartwheels straight across the playing field and over the goal line, right in front of those hundreds of pairs of eyes.

I was looking for Poole in the crowd. She was the only one I was wary of. I told you about those spiders that bury themselves in the sand. They lie in wait there. The spider is a predator. It is not original to compare someone to a spider, but I am doing it anyway, because a spider is a terrible creature—the worst I know. It has strong jaws. It is swift and almost invincible. It is a total hunter, and when a creature like that catches you, you won't need next year's calendar. Unfortunately Poole was capable of anything. That was why I was looking for her in the yard among all those children staring at the sports hall window. But she was nowhere to be seen. The headmaster was in the yard. He stood in the crowd of children and trembled. Rob Reed was there, too. Rob stood next to the headmaster, clutching a megaphone. They were both shouting threats into it and ordering me to surrender.

"Come out of there, Storm! Stop this clowning around," they bellowed one after the other, then in unison. It sounded quite funny.

I was still trying hard to spot Poole. I was afraid that she had dug herself into the sand. If you knew her, you'd have been afraid, too. Where was she? Where had she gone?

It was around then that it happened.

The whole school went dark.

All the hundreds of school windows went dark. The television screens went blank. The lights in the corridors, classrooms, and cleaning closets went out. The loudspeakers fell silent. The school became a black abyss. The sports hall vanished into darkness. Both of them became darker than dark holes in the night.

The air was filled with sound. Rob shouted into the megaphone. He yelled all sorts of instructions, but it was impossible to hear any of them, because the children had started shouting. They were shouting together and over each other. Some screamed. Some just cried. Someone was shouting for help. They huddled against each other. There was a sense of imminent catastrophe. If a typhoon had swept the country, if the earth had begun to crack and huge waves had swallowed the city, the confusion could not have been greater.

Everything was dark. I had never before seen any school that dark, and I'd seen a lot of schools.

"It's the school's heart," I whispered seriously. "Its heart is broken."

That sounded awesome when I said it out loud.

The school's heart is broken.

What was it that had broken exactly?

We took each other's hands and squeezed.

"The school's heart?" Moon whispered. "What does it mean?"

"Who broke it?" Ra whispered.

I shook my head. I didn't know. No one knew yet. I realized now that none of us would ever know the whole truth—not all of it.

We squeezed each other really hard. Then we started to run toward the school, which was darker than any night had ever been.

63.

It was hot in the basement. It was even hotter than the storeroom just above us. It was as stifling as a sauna or a rainforest. It was as if the air was rippling. It made us sweat. Our clothes stuck to our skin, and it was hard to breathe.

"Something's wrong," Mew whispered. "It smells odd."

It was true. There was a strange smell—quite a nasty one—and the smell grew stronger with every step.

I had seen the masks only a short time ago in the glass cabinet. At least I had assumed they were there under the glass domes. When I saw them for the first time, I had almost preferred them to the real children of the School of Possibilities. Or maybe, as usual, I was exaggerating. At least the masks knew how to keep their mouths shut. At least they breathed like real people.

But now I couldn't hear any breathing.

That was significant.

The masks were not breathing anymore.

"The air conditioning is off!" I cried out loudly when I noticed. "They're not breathing."

A cold silence followed.

"Get some light in here!" Mew ordered. But when Moon flicked his lighter, Mew snatched it away quickly.

"No fire, idiot. There could be something flammable in here."

Because there was no other light, we stood in the dark.

"I've got a light," we heard someone whisper timidly. "I've got a light on my cell phone. It's weak, but—"

It was Bridget.

"Bridget!" I interrupted her. "What are you doing here?"

"I came back to the basement," she said. "I thought they'd finish you off, so I came to destroy the glass cabinets. But then all this happened…the darkness. The electricity went off."

Then Bridget found her cell phone, and a weak light came on. In the dim light, we could see that something was really wrong. We all dashed to the nearest cabinet, but it was empty.

"They're gone!" I yelled.

I snatched the phone from Bridget's hand and leaned in to take a closer look. The others were right behind me. Someone had done the job for us. There was nothing in the cabinets, nothing to destroy. They were just empty, dirty cases.

"The masks have vanished into thin air?" Mew hissed.

"Or melted," Moon suggested.

I lifted my shoes off the sticky floor. I was beginning to understand what had happened. Until now it had been really cold in the basement. Now it was warm—hot even. Of course wax wouldn't stand that. It melted. It couldn't stand heat. No way could it stand sweltering heat like this.

I turned around to look at the others, all with serious faces.

"The masks have been destroyed. What are we going to do now?" I asked.

"Let's burn the school down," Ra suggested.

"Glass doesn't burn, stupid," Moon snapped and trod on his brother's toes.

"Should we talk to my father?" Bridget asked timidly.

"Your father? Why?"

"I don't know. I just thought that he might not approve of all this. I mean—I want to know whether he does or not. It would be good for me to know, because if he does, I'll run away and never come back."

It was, of course, ridiculous talk and didn't interest me. I couldn't be bothered and didn't want to talk about it anymore.

"I think I'll break my last chance contract," I said out loud, and as I said it, I knew that was exactly what I was going to do. I would do it, even if not a single school would accept me anymore. I would have to quit school and earn my living in a fish factory or as an onion chopper on some ship. "I am going to the headmaster's office. I will tear up the contract I signed and a couple of other papers. I resign."

There was silence. It was almost frightening.

"Me, too," said Mew beside me.

"And me," Bridget whispered.

"And us," said Moon and Ra together. "We'll burn our contracts."

Five hands slammed together in the dark.

Then we left the basement—for good.

64.

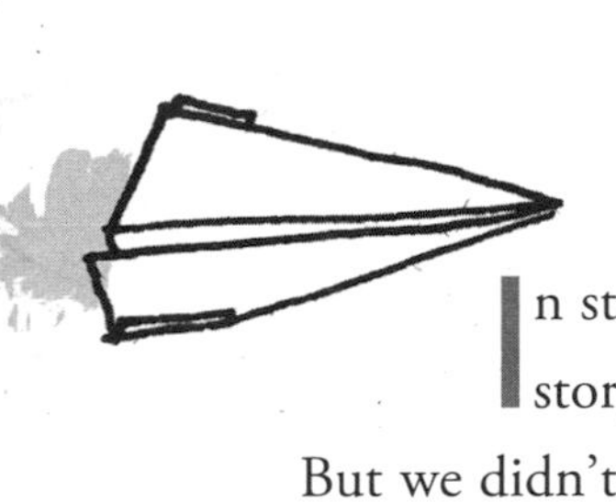

In stories fires sometimes start up. So it goes in this story, too.

But we didn't light it. In a way the fire was an accident, and in the end, it didn't destroy the whole school. In fact it only destroyed the watchtower and some things in the staff room and the headmaster's office. The windows blackened with soot, as well, and ashes floated around the yard for a long time after.

Did the air conditioning destroy the masks? Who turned off the world?

When we reached the corridor, we realized that something strange had happened there, too. At first, we could smell smoke, and soon we heard distant shouting from the yard. The school had been invaded. Children were running around the corridors. They were not doing cartwheels—they didn't know how to do anything like that. They just ran around.

When we saw the flames outside, we immediately dashed to the window. The yard was full of shadowy movement. The children were running to and fro and doing other things, too. They didn't look scared anymore. They weren't afraid of a tidal wave anymore. They had started one. They had collected books, papers, and arrest warrants into a heap and set fire to it, and they were now throwing all sorts of things into the bonfire. They jumped around like a wild bunch and were waving their coats above their heads like flags.

I whistled.

"What the heck happened here?"

"The masks have been destroyed," Bridget replied cautiously.

I glanced at her, astonished.

"That means—no one has died," I said, breathing easy.

Then Mew took hold of my shoulders from behind and shook me.

"This is a revolution, kids!" she said solemnly.

"Blood!" Ra shouted and pressed his nose against the glass.

"Flames!" his brother echoed alongside him.

Everything was in chaos. Only the hall at the back of the yard was as dark as night. The adults were nowhere to be seen.

"Could we burn in here?" Ra asked and took my hand.

I shook my head. "Glass doesn't burn. It just goes black and melts if it's really hot. It might break, but it won't burn," I said and beckoned to the group to follow me. "There is still something we need to do."

We ran into the office and did our final duty. We broke the windows, scooped the contracts out of the safe, and threw them out the windows. In the yard they caught fire and flared up for a moment before turning into ashes, which fell onto the screaming, running kids.

The air was filled with the piercing sound of the school alarm and the wailing of approaching fire engines.

I climbed on the table in the office with a contract in my hand. I folded it into an airplane. I, Storm Steele, rejected the future that was chosen for me. Then I moved nearer the edge. Mew and Bridget jumped down to the yard. Moon and Ra jumped, too. It wasn't much of a drop.

I was poised, ready to jump. Then just before I did, I saw Verity Poole. I saw her image in shards of glass.

"Storm!" she said.

I turned around and saw her. She was standing at the door of the headmaster's office, looking at me.

"Where are you going?" she asked. "Are you going to take off and fly?"

"Don't come any nearer," I said. I stared at her and thought no one would ever get me again—not even a spider like Poole, not when I was flying, not until I stopped. And I was never going to stop again.

That was why I nodded. "I'm leaving now," I said.

"There goes my beautiful creation," she said. "You destroyed it."

"You destroyed it yourself!" I shouted.

"Oh, I am so tired of little brats," she sighed.

Then Poole looked around the headmaster's office for a moment. She sighed again deeply. She sighed the way adults sometimes did. "This was a good experiment," she said.

Around then a burning paper plane landed on the floor. It turned to ashes in front of our eyes. But before it went out, it lit the papers strewn on the floor.

That was when I jumped.

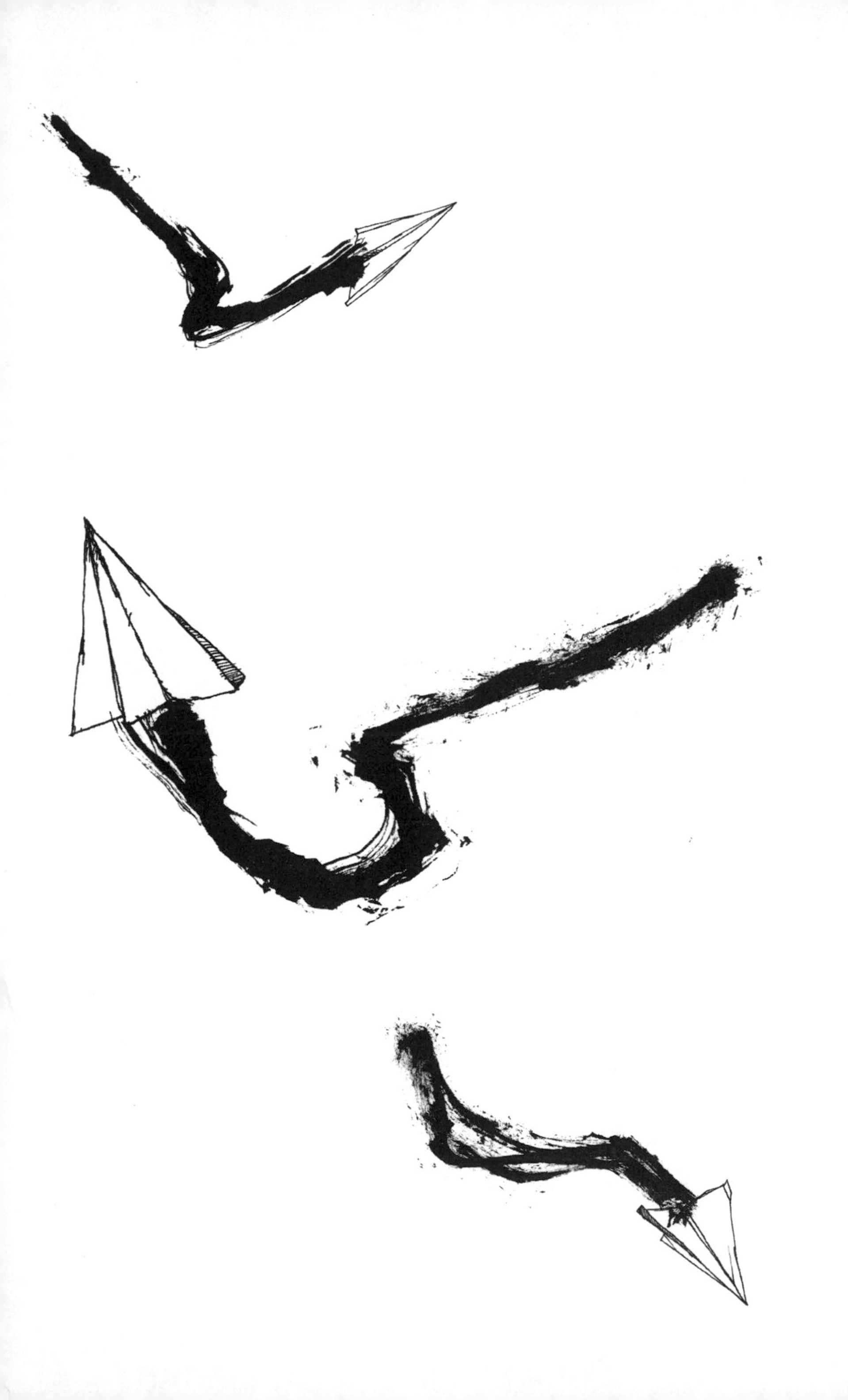

EPILOGUE

Every night comes to an end. And so did this one.

This is what was written in the local newspaper a couple of days later:

> *A crowd of children ran amok on Thursday night at the school known as the School of Possibilities. The school suffered some minor damage in the attack. The attack also revealed that the school's award-winning methods of education have not worked and have made the students stressed. An investigation into the school has been started, and some of the teachers have been suspended. One of the chief instigators, the school counselor, has disappeared. Her whereabouts are unknown…*

And so on.

There were plenty of these stories.

When the townspeople talked about the school and the night's events, they forgot about the masks. Maybe it was because there was nothing left of them. Talking about them would sound like superstitious nonsense. The adults said that we children talked about the masks because we were in shock. Traumatized children always imagine all sorts of things.

I know better now. The masks were important, and they were destroyed. Getting rid of them meant the children were freed. The school students believed that I had destroyed them. I became something of a hero. To adults, however, I was still the disobedient boy who uncovered the counselor's methods—I may have been a hero, but they still had their doubts. They weren't angry with me about the damage the school suffered or about the rewiring that had to be done or that the School of Possibilities had to start the next term in borrowed premises in a nearby elementary school. To those who asked, I tried to tell my own version of the night's events, but they were more interested in the Cinderella story of a naughty boy.

Mew told me to keep quiet, as well. She didn't want to talk about India. "India belongs there," she said and pointed at the factory—or maybe she didn't point at the factory but at the city.

So what did happen?

This is what I know. The rest I have imagined.

Someone turned off the electricity and the air conditioning that kept the basement cool. As you might recall, wax can't stand heat. It can't even stand warmth. When the temperature rises, it soon loses it shape and form. When it loses its form, it becomes liquid. Sometimes even lamplight is too much for it. It's always cold at the waxworks—as cold as a refrigerator.

Who turned off the school's power? There are only two possible answers.

India did it. That was one alternative. That night India was in the sports hall, the pride of the School of Possibilities. The school's power center was also there. The other alternative was Verity Poole.

She may have done it because she wanted to cover her tracks or for some other reason. Perhaps she wanted to free the children before she disappeared. Who knows? People never stop surprising you—especially adults. Evil is never all evil. There are always two sides to it—in the same way that good has another side. If anyone knows that, I do. I'm not a bad boy, but I'm not good, either.

It's also possible that the heart of the school overheated and exploded. That sort of thing happens, too.

Those who know the answer won't say. We will never know.

What happened to Verity Poole? I have thought about her at times. I have talked about her with other children. Not everyone wants to talk, of course. There are some who still draw black spiders. They have dreams. After Poole resigned as school counselor, she just disappeared. She packed her things and left the city. She took Mona with her. She left Dad's things and mine on the staircase. We found them there when Dad returned from a camp for students' parents a few days after the revolution.

Because the school was the center of the city's attention for a while, the papers were full of articles, interviews, and letters from townspeople expressing their opinions. The children were asked about what they thought made a good school, what made a teacher successful, what teaching methods worked, and what prizes and punishments were reasonable. Some articles talked about chances and futures, genius and disobedience, education and punishment. Some called for strict discipline and complained about graffiti. Others advocated gentler methods and demanded a new name for the school. In the end the school kept its old name.

You heard right—the school continues to operate. It is still an experimental school, although, of course, the headmaster and the teachers have been replaced. The new teaching staff adheres to "green methods." That's what they call them. On Fridays they hug trees. The teachers treat the children as though they were delicate plants. When the new teachers started at the School of Possibilities, the black chalkboard was replaced with a green one. The asphalt was torn up in the yard, and daffodils were planted instead. The sports hall was converted into a greenhouse. The students started to wear green school uniforms, each with a flower in the buttonhole.

While all this took place, I was already somewhere else.

Perhaps I have grown up. Perhaps I design cities. Perhaps I have continued flying or running after a ball. Perhaps I paint messages on walls. Or I build bridges across rivers like the Missouri or the Amazon. Perhaps I wander in the desert on the back of a camel. Sell tea in China. Search for treasures in Egypt.

Before I finish the story, I have a few further conversations.

I talk to Mom and Dad. They both returned from the parents' camp, where they hadn't begun to love each other again but had quarreled all the time while scrubbing floors and folding laundry. After hearing a sort of shortened version of the events at school, they were ashamed, because they had trusted the school. They were proud of me—proud that I had been disobedient about the right things. "You shouldn't obey misguided rules. That's what I've always told you," Dad said, although that wasn't true. He had never said that. What he did say, among other things, is that you must keep a low profile. In the same breath, he confessed that he had believed in the Guide to Possibilities given to all parents. "It seemed genuine enough. We wanted to give you the space to re-form. We were probably foolish."

Of course they were. I love them despite that—or perhaps precisely for that reason. Sometimes you have to look after adults. They are so easily taken in by others. They want to believe in things, and so they do. Ads and catchphrases work on them. Now, Mom and Dad understand me. They don't understand each other, like I said before. I can't offer you a happy ending like that, for this is not a fairy tale—at least, not that kind. I'm still traveling between two homes, which isn't all that bad—especially now that Dad has given up looking for a mother for me. I'll make sure he sticks to that decision. I'm not nice to any potential candidate who tries to infiltrate our life. I'm good at that. Nowadays Dad lives fairly near Mom. He bought the old practice room on Mom's block and converted it into a restaurant. Mom helped with the interior decoration. We don't mention Verity Poole. "Everyone is allowed one mistake," he says when I do try to ask about her.

Mona sends me postcards. At first they were irritating. Then I started to feel pleased about them. She lives quite a nomadic life. The latest card came from Kuala Lumpur, which is a city in Asia. This is what it said:

You would like this city, little prince. Here the trains run on tracks above the city. I miss you. Although really I detest you, of course. As you know.

My story will end soon.

The last chapter is about guards. It's about India.

India exists. She is a girl, not a country or a subcontinent. She can skate better than anyone else. She is a guard. I know her well, and she's not what you'd call ordinary.

She went to this school for a while. She sat next to the window and looked at the same factory I looked at later on. Perhaps she has been in your class, too. She is the girl who sat behind you, in front of you, or next to you, and was always a bit different. India appears from time to time, a bit like angels do. But she is not an angel. Perhaps she's more like an urban guardian. If you live in our city, you can see her colorful signs in subways, by railroad tracks, under bridges. They are signed *In©dia*, which is sometimes written so small that you can hardly notice it. India sleeps on staircases and in abandoned buildings. She knows the street door codes and knows where the showers and washing machines are and knows the best attics and storerooms. If you have your window open at night, you might hear her skateboard wheels rolling down the street. You might hear the ball bearings in her spray paint can—or smell paint. If you look out the window, you either see her or you don't. She knows how to become transparent and vanish, which means she's as free as anyone could ever wish to be. I didn't dream up India, and neither did Mew.

Sometimes a child gets fed up with his parents or something else happens, and he runs away from home. Then India takes him in, and he joins her troops. She looks after him until he learns to fly solo. Sometimes such children return to their parents, but not always. I returned. So did Mew, Moon, and Ra.

We don't talk about India, but we all think about her. And none of us will ever forget.

We like it in the factory. It has the best ramps ever.

Everyone can decide for themselves whether to believe me or not.

And finally…

Let's return to that night in the schoolyard for a moment.

The children aren't halting on command anymore. They are not obeying Rob Reed's whistle, even though he's blowing until his cheeks are almost the size of melons. I reckon he's going to pass out soon, like when you blow up an inflatable raft and blow for too long.

The children don't care. They are screaming, or perhaps they are singing. They are painting everywhere—on the school fence, on the walls and the windows, on the trash cans and the watchtower. They are painting on the glass walls of the sports hall. They are no artists. They are not as good as India or me, and the pictures are a bit hit and miss.

A group of soldiers is throwing contracts from the tower. They are folding them into paper planes and letting them go. They fly in the air like bombers or fiery butterflies. Alexander has smeared three stripes on each cheek. Minerva is screaming like a Navajo. It's as if everyone had just decided to toss their contracts in the trash.

Every child is breathing. Everyone is taking deep breaths.

About then India takes hold of my shoulder.

"I'll be watching you," she says.

She is standing right behind me. She is as close as a shadow—or a guard.

"We're not coming," Moon says. "We're going home now."

"If that's all right?" Ra asks to make sure.

India nods her head so that the lollipops, bones, feathers, and small birds fall down on the asphalt. Then she turns around and runs away.

"See you at the factory!" she shouts without looking back.

She runs away, and we can't hear her anymore, because she is too far away and because all over the yard, the children are shouting, and the air is full of airplanes with their wings on fire.

ABOUT THE AUTHOR

Seita Parkkola lives in Turku, Finland. She is a writer, teacher, and mother of two. She teaches graphic arts, photography, and writing, and she has also worked as a reporter and photographer.